ROSE EDMUNDS

Concealment

CRAZY AMY THRILLER 1

Published in Great Britain by Mainsail Books in 2017
Second Edition

Paperback formatting by Clare Davidson www.claredavidson.com
Proofreading by Julia Gibbs www.juliaproofreader.wordpress.com
e-book formatting by Ben Bryant www.makemyebook.com
cover design by Ana Grigoriu www.books-design.com

In memory of my sister Bryony, who deserved better

1

There were too many brown-noses on the Blue Skies Brainstorming Group for any good to come of it.

New boss Ed Smithies chaired the meeting. He was a pudgy, oily man with sinister white teeth, and a grating nasal whine of a voice. Few participants spoke, let alone challenged him. Instead, the gutless toadies dutifully transcribed his bombastic droning with their Pearson Malone plastic pens.

I'd been flattered when they asked me to join—it meant I was passing as normal. But an hour into the opening session, the urge to pass as normal was waning fast.

Smithies wittered on about diversity, though we already employed opportunistic robots of every imaginable colour, religion or sexual orientation.

'*And you're one of them.*'

I jumped at the eerily familiar female voice, which came from by the window. Everyone else carried on, oblivious.

'*Go on—prove you're not—tell them what idiots they are.*'

Not a wise idea, I thought, *whoever the heck you are*. And yet the suggestion was strangely appealing.

'*You do realise playing safe might be a high-risk option.*'

Yes—I'd felt that lately—not high risk for my career, you understand, but somehow high risk for me, as an individual.

'Look, you guys,' I said, succumbing to temptation. 'Diversity doesn't mean filling every job vacancy with a black lesbian in a wheelchair. It's not some box-ticking formulaic exercise—it's about people.'

A torpid wasp buzzed round the curled-up remnants of the sandwiches, breaking the silence as everyone waited on Smithies for their cue.

'Does anyone else find that comment offensive?' he asked, wrinkling his nose in disdain.

The puppets bobbed their heads in unison.

'That's bonkers—how can you hire disabled black lesbians if you're not allowed to mention them?'

An excellent point.

'I think Amy meant to say diversity isn't necessarily visible. You can't always see why someone is different.'

This trite observation came from Isabelle Edwards, the most junior committee member. She was a doll-like blonde who'd captained the women's hockey team at Oxford and still emerged with a double first. Who asked this little upstart with her flawless French manicure and prissy pearl drop earrings to act as my unofficial interpreter? If I'd meant that, I'd have said it. I was, after all, the world's leading expert on appearing the same and being different.

'Egg-zackly,' said Smithies. He gave Isabelle an appreciative little glance. 'Although why Amy couldn't have expressed herself less provocatively...'

He broke off, as his bleak lizard eyes fixed on me, penetrating through the bravado to the quaking mess within. The invisible speaker cast her shadow onto the board table and then retreated.

And that was the moment, before Isabelle was even dead, when I peered down into the abyss and realised I was running on thin air.

2

No way would I let Smithies spook me again—he might be the boss, but I was no underdog. More than a hundred people reported to me as head of the Entrepreneurs Tax Advisory Group, and you don't end up in a job like that by being a pushover.

Mind you, Smithies was no patsy either. Since moving from the Manchester office two years before, he'd systematically clawed his way into the role of Head of London Tax. Already, his "decisive management style" stood out in sharp relief against the non-interventionist approach of his predecessor, John Venner. And I knew, as you always do, that my intense and visceral loathing of him was reciprocated.

A week later we sat in Rules, ostensibly to discuss the staff pay review over lunch. The place was full of paunchy, grey-suited men guzzling hearty meat pies and rotting game birds. As I'd specifically asked my secretary to tell him I didn't eat red meat, I could only interpret Smithies' choice of venue as a hostile act. But perhaps I was being oversensitive.

Plaice fillet.

'You can't come here and eat fish,' he said, appalled, before ordering roast rack of lamb for himself.

'If it's on the menu, I can have it.'

'Any starter?'

'Not for me.'

'Me neither. But I think I might stretch to a glass of wine—how about you?'

I waved aside this miserly token of his esteem—Venner would have ordered a bottle.

'Water for me, thanks.'

'Very wise,' he said, 'to keep the booze under control.'

Smithies made a ridiculous show of asking for tap water. On the face of it, his reluctance to part with three pounds fifty for a bottle jarred with the Savile Row suit and Rolex watch, particularly as he would charge lunch to the firm. But this was an exercise in domination rather than frugality.

'Certainly, sir,' said the waiter. His gaze met mine for an instant—the knowing contemplation of a man who was likely writing a PhD thesis on Wittgenstein when he wasn't waiting tables.

Now Smithies directed his attention towards me.

'So tell me, Amy,' he said, flashing his flawless teeth in a reptilian grin, 'are you destabilised by the management changes?'

They say never smile at a crocodile. But it's hard not to when it smiles at you.

'Why, of course not,' I assured him. 'Should I be?'

Smithies' predecessor had left in a hurry to join the board of a client, amid rumours he'd been caught downloading child porn on his computer. You work closely with someone for years and think you know him well, but sometimes you're mistaken—so his departure was surprising, but hardly destabilising.

'You seemed on edge in the meeting last week.'

'No, not at all.'

'Well, you know what they say—perception is reality.'

'But everyone's perception is different isn't it?' I countered, perhaps unwisely.

'Egg-zackly. And so when several independent people have the same impression, it's liable to be correct.'

Therein lay the power of this stale leadership maxim. Someone important formed a negative view, others "independently" followed, and it quickly became established as the truth.

'And while we're on the subject of perception,' he added, 'I'm afraid we'll have to let you go from the Blue Skies committee. A number of people complained to me afterwards about your inappropriate comment.'

The number was almost certainly zero, but I didn't care anyway.

'Fine with me.'

So far, I'd handled him with ease.

'Now, I *am* a bit tight on time,' I told him, consulting my watch. It was an Omega not Rolex, but then my profit share was less than half Smithies'. 'So shall we get down to the main business?'

But Smithies was reluctant to abandon his attempts to unnerve me.

'Yes, but naturally, it goes without saying that if you ever feel unduly stressed by things, just say the word...'

His fake avuncular concern grated as much as the tenor of his voice—after all, at forty he was only two years older than me.

'I'm perfectly OK, thanks.'

He held my gaze for a moment, probing the turmoil inside. But that only stiffened my determination—he couldn't see, he couldn't know the insecurity that plagued me. Sure, pretending to be normal was tough sometimes, especially when you had no clue what normal meant, but I'd done a pretty effective job of it so far. I would not allow this pompous, tubby little man to freak me out.

'Now before we talk about the promotions, I have some excellent news—a marvellous opportunity for you.'

'Oh yes,' I said, with a jaded cynicism I hoped he hadn't detected.

'You've heard of JJ Resources?'

I had. It was a large private company in the construction business and an established Pearson Malone client.

'Now Venner's gone we need a new tax partner. If you can pass muster with Jim Jupp himself, you're in.'

JJ would have been a plum client, but FTSE-listed Megabuilders Plc had recently bid to take them over. After the deal, Megabuilders' in-house department would take care of their tax work. And in the meantime, I would be stuck overseeing the responses to the purchaser's due diligence questions and reviewing dreary tax warranties and indemnities. It wasn't even as though the Jupp family shareholders needed any sexy tax planning done—that had long since been organised.

'The company's being sold,' I said. 'So it won't be a client for much longer, will it?'

'Such defeatist talk,' said Smithies. 'It's up to you to use this opportunity to develop a relationship with Megabuilders so they'll use us going forward.'

Unlikely.

'Can't Lisa Carter run with it?'

Lisa, the lynchpin of the JJ client team, was a director in my group. She was also my protégée and the closest approximation to a friend I had in Pearson Malone, or indeed anywhere.

'Not appropriate, in the circumstances.'

'I see,' I said, although I didn't see at all.

'Eric Bailey thought you'd be ideal,' he added, by way of encouragement.

I drew no comfort from this. Bailey, UK CEO of our firm, operated on a feudal system, handing out favours to his henchmen in exchange for their undying loyalty. It was dangerous to be the recipient of his largesse because of what might be demanded in return—particularly in this case. Everyone knew that Bailey and Jim Jupp, JJ Resources' CEO, were best buddies. And while this personal connection strictly precluded any involvement with the client account, Bailey had no time for such tedious technicalities. He would interfere when it suited him and there'd be hell to pay if something went wrong.

If that wasn't bad enough, Greg, my ex-husband, led the Corporate Finance team advising JJ on the Megabuilders transaction. I was bound to have a degree of contact with him during the process. Was Smithies trying to manufacture complications in my life? And if he truly believed I was 'on edge', why burden me with more work?

I quelled the internal sniping. What had got into me? This was a simple request to take on a client.

'I'm pleased to have the opportunity,' I said with Oscar-winning sincerity.

Yet still the queasy intuition gnawed at my guts.

'Fish alright?' he asked, his chubby fingers working to prise his meat from the bones and sinew. My stomach heaved—lamb was the worst for me.

'Lovely, thanks.'

'Tricky staying slim once you reach a certain age, isn't it? No surprise that so many women end up with eating disorders.'

'Not me,' I said, prickling instinctively. Could I have an eating disorder without realising it, which Smithies had identified? He had this knack of making me doubt myself.

'*Well, he's not suffering from an eating disorder, that's for sure,*' piped up the little voice from last week's meeting. '*Look at the size of that belly.*'

She was spot on—his rotund physique must have presented his tailor with a considerable challenge. Still, the moment had passed for a pithy response.

'On the whole, you've made a fair attempt at these promotions,' he said, at last getting to the main point of the meeting. 'Far from easy in an economic downturn, so well done.'

He had no more experience of recessions than I did, but this didn't stop him from patronising me.

'Though a couple of them jumped out at me as anomalous.'

'Which?'

'Ryan Kelly—promotion to manager. I struggle to understand how such a major promotion is appropriate after that dreadful business in Daly's wine bar.'

There was no reason for Smithies be aware of the incident, but somehow he seemed remarkably well informed about everything.

'You're talking about the last appraisal period—he's really got his act together now, and we graded him as "meets expectations" this time around. Anyway, Daly's was outside office hours.'

'*And it was your Jimmy Choos he puked on, so you should decide if it screws his career,*' came the little voice again.

'I'm sure I don't need to remind you Amy—we are all ambassadors of the firm, twenty-four-seven. And I made it crystal clear that only those graded "above average" would be eligible for major promotions.'

'Yes, but…'

I'd also understood some exceptions would be allowed, but he choked me off before I had a chance to say so.

'You should have pressed for him to be graded higher in his appraisal if you felt so strongly.'

'I wish I had now. Ryan is way better than some guys in other groups who were ranked as above average,' I said, thinking of the worthless sycophants in Smithies' old section.

'I very much doubt that,' Smithies said dismissively. 'And you do need to be unbiased, even though Ryan's related to you…'

Ah yes, I should have mentioned. Ryan was my ex-husband Greg's kid brother. But by God, Smithies was crafty, trying to manipulate me by suggesting nepotism was at work.

'I am unbiased.'

'And even Greg thinks Ryan's a moron, so no need for you to stick up for him on his account.'

'*All the more reason to defend him, I should have thought.*'

'Then there's Isabelle Edwards—you're promoting her from one manager subgrade to another.'

If Smithies needed proof of my impartiality, this was it. I hated the suave little bitch, but I'd recommended her for promotion anyway.

'You can't have an issue with her—surely. We graded her as outstanding...'

'*Plus she's cosied up to slimy Smithies.*'

'Precisely my point—we need to sort the sheep from the goats—we should double promote her to senior manager.'

Smithies had told us all "for the avoidance of doubt" that double promotions would be vetoed in these straitened economic conditions. So this latest U-turn caught me unawares.

'But I thought…'

'You evidently haven't thought at all, or used any imagination. The promotions process is not some box ticking, formulaic exercise—this is about people.'

'*Bloody cheek, pinching your words,*' piped up the little voice once more.

Too right—especially when done with no apparent irony.

'Is this from the man obsessed with Bell curves and normal distributions?' I challenged him, emboldened.

'That's different,' he replied, with a satisfying level of defensiveness in his voice. 'We had a significant problem when I took over—eighty percent of our people were graded "above average" in the previous appraisal round.'

'Hey—they might be if the other twenty percent are completely useless.'

'Mathematically, that's perfectly possible,' I said, without thinking.

He eyed me suspiciously. I wasn't sure where this cheeky disembodied voice was coming from and why I let her egg me on. Did I have some kind of subconscious death wish? For sure, if I valued my own survival in the Smithies regime, I would have to rein her in.

'We digress,' he said. 'I take it you're not happy with a double promotion for Isabelle.'

'It could cause some ill feeling. I guess you don't know Ryan and Isabelle are an item...'

'I did know—and I can't see it's relevant. If the relationship endures, which frankly I doubt, for various reasons—he'll have to get used to her leapfrogging through the grades.'

'But you said no double promotions...'

'There are always exceptions,' he said. 'And Isabelle Edwards is a most exceptional young lady, in all respects...'

He added the final comment with a trace of a smirk, despite his prudish hyper-awareness of corporate propriety. I remembered the little look he'd given Isabelle, and how a couple of days earlier I'd seen them sitting together in the canteen.

And the thought flitted into my brain and out, almost before it had fully formed. Were they having an affair?

'But...'

'You don't like Isabelle, do you?'

'How can you say that?'

'*Well, it's true isn't it?*'

'It was obvious at the brainstorming meeting.'

This flair for mind reading was not only disturbing but also puzzling. Obviously, he couldn't see inside my head, but the conclusions he drew were nonetheless unnervingly accurate. Now, I wished I'd second-guessed him better and suggested the double promotion myself.

'The double promotion is OK,' I said, avoiding any discussion of my feelings for Isabelle. 'But Ryan Kelly deserves to be moved up.'

You may reflect on this later and think I'm lying, but it honestly wasn't a big deal. Yes, Ryan's promotion had been marginal, but everyone falls one side of the boundary or the other, and Ryan fell on the right side. Why should I capitulate purely based on Smithies' snide remarks?

'We'll come back to that later, once we've dealt with your other questionable decisions.'

That alarmed me, no matter how firm my determination to stay calm.

'Which?'

'Well, for example, you've allowed six subgrade promotions to go through on the nod, despite my instructions to rigorously review each case.'

'I *did* rigorously review them.'

'I fear that your idea of a rigorous review may be not be the same as mine,' he said sadly. 'But hey—it's a fairly minor point and if you can agree to hold Kelly back, I'll let those stand.'

I pushed my plate aside. Who needed an eating disorder with Smithies' slimy cunning to blunt the appetite? The trade-off was clear enough—one pissed-off guy instead of six—a fair deal on the face of it. Yet the cynic in me knew Smithies had introduced the subgrade promotions as a pseudo bargaining chip.

Though I could only guess at why he was so keen to advance Isabelle.

'OK.'

If I had to rationalise, I'd say I'd taken a pragmatic approach, done the best job for my team. But that still didn't ease the sting of guilt at not having tried harder.

'*What a complete shit you've turned out to be.*'

'So are we done?' I asked, ignoring the voice.

I had no desire to spend a nanosecond more than necessary with the odious man, but my hope that the meeting had ended was premature.

'One more matter,' Smithies said. 'Lisa.'

We'd been considering Lisa for promotion to partnership, an elevation that would deliver a salary comfortably into six figures. I dreaded what was coming next.

'It's not me,' said Smithies, with a faux apologetic hand gesture. 'But questions are being asked, at board level.'

He might not have asked the questions—for a start, he wasn't on the executive board, but he'd doubtless prompted them.

'I'm afraid we've been forced to pull her off the partnership promotion list.'

He was such a consummate liar that his pain on delivering this news appeared utterly genuine.

'So sorry, but in the current economic climate...'

'*What excuse does he use for stabbing people in the back when the economy's booming?*'

'She's passed the first interview—she's jumped through all the hoops so far—it's not fair to...'

But he cut me short.

'It's perfectly fair. We're in a recession and everyone's wary of who egg-zackly we let into the partnership. Frankly Lisa is a bit too much of an Essex chav girl to cut it.'

'*What about diversity?*'

'Aren't Essex chav girls part of our diversity initiative then?'

The words tumbled from my mouth before I could stop them. He greeted them with a cold stare.

'If you and I are to work amicably together, Amy, you'll need to lose the habit of making flippant comments when I'm being serious.'

I felt my cheeks flush.

'Yes, sorry.'

'And I'll leave you to tell her. OK?'

I shuddered in anticipation.

'Look—I know it's a tough conversation,' he said, picking up on my hesitation, 'especially as she's your chum. But hey, we don't pay you half a million quid a year to have an easy life.' He wiped his mouth with his napkin and blotted the beads of sweat off his forehead.

No—they paid me half a million quid to be shat on from above and below simultaneously, dogged by self-doubt, striving desperately to play the part of a successful Pearson Malone partner.

'*Is it worth it—is half a mill the price of your soul?*'

I must admit, I'd been asking myself that question.

'Leave it to me,' I said, standing up to go before he had the chance to suggest coffee. 'And thanks for lunch.'

'My pleasure,' he replied with another Instagram grin.

Of course if I'd known how it would all pan out, I'd have played it differently. For one thing, I wouldn't have wasted my breath arguing about a promotion for someone who'd be dead before it took effect. I'd have refused to take on JJ due to immense pressure of work and I'd have told Smithies to speak to Lisa himself.

But as it was, I actually believed I'd handled the meeting well.

3

JJ's secretary must have been psychic—before I'd even arrived back at the office, she'd called to fix a meeting the next morning.

I'd been planning to impart the sad news about her partnership to Lisa during a quiet drink after hours, but I now realised it couldn't wait. I needed her help preparing for the meeting and she'd instantly twig why the client had been allocated to me.

Lisa bounded into my office with no inkling of her fate, wearing a purple trouser suit, far too full-on for her spiky red hair and green eyes. Her skull and crossbones earrings finished the outfit with a flourish—no convention of business dress too trivial to flout. Such non-conformist signals disturbed Smithies—no wonder he'd killed her promotion.

Her face crumpled as I broke it to her.

'Well, I told you Smithies doesn't like gobby cows,' was her verdict.

True, but neither of us had foreseen this—Lisa stood so far above most of the other candidates, we'd assumed she'd be safe.

'My position is untenable,' she said simply. 'I'll have to leave. And truth be told, it's probably for the best, given the way everything's panning out here.'

She had a point. For some time we'd been bemoaning how the firm had changed in the three years since Bailey had taken control and gathered his clones around him.

Ironically, amid all the pontificating on diversity, he'd created a culture where everyone was afraid to be authentic. Everyone except Lisa, that is.

By dint of her talent and sheer force of personality, they'd allowed her some latitude. But with Smithies in the driving seat, she'd finally paid the price for bucking convention. Her response surprised me though—how could someone with her drive and naked ambition capitulate at the first hint of opposition?

'Wouldn't it be better to fight, get the decision reversed, pass the assessment and then give them the finger? I'll do everything in my power to help.'

'What power?' she asked, with a roll of her eyes. 'You can't stand up to Smithies. It's only taken him a few weeks to make you toe the line. No—much wiser to quit while I'm ahead, before I end up the same.'

It was sad to hear her thinking this way. Once I'd been a role model—now she pitied and despised me for jumping through the hoops.

'I'm amazed you're taking it so calmly.'

'It's called being realistic.'

I wasn't wholly convinced by her stoicism. Whatever she said, I would try my utmost to help, and not just for her, but me too. Without Lisa, life at Pearson Malone would be intolerable.

Meanwhile, we had a meeting to prepare for.

Lisa rattled off a status update. Since Princess Isabelle Edwards also worked on JJ's affairs, it came as no surprise to learn that everything was under control. Queries from the Megabuilders' due diligence team—sorted. Review of draft sale and purchase agreement from a tax perspective—no sweat—Isabelle had already emailed off a raft of incisive comments to the lawyers. What a paragon of virtue the girl was.

I was beginning to think this would be a doddle, until Lisa casually mentioned there'd been a "slight problem" on the account.

The hairs on the nape of my neck prickled.

'Like what?'

'A risk management issue.'

"Risk management issue" was a euphemism for being sued. And although even Smithies couldn't find a way to reproach me for an error made before I took over, I still felt uneasy.

'Surely not an Isabelle cock-up?' I suggested in tones laden with sarcasm.

'No,' laughed Lisa. 'And not me either, thank God—it goes back years. But Isabelle's been the most involved in sorting it out—why don't we ask her to explain the details.'

Lisa picked up my phone and dialled Isabelle's extension. Seconds later, Isabelle stuck her immaculately coiffured head round my office door.

I'd been to school with girls of Isabelle's ilk. Flawlessly presented, they churned out straight A's, ran for the county and lived in spotless detached Tudorbethan houses, where the sheets were laundered twice a week. Nothing bad ever happened to them as they glided effortlessly through their perfect lives.

Twenty years on, the bile of envy was as caustic as ever.

She sat down next to Lisa, her sober grey skirt suit and pale blue silk blouse in marked contrast to Lisa's outlandish outfit. The image was shrewdly calculated—Pearson Malone men responded better, if only on a subliminal level, to women who played it safe sartorially. I absorbed every detail—the nude ten-denier tights, the skirt an inch below the knee, the medium-heeled navy pumps…

'*What a worthless, shallow bitch,*' said the little voice, leaving me unsure if she meant Isabelle or me.

Isabelle sensed me peering at her, and flushed almost imperceptibly.

'You wanted to know about the potential lawsuit on JJ?'

'Yes please.'

'OK—a few years ago, JJ carried out a reorganisation, and all the business divisions were moved into one company. They have a slate quarry and mine, which had always been unprofitable, and the tax losses brought forward were transferred to the new trading entity.'

'Yes,' I said. 'Go on.'

'JJ first claimed the losses two years ago, when the slate division turned the corner. Then the Inspector of Taxes raised an enquiry. He thought profits might be overstated.'

While it's unusual for HMRC to suggest that the declared income of a business is excessive, they may do if they suspect manipulation to maximise loss relief.

'Don't tell me—queries on the allocation of divisional overheads?'

'How did you guess?'

'Been around a bit, kid—seen it before. Be all too easy for JJ to move expenses from the slate division to another part where there's no losses available.'

'He also thought there were bad debts which they should have provided against.'

'And what's your view?'

'The apportionment of overhead expenses is always subjective,' she said with her customary diplomacy, 'but there were some robust counter arguments we could have deployed. And the questions on the bad debt provision were plain silly, in my opinion.'

'You said arguments *could* have been deployed?'

'We never got the chance, because Charles Goodchild identified a mistake we'd made in our advice so that the losses weren't actually available.'

Goodchild was JJ's finance director, who I'd also be meeting in the morning.

'What mistake?'

She proceeded to describe a highly technical tax pitfall of group reorganisations—one I'd faced many times before. We usually found a work-around if the issue was identified upfront, and it would have been shocking negligence if we'd failed to spot it. Our clients paid us to recognise and sort out these conundrums.

'I can't believe we missed it. We'll mount a vigorous defence...'

But both Lisa and Isabelle were shaking their heads.

'You needn't bother,' said Isabelle.

'Why on earth not?'

'Because Jim Jupp and Eric Bailey are such good friends, JJ's agreed not to sue,' she explained.

I must say this didn't ring true, but I let it go.

'So in other words, the matter is now resolved,' I said, breathing a little easier.

'Egg-zackly,' she said. 'But Goodchild will be expecting to see a letter to HMRC, explaining why we're dropping the loss claim. I've drafted it up, if you'd like to review it before tomorrow.'

'Thanks—I will—that's all, Isabelle.'

Isabelle shimmied off, graceful and self-confident, leaving a discreet fragrance behind her.

Of course, she might not have been quite so poised if she'd known she only had four days to live.

***

'Convincing little liar, isn't she?' remarked Lisa after Isabelle had gone. 'I predict a glittering career ahead for her.'

'How do you mean?'

'Because Jim Jupp and Eric Bailey are such good friends, JJ's agreed not to sue,' she said mimicking Isabelle's voice.

'I agree—it doesn't sound at all in character. JJ's not a man to put friendship above business. Bailey must have offered him some inducement.'

'What about the Pearson Malone Entrepreneur of the Year Award—Jupp *is* on the shortlist?'

'Could be. But to sacrifice several millions of tax losses for a poxy trophy—even for an egomaniac like Jupp…?'

'Agreed. It only makes sense if for some reason the losses *are* unavailable.'

'Oh I get it,' I said, the light beginning to dawn. 'The *client* screwed up the implementation.'

It was by no means unusual for clients to attempt to blame us for their own shortcomings. Jupp had merely gone one step further by twisting the truth to wheedle a concession out of his old chum Bailey.

'And you reckon Isabelle knows the client messed up?' I asked Lisa.

'I'm *certain* she does. She checks the files, she's little Miss Perfect.'

'So why's she lying?'

'Search me. I believe she raised the issue with Venner when I was on holiday but he told her to back off.'

'Should I speak to Venner?'

I was reluctant to do so—he hadn't even bothered to s. goodbye properly, hadn't given me the chance to tell him I didn't believe a word of the allegations against him. Which made me wonder…

'You won't be able to reach him. He's gone on a month-long cruise before taking up his new job and he's uncontactable.'

Or rather he didn't want to be contacted.

'Mind you,' I said, 'you've not made much effort to set the record straight either.'

'Nobody's suggested I lie about it,' she retorted, a shade defensively.

'I should think not, because you never lie, do you?'

She knew as well as I did that there was often little moral distinction between a lie and remaining silent.

'No, but equally I'm not on a kamikaze mission—if I'm leaving I need a reference.'

It wasn't even much of a justification for keeping quiet. Everyone who left received the standard reference, except for the crazy guy who'd lasted a week before he glassed someone in the pub on the Friday night.

'Oh come on,' she said, sensing my disapproval. 'If I drop Goodchild in it, Smithies'll be out for revenge big time.'

'Why would he be bothered?'

'Ah,' she said. 'You haven't been told, have you? Goodchild's married to Smithies' sister.'

Dozens of demonstrators barred the entrance to JJ's headquarters as I arrived.

'*Stop Capitalist Pigs Now*,' read one of their placards. '*The 1% are killing the rest of us*,' proclaimed another. And, in a more direct jibe, '*Pay Up Jim Jupp*.'

The protestors hadn't targeted JJ's offices at random. JJ's wife, an Isle of Man resident for tax purposes, held all the family's shares in the company—she would pocket nearly five hundred million tax-free when the Megabuilders deal went through. No matter that this brand of tax planning was within the law—the media had been relentless in their condemnation and had whipped up a tidal wave of public hysteria. Now everyone was baying for Jim Jupp's blood.

As I elbowed my way past the demonstrators, they stared at my navy blue Armani suit and peach silk blouse with grave mistrust, but let me pass unimpeded. Maybe they saw through the costume to the weirdo underneath.

The JJ building showcased the work of their office construction and fit-out division. Behind the elegant Art Deco façade, it had been gutted and subjected to a hi-tech remodelling. An imposing marble reception area with ornamental fishpond led to a glass-roofed three-storey atrium. In the centre, a lavish space-age chandelier hung, apparently suspended in thin air, while glass elevators with flashing coloured lights whizzed up and down at terrifying speed.

Jupp's office suite occupied the whole of the top floor. In sharp contrast to the rest of the building it was traditionally furnished with leather sofas, antique tables, plush carpets, and works of art which didn't look like reproductions. And that was just the waiting room.

The sound of raised voices from behind the closed door of Jupp's office broke the illusion of tranquillity. I couldn't hear everything but I caught snatches of the words.

'Take my money… I'll honour my part of the bargain… won't answer for the consequences… wouldn't have the balls… nothing more to be said...'

At which point the door opened and a red-faced man in his mid-twenties burst out.

'Fucking parents,' he muttered, shaking his head.

Five minutes later Jupp's secretary escorted me into the room. Jupp stood up, took my hand in a vice-like grip and pumped my arm up and down as though trying to dislocate it. He beckoned me to sit at an oversized walnut veneered board table.

'Good of you to meet me so quickly. I'm sure you're a busy woman.'

The strength of his Geordie accent startled me. I knew he'd attended the same grammar school as Eric Bailey, but our CEO's speech carried only the faintest hint of a northern dialect. Sod diversity—Bailey must have spent a fortune on elocution lessons to eliminate every trace of his origins.

'No problem,' I replied.

'Any hassle with those losers outside?' he asked.

'None.'

'They call themselves anti-capitalists, but I'll bet if you gave them ten grand each they'd all piss off. Everyone has their price.'

He plainly regarded ten thousand pounds as a trivial sum. Did he have any inkling of what life was like for ordinary people, or their outrage at the way obscenely rich people like him slithered past the taxman?

'Ten grand might be over-generous,' I suggested.

'I don't see why they're so fussed anyway. If the money went to the government they'd only piss it up the wall paying middle managers in the NHS. My wife owns the shares and she lives overseas so there's no tax due when we sell the company. It's not rocket science, it's not illegal and it's certainly not immoral. It's just the way things are.'

In fact, Mary's emigration and tax residency status had been the result of extensive advice from the Pearson Malone private client team. But Jupp was correct in one respect—until such time as the law caught up with the shifting moral climate, what they'd done was perfectly legal.

'Her tax position is watertight,' I said. 'Provided she's followed our advice, that is.'

This was the nub of the matter. It was almost inevitable she'd have accidentally breached the complex conditions for offshore residence in the past ten years, and she'd be easy prey for an HMRC enquiry. After all, taxmen read the newspapers too. But I would gain nothing by voicing this prediction.

'And JJ Resources pays corporate tax too, not like some of these global firms who ship all their profits offshore.'

The arrival of Charles Goodchild, JJ's Finance Director, saved me from any potentially hypocritical agreement to this statement. His bloated appearance reminded me of Smithies, and on this basis alone I was minded to distrust him. And though his suit was more likely Austin Reed than Savile Row, he was equally supercilious.

On paper at least, he would be comfortably wealthy post sale. All his share options would vest and although some of his proceeds would swap over into Megabuilders' equity, he would get a reasonable dollop of cash on Day 1. With no easy way for him to avoid tax, he'd nevertheless be left with assets worth upwards of two million—vastly more than such mediocrity deserved. Still, he wasn't the first person to strike lucky on a takeover and he wouldn't be the last.

Goodchild removed his watch and laid it out in front of him, as though to emphasise how little time he could spare out of his busy day.

'Let's cut to the chase,' he said, before Jim's secretary had even finished pouring the coffee.

'Yes, please do. I can see you're in a hurry.'

'I imagine you've heard about the pig's ear your predecessor made of the reorganisation project.'

I smirked inwardly, recognising the blustering of someone who'd blundered but avoided detection. Somehow, I doubted whether even JJ knew the truth.

'Yes, I'm told the claim for the slate division tax losses will have to be withdrawn.'

'Indeed, and you were supposed to be drafting a letter,' he replied, with disproportionate aggression.

'I have it here.'

The letter, carefully worded by Isabelle, was a masterpiece of diplomacy. However much I loathed the girl, I had to grudgingly admit she was damned clever. We hoped that HMRC would now accept our explanations and withdraw all his enquiries. After all, he couldn't reasonably continue to argue that profits were overstated if they were taxable.

'This is well written,' said Goodchild, sounding surprised. 'But we have a new challenge. Now Megabuilders want to reduce the price for the company because the losses aren't available.'

'It's a try-on,' I said, making light of this apparently empty threat. 'Hardly anyone ever pays for tax losses upfront—there's too much anti-avoidance legislation to stop them being used.'

'No—you don't understand. They expect a price adjustment because of the extra tax due for the years already submitted.'

I cursed myself for not having foreseen this.

'And it's up to you,' chimed in Jupp, 'to find another way to save us tax and put the position back to what it was before.'

So not enough for us to take the rap for Goodchild's oversight—they expected us to rectify it to boot.

'Well,' said Goodchild, sensing my uncertainty and taking obvious pleasure in cranking up the pressure. 'Any ideas?'

I sipped at my tea, shamed by my inability to provide the instant solution they expected and desperate to buy a crucial few seconds' thinking time. The ticking of the antique carriage clock and Goodchild drumming his fingers on the table only added to my stress.

'Capital allowances,' I said, in a flash of brilliance driven by necessity.

Yes—they must surely have spent millions on capital expenditure on quarrying and mining equipment. The chances were no one had examined the tax allowances in detail with so many losses swilling around. And the claim could be backdated, which would nicely cover the affected years.

'My thoughts egg-zackly,' said Goodchild, sounding spookily similar to his brother-in-law, as he attempted to take credit for my idea. 'So we'd like a full review and agreement with HMRC, free of charge please.'

'I can't do it for free, but why don't we get one of our capital allowance specialists to do a site visit and an initial evaluation? Then we can see how much the potential tax savings might be before we do our quote.'

Goodchild opened his mouth to argue, but Jupp sprung swiftly to my defence, perhaps because he didn't care to jeopardise whatever deal he'd struck with Bailey.

'Sounds fair enough. But is a site visit really necessary?'

'I think it would be best—yes. But don't worry—we won't charge for that.'

I thought I saw a flicker of worry clouding Jupp's face, but I might have been wrong.

***

Lisa was less than impressed as we debriefed on the day's events on the treadmills in the Pearson Malone gym.

'Bloody amazing,' she puffed. 'They screw up… we take the rap… and they expect… us to re-save… the tax… they shouldn't have… paid… in the first place.'

'That's about the size of it. Still, we should get a decent fee for sorting it out.'

This was Lisa's first session in the gym. She'd reluctantly started on the fitness trail, in case she needed a medical for a new job. I was still hopeful I'd persuade her to stay and turn things around, but it wouldn't do her any harm to slim down however her life panned out. She switched off the machine and wiped the sweat from her face with a towel.

'God... I wish… we'd gone… to the pub instead… this is torture.'

'You'll love it when you get into it,' I promised her, although I feared my efforts to encourage her to keep fit were doomed to failure.

'Nah… only until… I've had my… medical… bloody hate it. Actually… don't think… you're fitter than me…' she gasped. 'Not with all the booze you put away…'

'You're a fine one to talk. And smoking will kill you first.'

'Ah, but you quit… when you were older… than me. At least… I'm not in denial… about any of my vices… only reason you do this… is to stay a size eight…'

OK—being fit was overrated. Who wanted to live forever? But being in control of your body shape was a matter of pride.

'Doubt there's enough… capital allowances claim… to cover those losses,' she continued breathlessly, as we made our way to the changing room. 'Meanwhile… we take… the meeting and travel time… on the chin. You do realise… the slate mine's... in the middle of nowhere… in Wales.'

'I know, but I had to offer them something for free.'

'Oh well, I suppose we can send Isabelle… to support the specialist… it'll be cheaper than us going… and her folks live about twenty miles away.'

'Really? I assumed she was Home Counties through and through—she doesn't sound Welsh.'

'I expect she went to a posh school, like you. But she told me her grandfather worked in the slate mine… which is why she wanted to be on the JJ service team.'

'Incredible. Just think, in another two generations your family might be all polished and poised like her.'

She fixed me with a beady stare.

'So we'll organise the meeting for a Friday and … our little princess can enjoy a weekend at home.'

And she probably would have done, had she lived to make the journey.

5

The night before the pay review I had the dream.

Teetering piles of rubbish surrounded me, encroaching on my space before collapsing, entombing me beneath them. I clawed in vain at the debris above me as I struggled for breath.

Clammy and fearful, I woke to the pungent odour of garbage, and the sensation of insects crawling on my skin. I threw off the duvet and examined the bed in detail. No bug in sight, but the fear and smell both lingered.

I hurried to the shower and stood under near-scalding water, speculating on what might have precipitated this bout of dread. Sure, there would be some challenging conversations today, but I hadn't been conscious of any worry about the pay review. Yet what else could have triggered the familiar nightmare?

Ten minutes later, and satisfied that I'd removed the last vestiges of imaginary squalor, I set about blow-drying my hair.

Now for the next challenge—who should I pretend to be today?

Who I was came down to what I wore. I possessed a whole double wardrobe of designer outfits—my corporate armour. People saw the clothes first and made assumptions about the person who wore them. They were the props of the gigantic con act I perpetrated every day, pretending to be this savvy successful woman. In truth, that woman was a stranger to me.

Black Max Mara trouser suit? No—too mournful, or even aggressive. Navy Armani? No—far too expensive to wear while explaining to staff why we couldn't afford a raise. Red Luisa Spagnoli skirt suit? God no—why did I even *possess* a red suit? I quickly transferred it to the bag for the charity shop—I knew the perils of keeping stuff you don't use. Not a suit at all, then. My eyes lighted on a Nicole Farhi silk jersey wrap dress in a floral print, and I selected a carefully coordinated cardigan. Yes—spot on—I came across as a touch vulnerable, verging on mumsy, but empathetic. Empathetic was perfect for giving bad news. I sprayed myself liberally with Eau De Lancôme, just in case, and painted on a happy face.

I'll be straight with you. Number one priority in a downturn is to maintain the partners' profit shares. And if revenues are static, the easiest fix is to hold down payroll costs. To justify our stinginess, we waffled on about "market forces in the current economic climate". But everyone we employed was way too smart to be duped—they knew they were footing the bill for our Porsches and Mercedes—so the pretence was futile.

I guess I could have handled the one-to-one meetings differently and avoided the bullshit, but I had a hundred and twelve to see—everyone in the group, apart from the partners. To finish the exercise in one day as stipulated gave me a bare couple of minutes with each person, and it was quickest to parrot from the approved crib sheet.

The Pearson Malone offices (built by JJ) were ill-designed for the delivery of bad news, being constructed almost entirely of glass. Erected in the hubris preceding the worst financial collapse in living memory, this magnificent edifice was supposed to symbolise the transparency of our innovative approach to professional services. And though, in this age of diversity, there was no metaphorical glass ceiling, we had real ones here. All the ventilation ducting and other pipes were plainly visible from below, and the meeting rooms came equipped with glass floors. To break the monotony of this sea of reflectivity, and give a reassuring solidity, islands of stone or carpet had been inserted at random in the design. The walls only added to the bizarre ambience—mirrored partitions alternated with glass screens and windows, juxtaposing interior reflections with framed glimpses of the London skyline.

Rumour had it Jupp and Bailey got hammered together and Jupp promised him a creation to set Pearson Malone apart from all other major accounting firms in the City.

He had indisputably delivered that, and the building had garnered awards and accolades along the way for the architects who'd taken on the challenging brief. None of these people cared that the offices were a pig to work in, with no blinds to pull down to allow solitude or privacy. Perception is reality, as we all know, particularly when viewed through a hall of mirrors.

At the tail end of a recession, there wasn't much fat left to trim on the payroll. Already, our programme of redundancies had laid waste to many who were basically competent. Now we were forced to restrict promotions, pay rises and bonuses for people who performed well.

At least the six who'd received their subgrade promotions would be reasonably satisfied, until next year when denied their main grade promotions. Still, I thought gloomily, Smithies would probably have fired me by then. And one person would be ecstatic—that self-satisfied little bitch Isabelle Edwards.

But first I had to face Lisa.

Smithies had tried to "make it up to her" for pulling her promotion by giving her a five percent pay rise and a twenty thousand pound bonus—in reality, this was a clumsy mechanism for letting her know how little he cared whether or not she stayed.

Not surprisingly, Lisa was unmoved by the gesture.

'Only Pearson bloody Malone would have the brass neck to buy off a hundred thousand a year pay rise with a twenty thousand lump sum. That's it—I'm definitely leaving.'

She knew better than anyone that I had no slack in my schedule to commiserate with her, and left without saying another word.

When her turn came, Isabelle trotted in laden down with JJ files, showing off her multi-tasking ability in her usual irritating manner. Most of our files were electronic, but these went back a few years—I cursed her for cluttering up my office.

'I've brought you these, so you can review the revised tax computations for JJ before they go out.'

Unaccountably, conscientious types like Isabelle invariably assume the partner wants to scrutinise everything in minute detail. We don't—we employ battalions of clever people like her precisely so we don't have to triple check everything ourselves.

'Lisa said she was too busy,' Isabelle explained, perhaps picking up on my annoyance.

I thanked her for dealing with it so promptly, although I could have thumped the stuck-up cow. And then I gave her the good news.

The little creep made all the appropriate noises, as you'd expect. She gushed on about how grateful she was for all the opportunities she'd been given, blah, blah, blah. But the more she said, the more hollow and insincere she sounded. Mystified, I choked her off sharply for the sake of my timetable.

I zipped through the next few staff. Smithies hadn't discussed these with me, because I'd arrived at the "right" answer without his intervention—I'd held them all back. They were disappointed, I sympathised, and they slunk off, no doubt to stick pins in a wax effigy of me.

Then came Ryan.

I'd sacrificed him like a pawn in a game of chess. Now, as he stood in my doorway, the multiple reflections of his sheepish grin filled me with guilt. It was as if he anticipated the impending disappointment, but believed that by putting on his best behaviour now, he might magically change the outcome.

Physically, Ryan was essentially an unfinished version of his older brother Greg—his asymmetrical features moulded by a less accomplished sculptor. To compound his physical imperfections, he wore his clothes sloppily, so that even a designer suit looked scruffy on him. But his troubles ran deeper still—his attitude was flawed too. Whatever Greg's faults, he had quickly identified that the nebulous quality of "gravitas" was essential for an Irishman to progress in life, and worked tirelessly to cultivate it. By contrast, Ryan basked in his role as the team's cheeky buffoon.

'No promotion—no pay rise?' he said, plaintively echoing what I'd told him. The news must have been hard to stomach, especially if he'd already heard that his girlfriend had scooped the jackpot.

'I'm afraid so, Ryan. If it makes you feel any better, there are plenty of your peers in the same position.'

'It doesn't make me feel better.'

'And in your case, the decision was extremely marginal.'

'Jesus,' he said. 'If it was so marginal, why didn't you let me through?'

'I'm sorry, Ryan, but you fell the wrong side of the line.'

'I hope this isn't your way of getting back at Greg.'

'What?'

I was astounded by this suggestion. Smithies had pretty much accused me of nepotism, and now here was Ryan claiming I was biased against him.

'You heard.'

'Ryan,' I said sighing. 'Do you seriously think I can't view your promotion objectively because I was once married to your brother?'

'Well, there's something behind all this I'm not getting.'

'For the avoidance of doubt,' I said, taking refuge in the protective mantle of Smithies' jargon, 'it has nothing to do with Greg. Even if I minded about Tiffany, which I don't, it wouldn't affect my judgement.'

Ryan seemed doubtful, maybe because he somehow recognised that Greg's remarriage did in fact rankle.

'So it's because I puked on your shoes?'

'You're kidding—that was last year.'

'But there must be a reason.'

'The reason is simple. We have to examine promotions extremely carefully in the current economic climate, and having considered all the evidence from the appraisal process, we couldn't justify your case.'

'Bullshit. I don't believe you.'

'What—that we have to examine promotions carefully or the case couldn't be justified?'

'I've pulled my socks up in the last twelve months—you said so yourself. I did a grand job on the hotel client spotting all those unclaimed allowances, didn't I? And on Project Rocket.'

'You did,' I agreed. 'But your appraisal grading was "meets expectations". You did what we would expect someone of your grade to do.'

'Which means there's no reason not to move me up.'

'No,' I said, shaking my head. 'It means quite the opposite.'

'But usually if you get meets, you automatically…'

'It's never been automatic,' I put in quickly. 'But you're right—we have been tougher with the promotions this year. And we told everyone all this beforehand.'

'I don't recall being told. If I'd known it'd be such a struggle to get moved up I'd have challenged my grading.'

'But you were very happy with it. Now let me see.'

I pulled up a copy of his appraisal form on screen and read.

'This was a fair grading and I'm keen to build on the progress I've made in the upcoming year.'

Checkmate.

'*What a lousy piece of shit you've become,*' came the little voice. '*I hate you.*'

I guessed I was lucky she'd kept quiet up till now. Who the hell was she, and what was her problem?

'You tricked me into accepting that appraisal,' said Ryan, with contempt. 'Greg always said you were cold, and he was spot-on.'

'Let's talk Monday when you've calmed down,' I replied, trying not to rise to the bait.

'Let's fucking well not.'

He walked out, disgusted at the idea, and leaving me to deal with my conscience.

But by Monday, Ryan's promotion would be the least of his problems.

6

The monthly group drinks was a Smithies innovation.

'You must do more to bond the team together,' he'd chided, having swiftly identified this as a "weakness" in my management skills.

In my view, we were close knit enough without any enforced jollities. But Smithies always put on an elaborate show of caring about his people and expected others to follow his lead. Reluctant to fight over such a trivial difference so early in our working relationship, I'd fallen in line.

Most of the team had now assembled in the tatty Fleet Street pub, where we'd hired the upstairs room. They'd laid on a plentiful supply of weary samosas and chicken drumsticks to soak up the unlimited free celebratory wine and beer.

It ought to have been a fun get-together, but for one small hitch. Few had cause to celebrate tonight.

'Damned if you do and damned if you don't,' Smithies had said unsupportively when I'd pointed out the poor timing. I was certain he'd known the party would clash with our pay review when I'd set the date. But instead of alerting me, he'd let me go blindly ahead. These sneaky, destructive little ploys were, I was rapidly learning, typical of the man.

He insisted on attending himself "to get a feel for the mood". That his mere presence might alter the dynamic had not occurred to him, but people were wary for sure. Smithies drank little alcohol, but often feigned intoxication to encourage others to shed their inhibitions. He then viewed their antics from a position of complete sobriety, while logging down the details to undermine them later. Sometimes he would even take pictures, to be exhibited (accompanied by jokey banter) at away days. But folks were quickly wising up to his techniques and besides, the low team spirits made high jinx unlikely tonight. In fact, it promised to be a depressing evening all round.

Mercifully, Ryan hadn't shown up. If he'd still been in the same truculent frame of mind, he'd have been a catalyst for discontent, perhaps re-enacting his projectile vomiting. I'd heard he and Isabelle had rowed furiously in the office and guessed he was sulking. Isabelle came though, but didn't look ecstatic, especially when Smithies advanced towards her.

'Jolly well done on your promotion,' he said, slapping her enthusiastically on the back. 'You must be thrilled.'

Her smile was convincing, if you didn't catch the melancholy in her eyes. She seemed sadder even than earlier in the day, so sad that I felt a momentary pang of sympathy for her. Maybe she'd twigged that as Top Banana there was only one place to go, or was still reeling from Ryan's obnoxious outburst. Either way, you would never have imagined she'd recently benefited from a massive hike up the greasy pole.

'Oh yes,' she said, in a flat voice. 'I really appreciate the opportunity—can't wait to get stuck into the new role.'

'Great stuff,' said Smithies, either not noticing or ignoring the non-verbal cues. 'Let's get something to eat, shall we?'

I wasn't hungry, but remembered his little dig about eating disorders. Shame to give him more ammunition.

'Yes, let's.'

'What a super attitude Isabelle has,' he said, piling food onto his plate, indifferent to its poor quality.

'Yes, super,' I replied, wondering if his comment was an implied criticism of me.

I estimated the minimum amount of food necessary to avoid appearing hung up about it, and picked up a chicken drumstick with a serviette. Instantly, I replaced it—without investigating too closely, it smelled unpleasant to me.

'Does chicken count as red meat?' he asked, proving he'd been aware of my preferences all along.

'I think it may be off.'

He sniffed at his own chicken.

'Seems alright to me.'

As if to underline his opinion of my judgment, he helped himself to a second piece.

'Your call—I'm not touching it.'

I took a few of the pastries instead.

'I suppose I ought to say something to Lisa,' he said, the precarious pyramid of food on his plate wobbling dangerously as he moved away from the table. I couldn't help but notice the lack of enthusiasm in his voice.

So far Lisa had been doing a brilliant job holding court in the corner with a huddle of disaffected junior staff. I admired the way she buoyed them up despite her own disappointment. Still, it was easy for her—she hadn't played any significant part in the tough decisions taken. If she ever made it to partner, she'd have to change her tactics. After all, it's not so easy to slag the bastards off if you're one of them.

'I am *so sorry* to hear the disappointing news on your partnership,' Smithies said, reinforcing the fiction that he was wholly disconnected from the process.

'Me too.'

'I trust Amy explained the reasoning behind the decision.'

'Oh yes, but we both know the real reason, don't we?'

'Indeed?'

'Yes, you think I'm a gobby cow.'

'I must fetch a drink,' I said, desperate to escape. Lisa's natural belligerence fuelled by an excess of wine was a potent combination—the conversation would be constrained only by her need for a reference. That meant glassing Smithies was out, but practically anything else was permissible. Listening to her rant would be insufferable.

'Ah well, it is Friday, isn't it?' Smithies replied, spotting my empty glass. 'Although you should take it easy—we don't want to stray off message do we?'

The implication was clear—he believed it was me who'd coined the phrase "gobby cow". And his snide little remarks about my drinking were beginning to grate.

Drunk or sober, I wasn't likely to stray off message. Smithies might not know it, but I could drink the bar dry to the point of falling over in a stupor but still stay on script. I was used to acting a part.

'Well, *I'm* going off message...' I heard Lisa say, and left them to it.

It may have been Smithies or the pervasive low mood, but by nine o'clock the last hangers-on were leaving, despite the lure of a free bar.

'No drinking stamina, this lot,' bellowed Smithies, in his pseudo drunkard's slur. 'You should have them better trained.'

'They weren't in the best of spirits.'

'Ah yes,' he said, draining the half pint of beer he'd been carefully eking out all evening. 'I told you the timing of this was questionable, didn't I?'

I was about to give a spirited and indignant response when I spotted Lisa hurrying towards me, carrying my jacket.

'We must go,' she said, without giving a reason.

'So soon?' replied Smithies, apparently crestfallen.

'Yes, we have to.' She steered me firmly towards the door.

Once outside, she rummaged in her bag for a cigarette.

'Bloody hell—had to get out of there before I killed that scumbag Smithies. And he was moving in on winding you up too.'

'Thanks for rescuing me.'

'Go somewhere for a last drink?' she suggested.

'And you tell me *I* put away too much booze,' I reminded her, as we strode purposefully towards Daly's.

'Oh never mind that now – you can always cut down next week,' she said. 'You've had a tough day, and I haven't made it any easier for you. But that lousy bonus wound me up. Anyway, I've got it all off my chest with Smithies now.'

We pushed through the throngs of Friday revellers to the bar, and ordered a bottle of Pinot Grigio.

'Hope you didn't go too much over the top,' I said, with little optimism. Didn't she realise her gung-ho approach would reflect badly on me?

She probably did realise, because she rapidly changed the topic of conversation to Isabelle.

'That self-satisfied little cow was acting a bit glum, wasn't she, despite her double promotion?'

'Guilty conscience.'

'Sorry, I've lost you.'

'Oh keep up, Lisa. She kept mum about Goodchild's mistake, didn't she? That's how she got the promotion.'

This had only just occurred to me as a rationale for Isabelle's muted reaction, but the more I thought about it, the more sense it made.

'Oh I doubt that's the reason,' said Lisa quickly.

'But you told me she knew…'

'I was speculating, that's all,' she replied, cutting me off abruptly. 'In fact, I'm thinking she and Smithies are having it off, and *that's* why he promoted her.'

I'd forgotten that the same idea had previously flashed through my own mind, but it still seemed just as ludicrous now Lisa had suggested it.

'No,' I said.

'They were in the archived file store together the other day, which was strange.'

Maybe not so ludicrous.

'I saw them in the canteen, and he gave her the eye in the brainstorming meeting.'

'There you go, it's obvious,' said Lisa, with a splendid disregard for the paucity of the evidence. 'But he's so gross though. How could she do it? And Ryan's so cute…'

'Ryan—cute? You wouldn't say that if you'd been a fly on the wall in his one-to-one meeting today.'

'Aw, cut the guy a bit of slack. You can understand him being sore, plus it must be so annoying to have a girlfriend as perfect as Isabelle.'

'Isabelle reminds me of the posh girls at school,' I said, using up most of the wine in pouring out two generous glasses.

'I wouldn't know,' she laughed. 'There weren't any posh girls at my school. Anyway, you're posh too.'

If only she knew the truth. At least Lisa never had to pretend she was anything other than a chavvy girl from Basildon.

'That's what you think,' I said, laughing hollowly.

Lisa stared at me, puzzled.

'I hate these cryptic little comments you keep making about your family. Wish you'd come out with it and tell me the whole story.'

'It honestly isn't important.'

'Aw—come on—if it wasn't important you'd share it.'

'Actually, it's so *unimportant* there's no need to explain.'

'Disagree—must be bad shit if you've fallen out with your mum forever. I mean, I fall out with my mum all the time, but we always patch it up.'

'Your situation's totally different.'

'But we're mates, aren't we? You tell your mates stuff—right?'

I wasn't used to having friends you got close to—my survival tactics had always involved keeping my distance. Hell, I'd told no one, not even the man I'd married.

'I'm sorry—I can't talk about it.'

But Lisa had no intention of letting it go, and continued interrogating me unabashed.

'Your stepfather tried it on with you?'

Oh, how I wished it were so simple. People "got" sexual abuse.

'No stepfather.'

'Or your mother's an alcoholic…'

'She's teetotal.'

'Or she beat you black and blue.'

'Wrong again.'

'I can't imagine what it is,' she wailed.

'No,' I said. 'You can't.'

I had erected a barrier in our friendship, but the more Lisa pushed, the more I resisted. And no, she couldn't imagine, because normal people lacked the capacity to do so. I wished she'd stop probing and prying and leave me alone. Nobody else asked me all these questions.

The wine disappeared disturbingly fast, especially given the amount we'd already drunk, but hey—it was Friday night, and it had been a stressful kind of day. Even so, although we were swaying slightly when we left Daly's, I felt almost sober. So what happened next took me utterly by surprise.

As we turned into Arundel Street to head for Temple Tube station, the last person I expected to see was walking towards us.

Me.

Not me as I am now, you understand, but me aged—oh about fourteen. At least, that was the age I remembered wearing the baby blue batwing sweater, black leggings, and the little preppy ballet pumps. I also vividly recalled the hooped earrings fully two inches in diameter. Ah well—you can't expect a teenager to have impeccable taste in everything. She had her hair tied back in a neat ponytail—clean and shiny—consistent with the tidy, middle-class image. But looks can be deceptive.

And I suddenly recognised the source of the pesky little voice that had been bugging me.

'You see that girl heading towards us,' I said to Lisa, tugging at her sleeve to grab her attention.

But Little Amy had already melted away.

'What girl, where?'

It seemed too silly to explain, too spooky even.

'Do you ever see things you know aren't real?' I asked. 'Or hear voices nobody else can?'

'Never.'

'You see, lately I've been feeling strange, seeing shadows and hearing voices, but now...'

Again, I hesitated to confide in Lisa, especially when she laughed and wagged her forefinger at me. 'Jeepers—you've definitely had one glass of Pinot too many tonight—me too, come to think of it. Time to go home.'

7

Try as she might, Isabelle couldn't take any pleasure in her promotion. And playing the part expected of her, knowing what she did, had been excruciating.

First there'd been Amy, brimming with barely concealed hostility. While Amy was never anything but uber-professional, Isabelle had always sensed an underlying resentment. None of these top women ever helped others up the ladder, but today had been the worst. Smithies must have twisted Amy's arm to deliver on his promise.

Ryan's reaction, though predictable, had been tough to take too. The way he'd mouthed off at her in the corridor had been mortifying. She understood that his male pride had been dented, and sympathised, but it didn't excuse his boorish behaviour. Trouble was, his angst ran deeper than resentment at her earning almost thirty thousand a year more than him. At the same age Greg, Ryan's brother, had also been awarded a double promotion and four years later he'd been made a partner. Ryan had spent his life trying to emulate his brother's achievements, yet perpetually found himself on the back foot. Isabelle's success merely underscored his failure. And when she'd tried to play it down, to hint at how she hadn't really deserved it, he'd gone ballistic, frightening her with his rage.

Then at the group drinks, everyone had congratulated her through gritted teeth, as she strained to act normal with Smithies…

Ryan wasn't picking up his phone—where the heck was he? Still mad, she guessed, and drunk. Drunk was bad news, because he'd taken the car. Unless he'd gone to visit Greg, which was always possible. She'd called Greg to check—he hadn't answered either but she'd left a message.

The knowledge that she'd come by her promotion dishonestly ate her up—this was the first time she'd cheated in anything in her life. But she felt even worse now she realised, too late, precisely what she'd got tangled up in. She was doing her best to correct the position, naturally, but handing back the promotion wasn't an option. Only living up to it would salve her conscience.

Isabelle popped open a beer. She seldom drank at home, but tonight she needed to slow the swirling vortex of negative thoughts threatening to engulf her.

The doorbell rang.

She opened it on the chain, although it was probably Ryan forgotten his keys. She loathed answering the door at night when alone in the flat. You read too many newspaper articles about dreadful things happening.

'Oh,' she said, 'It's you,' relieved but mortified to have been caught out in neurotic security precautions.

And she took off the chain and opened the door.

8

Home was a spacious Victorian terrace house in Chiswick, bought with Greg in a fever of optimism for the future. I'd joined Pearson Malone as a new partner six years before and met Greg at a conference. A year later we'd been married, and within three years we'd divorced.

I found it painful now to remember how happily it had all started. We'd had such great plans, Greg and I—the golden couple who'd produce amazing children and live the picture-perfect life I'd always coveted. The house represented a tangible symbol of the dream.

Interior design was a mystery to me. This surprised Greg—after all, as he pointed out, I dressed snappily enough. Surely decorating a house must require similar skills? Not really, I'd replied cagily.

Instead we hired designers and a few months later were surrounded by stylish furniture and dramatic colour schemes. The crowning glory was a futuristic kitchen with black granite worktops and sleek white cabinets, and filled with hi-tech gadgets. Most poignantly of all, we had decorated the nursery.

We threw dinner parties, with elaborate menus cooked by outside caterers. This concept of entertaining and proudly showing off the house was alien to me. But a few stiff gin and tonics reliably saw me through the ordeal.

Children were problematic, though.

Greg must have speculated about what terrible event had

triggered the estrangement from my mother—she'd even been excluded from our wedding. He may have suspected a link between this and my second thoughts about starting a family, but we never discussed it. Fact was, I dreaded passing down the crazy gene I felt sure was lurking somewhere inside me.

Greg came home one evening and announced he was leaving me for Tiffany, his blandly pretty twenty-one-year-old secretary. Our life together was so false I'd suspected nothing. Once I'd recovered from the shock, and the rage at Greg for becoming a walking cliché, relief kicked in. His departure had released the mounting pressure to tell him the truth, like a boil being lanced. At last I was free from the terror of being watched and found wanting.

When he left, he bought a much larger house several streets away and took much of the furniture with him. I'd heard Tiffany was pregnant, so Greg now had the life he aspired to and a mind-numbingly normal person to share it with. But despite the relief, it still hurt that he'd discarded me so callously.

I should have moved, instead of staying in a house that served as a constant reminder of an unattainable ideal. But I couldn't do it. Paralysed by fear and indecision, I rattled around in a beautifully decorated, semi-furnished house—its emptiness echoing the bleakness of my emotional life.

All in all, another drink was inadvisable, but in a physical act divorced from any brain activity, I poured an enormous gin and tonic. I flopped onto the sofa—lacking the energy even to get ice from the freezer. I told myself it would help me sleep—a flimsy excuse—I needed it to smooth the jagged edges off the day.

Just as I applied my lips to the glass, the doorbell rang.

I froze. Not that I'm an overanxious woman afraid to answer the door at night—I'm a deranged woman who hates unexpected visitors violating my personal space at any time. It was an anxiety hard to unlearn in a mere twenty years, but in a supreme effort at normal behaviour, I opened the door on the chain.

'Ryan. What a surprise,' I said, forcing a rictal smile.

Surprise was an understatement. Ryan had only visited the house a few times, and not at all since Greg's departure. On reflection, remarkably few people had visited since then.

'I was passing,' he said, 'on the way to Greg's.'

'Really?'

Funny how often he called on his brother now he was with that slag.

'OK, I drove over to see Greg, but Tiffany's away at her mother's, plus he's out somewhere and not answering his phone. Then I went for a few drinks and he still isn't answering.'

So you came to disturb me instead, I thought sourly.

'Aren't you going to ask me in?'

Leaving aside my visitor phobia, there were a couple of good reasons not to. Clearly, it would be unprofessional to invite a male staff member into my house so late at night. And if his dissatisfaction with his pay review wasn't the main reason for his visit, he'd be bound to raise the topic and I was in no state to respond.

'Sure,' I said, despite all the years of practice at shooing visitors away.

Once inside, Ryan stared, perplexed by the bareness of my lounge.

'You don't have much stuff, do you?'

'It's the way I like it.'

This was a semi-truthful answer. Although I did relish the vast expanses of open space, uncertainty over what to choose was the main reason for not replacing the furniture. All the lounge contained now was the sofa, a coffee table, the television and a lone picture over the fireplace.

'But this is a huge room.'

'What else do I need?'

'Well…' He wrinkled his brow. 'Nothing I suppose, but most people have ornaments, flowers, photographs, books… I mean, you had them before, when…'

'Greg took stuff when he left,' I said, although there'd been ample time for shopping in the two years since.

'Any chance of a drink?' Ryan cast around, as if the emptiness of the room might extend to the contents of the fridge.

'Hope you're not driving.'

I recalled Ryan's pride and joy, a 1977 Triumph TR7, in a ridiculous yellow colour—not for him a bland executive model. The quirky choice of car somehow symbolised all Ryan's troubles at work—despite all the fuss they made about diversity, if you were a white heterosexual male you were expected to fit the template they'd cut for you.

'Don't worry—I left the car round the corner from Greg's place, and it's not moving an inch till the morning.'

'OK, I'm having G and T,' I said, 'more of the G and less of the T. But I expect you'd prefer a beer.'

Unbidden, he followed me. I hate guests assuming they can wander at will in my home—from habit I suppose.

'Wow—I'd forgotten how awesome your kitchen is.'

'Yes, it is amazing.'

Ever since moving in, I'd always felt like a visitor at someone else's house, and nowhere more so than in the kitchen. My inability to cook, overlaid with a nagging suspicion that I was unworthy of such luxury, left me fearful of being exposed as an imposter. But tonight I viewed my surroundings through Ryan's eyes, for the first time allowing myself to take in its glamour without any sense of inadequacy.

I handed Ryan his beer and he took a hefty swig.

'Issy and I had a terrible row today,' he began.

'Yep, I heard. I'm sorry.'

'I think we're through.'

'Can't you patch things up?'

'No. I made some spiteful comments—and I was rude to you too.'

'It's OK—I understand.'

It had been totally unacceptable for him to swear at me, but I guessed the time to complain was long gone.

'Everyone thinks I'm sore because she got such a humongous pay rise and promotion, while I got nothing.'

'And aren't you?'

'Well—a bit pissed about that stupid line you drew above me, but best let that lie.'

He swilled down another mouthful of beer and gave a loud belch.

'But Issy's awesome,' he said. 'She royally deserved everything.'

'So what's the trouble?'

'When she told me, she played it down, saying she wasn't worthy of it—like she was worried I couldn't handle her success. It made me incredibly angry—the way she was pussyfooting round me.'

'I can see that might be annoying,' I sympathised. 'But you know what? When I told her, she didn't seem at all pleased. Maybe that's how she truly feels.'

'Yes, that's what I decided when I'd calmed down. Which is even worse, because you have to ask yourself—*why* would she feel that way?'

'Why do you think?' I asked, intrigued.

'The answer's obvious—she's been shagging Smithies, and she believes that's the only reason she got the promotion.'

My head spun. The small part of my brain still functioning screamed out a warning. If this was a serious allegation, it ought to be discussed sober. And if not—we shouldn't discuss it at all. But how funny he should bring it up.

Ultimately, curiosity triumphed over common sense.

'What makes you say that?'

'It sounds stupid, but she's been acting oddly—taking phone calls outside. And when I checked her phone, his number came up. I didn't think anything of it at the time, but now...'

The evidence in favour of this improbable liaison was mounting.

'Did she give any explanation for the calls?'

'Yes—she claimed she had an issue on a client.'

'Which one?'

'JJ.'

My brain whirred—Smithies shouldn't have been discussing JJ with a member of the client team, given his close relationship to the Finance Director. So either he'd broken the rules on client independence, or Isabelle had lied to Ryan.

'What issue?'

'It was about tax losses, but there was other stuff too I didn't hear properly.'

'There *was* a technical query over some loss relief,' I told him.

'So you reckon she was telling the truth?'

'For sure.'

I didn't necessarily believe the two words I'd just uttered with such certainty, but closing down the discussion now seemed the wisest course. I mean, who wants to report her boss for inappropriate behaviour with a team member?

'But why would she say she didn't deserve the promotion, if she hadn't done something dodgy to get it?'

'People are complicated, Ryan—and not always as confident as they appear. The explanation may be as simple as that. She's probably feeling hurt—she tried to open up to you about her insecurity and you blew your stack. Why don't you give her a call and try to smooth it over?'

He whipped out his phone.

'No answer,' he proclaimed after a short interval. 'Which tells me all I need to know.'

'You don't seriously think they're together now do you?'

Ryan didn't answer—he waved his empty beer bottle in the air.

'Shall we have another?'

I was already woozy from an excess of wine and gin, but before I could refuse he headed off to the kitchen, returning a few minutes later.

'Blimey, this is strong,' I said, after taking my first sip and finding it even more alcoholic than my own industrial-strength concoctions.

'Well, you did say more of the G and less of the T.'

He slumped onto the sofa and, filled with an inexplicable apprehension, I sat down tentatively beside him.

'And you,' he began. 'Are you as confident as you appear to be?'

For a moment, I lost my nerve. Had he, like Smithies, seen through to the inner Amy?

'Oh yes,' I replied, brushing it off. 'More so.'

'Then why keep so much of yourself hidden?'

'I don't keep anything hidden,' I lied, my defences rising.

'You do, and I never noticed before today, but you're so sad.'

'Not sad—not really.'

'I'm sorry if I gave you a hard time earlier.'

'You were upset and disappointed—I understand.'

'Is it really the economic climate?'

I switched back into professional mode.

'Honestly—yes. Five years ago we'd have promoted you, no question at all. And this isn't the end, Ryan—this doesn't mean we've written you off.'

'You're different from the others, Amy. You spout off all the corporate bullshit but underneath you don't believe it.'

'I don't think anyone believes it,' I laughed, gulping at my gin, 'neither the people who deliver it nor those on the receiving end.'

'But the others don't *care* whether it's true or not. You do care, and some would say it's a weakness, but I don't agree.'

'This morning you said I was cold…'

'That was meant to hurt you. Greg never said it either. But he always thought you kept secrets from him.'

'Only one,' I said, before I could stop myself.

'Something to do with your mother.'

'I'm no longer in contact with her—we don't get on.'

'Yes, I know, but why?'

In retrospect, it seemed extraordinary that Greg had never asked this question directly. But maybe it wasn't so strange. I'd constructed my whole life around avoiding awkward questions, not only avoiding answering them, but somehow making people reluctant to enquire. Only Lisa, in her fearless quest for the truth, had probed. Until now.

A strand of hair fell down over my face. Ryan gently flicked it back.

'You wouldn't understand.'

'Give it a go.'

'I can't.'

'Shame,' he said. 'Don't they say the truth will set you free?'

Strangely, the temptation to unburden myself to Ryan almost overwhelmed me. Perhaps the effort of holding onto a secret eventually became too much. But I checked myself—it wouldn't be appropriate to spew it out drunkenly to him now. And why discuss it anyway? Here I was, a successful professional woman—my mother's problems hadn't affected me at all—apart from those occasional silly dreams.

'Perhaps you're so sad because you can't be true to yourself.'

I paused for a moment's reflection, then sat bolt upright, as the full force of his insight hit me. He'd nailed it—this jokey little Irish wag. It physically pained me to hear him say it, but he was spot on. I'd been acting, one way or another, pretty much all my life, so much that I sometimes I questioned who lived underneath the veneer. All I knew for sure was that the real Amy didn't deserve the nice house or the mega job, so she had to pretend to be the woman who did.

But I couldn't admit any of this to Ryan.

'That's ridiculous.'

'No—it's not—it's the truth and you know it. I could see by the way you just reacted when I said so.'

He nuzzled up against me; so close I felt his breath on my face.

'I never realised you were so human before. I like that side of you—it makes me want to...'

'Want to what?'

Despite the strength of the signals, I could scarcely believe I was reading them accurately. A heady cocktail of fear and desire overwhelmed me as I sank back into the cushions of the sofa.

We hesitated, but the time for analysis and sober reflection had passed. Our lips met and my stomach lurched in anticipation of the inevitable.

Surely I should stop this madness...

***

I woke at eight to the sound of the front door banging shut. Ryan had gone.

The brutal force of my hangover floored me as I dragged myself out of bed. I crawled to the bathroom on all fours as if crippled, and gulped water from the tap on the bidet. It came straight back up, along with undigested scraps of the previous night's food. I sat on the floor, gasping for breath and filled with self-loathing.

Fragmentary but shocking memories jabbed at the edges of my perception. Ryan's tenderness had vaporised in the instant I'd regained my sanity and tried half-heartedly to push him away. He'd been determined to have me and prove which of us was the real boss. The inside of my thighs ached dully, as did the developing bruises on my arms where he'd pinned me down.

I'd been so weak—I'd surrendered. The Nicole Farhi dress lay in a wrinkled heap—yes, it had made me vulnerable alright.

What had possessed me to be so feeble and stupid? My brain had said no, but my body had overridden it—I'd allowed myself to be used, like a loser with zero self-esteem. I could have stopped him, should have stopped him…

And most shaming of all, I'd boosted his ego by enjoying the experience.

'Boy—you needed that, didn't you?' he'd said after it was all over, as though he'd done me a huge favour. And then, in a statement that simply begged for psychoanalysis, 'You're not the first woman I've shared with Greg, you know.'

I shuddered. Was that it, simply wanting what his big brother had already sampled? Even if it was only his sad old minger of a boss?

I pulled myself to my feet and peered in the mirror. Sad old minger was about right. My tangled hair lent a startling intensity to my wild, baggy, panda-rimmed red eyes, while fresh lines and wrinkles had etched themselves in my face in the dead of night.

'*You disgust me, you slag,*' said the little voice, from behind me. I turned, but Little Amy wasn't there.

I hoped to God Ryan wouldn't tell anyone.

9

In the following forty-eight hours my mind obsessively circled the same ground.

Easy to blame the drink—I must have been off my head to see the weird image of Little Amy. But alcohol didn't absolve me of responsibility—it only added to the shame at my stupidity. Letting Ryan into my home while plastered—what had I been thinking? The minute I'd opened the door I'd shown I was up for it. What a fool.

By Sunday, the humiliation was superimposed with a churning anxiety over what Ryan might do next. With luck, he wouldn't ever refer to the incident again, but even that possibility unsettled me. Once my bruises had faded, I might as well have dreamt the whole episode. Still, feigned amnesia was a better outcome than him bragging to his mates, or confessing all to Isabelle, or the Armageddon scenario of a harassment claim against me.

God—no.

On balance, a claim seemed a remote possibility. Despite equality in the workplace, men who reported women were still generally considered to be wimps. But Ryan might see a complaint as a tactical move to have his promotion reconsidered. And who knew, Smithies might even back him if it gave him a stick to beat me with.

No, the greater risk was of Ryan telling his chums, and me being landed with the reputation as the office slut, my authority irreparably weakened. The whispers would go round at lightning speed, quickly reaching Smithies' ears, and I'd be finished. Still what did it matter? I was done for anyway—six years must be time to move on—before they all saw that I'd climbed higher than I deserved to.

Several times I began to dial Lisa's number and stopped midway. Sure, she'd keep my shame a secret, but how do you admit to your protégée that you've fallen so short of your own standards? And heck, I'd been too feeble to stop Ryan when I came to my senses. Feisty Lisa would be appalled at my weakness.

I trusted no one else at work—my fellow partners were colleagues rather than friends, and several had ambitions to usurp my leadership role. The climate of suspicion created by our CEO not only prevented people from uniting to depose him, but made it impossible to trust anyone. I wished so much I had a close friend, someone unconnected with work, to confess my idiocy to. But close friendships didn't come easily to me, and nor did confessing my deficiencies.

So I toughed it out, unaware that Monday's events would render all my worst imaginings trivial by comparison.

***

I'd been in work for all of five minutes when I spotted Lisa ambling towards my office, carrying coffee for both of us and obviously keen to talk. I hoped she'd reflected over the weekend and decided to fight for her promotion after all, because the place would be unbearable without her.

She was almost at the door when a visibly distressed Ryan shoved her out of the way in his haste to reach me first.

'Piss off, Ryan,' Lisa said. 'Didn't anyone ever tell you it's bad manners to push?'

'I need five minutes to tell Amy something,' he shouted.

A sudden nausea hit the pit of my stomach. Ryan's appearance suggested he'd lain drunk in a gutter since Saturday. His red eyes hinted at raw emotions. Had I been responsible for this?

Lisa opened her mouth to protest, but Ryan cut in.

'It's bloody urgent,' he snarled.

Lisa gave me a knowing glance, smart enough to recognise when she was onto a loser.

'OK, keep your hair on. If it's so important, you go first,' she said.

She handed me my coffee, although I fancied I'd need something stronger to get me through this particular encounter. My heart pounded faster than on the early morning treadmill session I'd just endured.

I closed the door and invited him to sit down. The formality of the office setting accentuated the stupidity of Friday night's events, as everyone watched us through the glass with curiosity. Ryan's reflections in the mirrored panels embodied an infinity of anguish—an anguish of my creation.

'You look dreadful,' I told him, unhelpfully, as I braced myself for the coming outburst.

There was a long, painful silence while he fought to control himself.

'Issy's gone missing,' he said at last.

I held my breath. They'd rowed about me—she'd stormed off. Shit.

'Missing? Since when?'

'I'm not sure exactly—she arrived home after the party on Friday, because her jacket and phone and everything were inside the flat on the dining table. But when I got home last night, she'd gone.'

My mind raced.

'No contact during the weekend?'

'Nope.'

My relief was both profound and selfish as I discounted the possibility of any connection between her disappearance and my idiotic fling with her boyfriend.

'You said you got back *last night*? What were you doing since Saturday morning?'

'Now see,' he said, 'I spent the weekend with Greg, like I told the police.'

'The *police* are involved?'

'Yes—that's what you do when someone's missing—you report it to the police.'

'And you told them you'd been with Greg.'

'Yes.'

'But…'

'But nothing,' he said nastily. 'I stayed *most* of the time with Greg, after all. What the bloody hell difference does it make?'

Quite a lot, as it transpired.

'You didn't tell Greg about…'

'How can you be so egocentric? Issy's missing and all that bothers you is people finding out what a slut you are. Issy is *missing*,' he repeated. 'This is serious shit.'

'So where does Greg believe you were on Friday night?'

'Christ—will you shut up worrying about yourself.'

'I wasn't,' I lied.

'You don't get it, do you? No one has seen hide nor hair of Issy since Friday. She's gone—vanished.'

He spoke with deliberate slowness, as if to a foreigner.

'OK—I hear you. Are you sure she didn't go somewhere to cool off after your row?'

'I checked everywhere, and besides her phone was there, her handbag, jacket and everything. She wouldn't go out without her things. And the flat… it was different somehow. That's why I called the police.'

'I'm positive she'll turn up soon,' I said in a vain attempt to soothe him. 'Why—it's only just gone half nine—she might walk in here at any moment.'

'Believe me—she won't. To be honest with you, it looks like…'

He paused as he wiped away a tear from his face and gave a strange hiccupping sob.

'It looks like… she's been abducted.'

'*Abducted*?'

I hadn't meant to sound disbelieving, but the idea did seem farfetched.

'There's stuff the police told me not to mention…'

Until this point, I'd suspected Ryan of overdramatizing. Now, the gravity of the situation hit me full on. It wasn't Isabelle's style to flounce off and miss work. The suave little bitch would show up and put on a professional performance irrespective of her personal life. The police were taking her absence seriously, plus Ryan's grief was real and visceral.

'Is there anything I can do to help?' I asked, switching into my professional sympathy mode.

'Nothing, apart from keeping your mouth shut,' he said baldly.

***

'Charming,' said Lisa after Ryan had left. 'What the hell was all that about?'

'Isabelle's gone AWOL. He's beside himself.'

'I'm not surprised,' she said, 'after the way he spoke to her on Friday. But fancy little Miss Perfect being late for work, because of a row with her boyfriend...'

She didn't even try to conceal her delight at the prospect of Isabelle having blotted her copybook.

'Ryan says she's been abducted.'

'By who—aliens?' she snorted.

'Apparently she left her jacket behind, her bag, her phone. He's called in the police.'

'I say there's nothing in it—I'd put money on it. Remember the guy who went missing after his stag weekend?'

Despite my sense of foreboding, I chuckled at the memory. The police were involved then too, and we'd all been worried sick. Finally, it transpired that his friends had bundled his comatose body onto the Inverness sleeper train for a prank.

'This is different,' I said.

'But it's far too early to jump to melodramatic conclusions.'

It puzzled me that Lisa was so unconcerned. I felt much less breezy. With hindsight, there'd been some nasty undercurrents swirling around for a while, which we'd all been too blinkered to notice.

'Who said I was?'

'You seem tense,' she observed. 'Is everything OK?'

I tried not to wince as she patted my arm on the bruises.

'Apart from this, yes.'

'But you had that stressed, haunted look even before Ryan came in, like something freaked you out.'

I obviously hadn't done as proficient a job as I'd thought in pulling myself together.

'No—no I'm OK. Anyway, how are you?' I said, spinning the conversation around to a safer topic. 'I assume you came to see me for a reason. Have you changed your mind about leaving?'

'No—I came to tell you I'm definitely off—that pathetic bonus is the last straw. Why fight a foregone conclusion?'

Why indeed?

***

I figured Smithies should hear the news from me rather than a distorted version via the office rumour mill.

He was speaking on the phone when I arrived—his back to the door, and admiring his reflection in the glass. I took in the details of his office as I waited for him to finish his conversation.

The desk was bare, either in compliance with the firm's 'clear desk' policy or because he didn't have enough work to do. One of the glass wall panels had been replaced by an opaque partition, now filled by a jumbo-sized portrait of his wife and children water skiing—tanned, beautiful, smiling and perfect in every way. Naturally, the shot did not include Smithies—his flabby pasty body could only have detracted from the flawless image.

The biggest bastards often favour conspicuous displays of family photographs in their offices, in which everyone is invariably grinning as though auditioning for a toothpaste commercial. It's a psychological thing—a means of saying—hey get this, I'm a nice guy, my family is happy and if you don't like me it's your fault. Smithies had taken this concept to a new extreme.

The picture disturbed me on various levels, yet I found myself inexorably drawn to it as Smithies wrapped up his discussion.

'Don't you worry,' came his quasi-sympathetic nasal whine. 'She's got far too much on her plate to focus on the detail.'

Silence, as the person on the other end of the line no doubt protested. I hoped he wasn't talking about me.

He abruptly stopped preening himself in the glass and terminated the call when he saw me loitering.

'Must shoot now—let's talk later.'

He spun his chair round to face me.

'Can't you see I'm busy,' he snapped.

'Yes, but this is important. Thirty seconds of your time.'

'OK—but calm down for heaven's sake. You're making me tense just watching you.'

So he thought I was on edge as well. I would have to redouble my efforts to act relaxed.

Smithies greeted the news with an almost infinitesimal movement of the eyebrows—he might have been a professional poker player in a previous incarnation.

'I heard she and that cretin Ryan had a big row,' said Smithies. 'Perhaps that's why she went off.'

'Perhaps.'

His extra-sensory antennae twitched, detecting I had something new to conceal.

'*Remember*,' said Little Amy. '*You mustn't allow him to psych you out.*'

I appreciated the reminder and steadied myself.

'Frankly, I wouldn't be too worried at this stage.'

'I'm not worried—I just thought you should be aware, especially as Ryan's involved the police.'

'What a complete jerk that guy is—the police never act on a missing person report for the first twenty-four hours.'

'From what Ryan said, they've launched a full-on enquiry. And it's more than twenty-four hours anyway—it seems she went missing on Friday, after the drinks.'

'I still reckon they'll sit on it for a while.'

'Ryan says she's been abducted.'

'Really—well, you were one of the last people to see her alive. You didn't like her much did you…'

A wintry smile signalled that he was joking. But it made my flesh creep to listen to him talking as though she was dead.

'Not as much as you, no,' I replied, with obvious innuendo.

No flicker of a reaction.

'I suppose you've tried calling her?'

'What's the point? Wherever she is, her phone isn't with her.'

He tut-tutted.

'*I'll* try,' he said. Clearly, dead or alive, and with or without her phone, she wouldn't *dare* to ignore a call from him.

'Do you have her number?'

'It's on the system.'

With some effort Smithies brought the number up on screen and dialled. So either she wasn't on speed dial on his phone, or he was bright enough to pretend otherwise, I thought.

'Voicemail,' he pronounced.

'Told you.'

'Well, I'm sure she'll be back before long,' he said. 'Although this is completely inappropriate behaviour from someone who's been double promoted. Hope it hasn't gone to her head.'

Two things struck me about Smithies' reaction to the news. First, if he was having a fling with Isabelle, he hid it astoundingly well. And second, whether he was or not, he seemed blithely indifferent to her fate.

'By the way,' he said, as I was leaving. 'You were right about the chicken. Been puking up half the weekend.'

'What a shame,' I replied.

10

Smithies' confident prediction of police inactivity proved to be somewhat wide of the mark.

A gorgeous young professional woman had literally vanished into the night. Moreover, she'd had the presence of mind to do so when little else of substance was happening in the world. The media found the story irresistible and the police responded with a high profile public campaign. By Tuesday evening every TV channel was saturated with images of our star tax consultant, her parents, her boyfriend, and their flat in Ealing.

A media encampment was hastily established outside the flat, where white-suited forensics experts picked through the driveway with exaggerated care. Occasionally, the front door opened to allow the removal of bagged items, but otherwise all was quiet. Undeterred by the lack of activity, the TV stations eked out their coverage with endless speculation. And in the background to the BBC reporter's inane chatter, the equally mind-numbing drivel of his counterpart from Sky could be heard.

Cut to the press conference, and a Detective Chief Inspector Dave Carmody of the Metropolitan Police gave a pre-prepared statement to the assembled pack of reporters.

'Isabelle Edwards was last seen at a social evening with colleagues from the accountancy firm of Pearson Malone in the Victoria Pub in Fleet Street, London at around eight-thirty pm. She took the Tube to Paddington, the train to

West Ealing and then walked the half-mile to her flat in Drayton Green. We know she reached home because we found timed receipts from local shops, and we're examining CCTV images to try to piece together her movements. She was reported missing on Sunday night by her live-in boyfriend, Ryan Kelly, who worked at the same company, and who'd been away for the weekend. Isabelle failed to show up for work on Monday morning, which her family say is out of character.'

I'd spoken to Carmody earlier in the day about interviewing the team. Over the phone, he'd sounded imposing, but the camera did him no favours. Uneasy and stilted, he resembled an insolvency practitioner announcing a major receivership with many job losses. His eyes darted nervously, as if seeking out a friendly face.

'I repeat—we're satisfied that Isabelle arrived home, but have no information about her movements afterwards. We're appealing to anyone who saw her on her way home, or early Saturday morning, or indeed at any point over the weekend, to contact us.'

Cut to Isabelle's grieving parents sitting next to Carmody. The father delivered an emotional appeal for the safe return of his daughter, describing how precious to them she was. The Welsh lilt to his voice added extra pathos to his plea. Isabelle's mother managed to maintain her elegance and poise to begin with, but broke down when it was her turn to speak. She sounded properly posh between the racking sobs—so posh it seemed amazing she'd wound up married to a Llandudno solicitor.

The obvious affection of Isabelle's parents stirred a stab of envy in me. After thirty years I scarcely remembered my own father and as for my mother—enough said. If they lured that bat-shit crazy woman from her lair to plead for my return, I'd never come back.

'Isabelle, we love you—please get in touch, or at least contact the police to tell them you're safe,' said Isabelle's dad in conclusion. But his voice sounded defeated, as if he'd reconciled himself to the worst.

Alongside them sat Ryan, unshaven and scruffy, like someone sent from central casting to play the part of prime suspect. He stuttered over his own appeal.

I slurped at my gin as I stared at the screen in disbelief.

'You stupid idiot, Ryan,' I shouted. 'If Isabelle's parents can get their shit together, why can't you?'

'*Maybe he's involved*,' said the Little Amy voice. '*After all, he hurt you, didn't he?*'

I shuddered, suddenly conscious of my bruised arms again.

Carmody summed up as a contact number flashed up on the screen.

'This is a level-headed professional woman, who had no reason to disappear. She vanished last Friday, taking none of her things with her. We've explored all the obvious avenues and drawn a blank. Now we need help from you, the public.'

When fetching ice for a second gin, I checked my iPhone on the kitchen counter and discovered two missed calls and three messages. One was from Charles Goodchild, hoping Isabelle's absence wouldn't slow up the sale process. What a narcissistic twat—I would call him in the morning, if he was lucky. The other two were both from journalists—I guessed they'd got my name from Carmody.

I ignored the journalists, assuming someone else in the firm had dealt with them, until I heard the News at Ten. They specifically mentioned that Pearson Malone had so far made no comment, in suggestive tones implying that we didn't care or might conceivably be somehow involved ourselves.

I called the twenty-four-seven hotline to the firm's Media Relations team, hoping they would have everything in hand. But a recorded message provided a selection of alternative contacts, depending on your department. I was supposed to call Smithies.

I steeled myself and dialled his mobile. Voicemail. Keen to exhaust all avenues, I called his home number.

A woman, his wife I supposed, answered. She claimed, pleasantly and plausibly, that he wasn't around, but the pompous droning of his voice in the background nailed the lie. She offered to pass on the message "when he got back".

Now what?

Pearson Malone's attitude to media exposure verged on phobic. They had such a big name that any coverage, except for their own orchestrated PR blitzes, was unlikely to enhance it. Consequently the firm had established an elaborate protocol for media contact, which required the authorisation of either Media Relations or a designated senior partner. Nowhere did it mention what action to take when you'd exhausted the official channels, but the underlying principle seemed clear enough—if in doubt do nothing.

I would have left it there, had the BBC woman not called back.

Danielle was unmoved by my bleating about Pearson Malone procedures, and knew how to turn the screws to secure the quote she wanted.

'I'm *so* surprised no one from the firm has commented yet,' she said. 'If you made a quick statement it would kill all the speculation dead.'

'*What* speculation?'

'About why you guys haven't released a statement.'

'No comment,' I replied.

'Oh dear, that doesn't sound good. If we were forced to tell everyone you *refused* to comment...'

She left the implications hanging like an axe ready to fall.

'You *are* a partner of the firm after all, and Isabelle's boss.'

I wavered. Failure to follow firm's procedures was risky, but equally I might be criticised for not being resourceful enough if Pearson Malone came out of this looking bad.

What use was an emergency hotline which led to a dead end? Why did bosses who tried to micromanage the minutiae of your working day always leave you in the doo-doo when you really needed them? What was the point of being a partner in a global firm if you had no freedom to act? But this internal maelstrom was senseless—I had to decide.

We were all at a loss to explain Isabelle's disappearance, I said. She was a happy, popular and talented team member, whose professionalism and dedication to duty made her sudden departure all the more baffling. Her team were all frantically worried, and we urged her to make contact, whatever the reason she'd left.

No one would have guessed from this bland, impromptu little piece just how much I detested the smug bitch. And who could legitimately object? After all, I'd followed the time-honoured tradition of venerating the vanished. Isabelle was a paragon of virtue, a princess in terrible danger, and the media were lapping up the story. I prayed to a non-existent God that I'd made the correct decision. Pearson Malone kept a record of non-compliance issues, which they dredged up as evidence of your incompetence if they decided to fire you.

'Oh great stuff,' gushed Danielle. 'Lovely. Any chance of a sound bite to camera early tomorrow morning—show the caring face of corporate Britain? Perhaps standing outside your offices?'

The damage, if any, must have been done already, so I agreed.

The Telegraph also required a short statement. I detected a hint of annoyance at missing the deadline to go to press, but they promised to update the website instantly.

That night I dreamed of junk again. This time, a mass of old newspapers and rags barred the entrance to the underground station. As I attempted to flee, the pile collapsed on me.

As I woke, gasping for air, the image of Ryan thrusting naked on top of me sprang unbidden into my semi-slumbering mind.

'*Oh God, you slut—you're loving it—you wanted it all along. You're so horny.*'

And then he'd put his hands round my neck…

I sat up with a start. Where the heck had that come from—memory, imagination or a combination of both?

11

Like most people who've grown up in a dysfunctional household, I'm brilliant in a crisis. So after my morning TV appearance, I convened a group meeting.

At this point, the general excitement at being caught up in the eye of a media storm outweighed any anxiety about Isabelle. Everyone was still optimistic of a benign explanation for her absence and a safe homecoming. People worried more about the way the press had vilified Ryan.

I told them the police planned to spend all day interviewing the team, and in particular anyone who'd been at the social on Friday. I added "for the avoidance of doubt" that this would include me. In keeping with the human touch which had recently become such a virtue, I said I knew how "destabilising" all this had been for everybody. But we needed to keep focussed and professional, and positive nonetheless.

When I'd finished, I discovered a voicemail from Smithies.

'Drop by for a quick word when you have a minute,' he said. 'We need to discuss a couple of minor matters.'

Matters plural. I guessed he'd sussed out that my media contact hadn't been properly sanctioned—but what else could be on the agenda?

In his office, I glanced at the mural of the water-skiers. Their eyes twinkled triumphantly today, particularly the wife's. Wasn't I so plausible when I told you Ed was out—had you totally fooled? And check out my body—size eight, with pert boobs and washboard tummy—all effortless—aren't you jealous?

Of the abs perhaps, but not of her lying underneath Smithies' heaving sweaty torso and simulating ecstasy. Even the thought turned my stomach.

'OK?' he asked, keeping the obligatory inter-personals to a minimum.

'Fine, thanks.'

'We need to talk about Ryan.'

I stiffened—an involuntary physical response he must have noticed.

'What about him?'

'What do you plan to do?'

'How do you mean?'

My voice shook with nerves. Smithies paused—long enough to make me think he knew everything.

'It's vital we exit him—we have to get him off the payroll before the shit hits the fan.'

'What shit?'

'Oh wake up, Amy. What is wrong with you this morning? It's quite clear he's as guilty as hell.'

'Guilty of what?'

'He's killed her, can't you see that, or are you so blinded by your relationship with him?'

'What relationship?' I asked, the panic rising again.

'Because he's family, of course,' said Smithies, fixing me with a penetrating gaze.

My pulse fell back to normal.

'Aren't you jumping a bit ahead of yourself? We don't know yet if Isabelle is dead and still less if Ryan had any involvement. And HR will do their nut about firing someone with no evidence…'

'I'm amazed you're continuing to defend him. Even Greg thinks we should sack him.'

I doubted Greg had said any such thing, though God only knew why I should attempt to argue Ryan's corner, having seen a more sinister side to him.

'On what grounds?'

'Oh come on,' he said. 'You're an experienced partner, not a bloody first year trainee—I don't have to explain how the world works. We compromise him out.'

In other words, pay him off and make him sign an agreement not to sue the firm for unfair dismissal. Pearson Malone management hated compromise agreements because they cost money, but they were miles quicker than a disciplinary process. And in this case, speed was evidently of the essence.

'What happens if he's not guilty?'

'Amy, sometimes you can be so naïve,' said Smithies. 'The Boston Strangler would have performed better in the press conference. He's finished here, however this plays out.'

'But he hasn't even been charged!'

'We can't take the risk.'

British justice might be based on a man being innocent until proven guilty, but Pearson Malone operated to much harsher standards.

'OK,' I said, more to avoid further argument than because I agreed. 'I'll contact him to arrange a meeting with HR, if that's what you want.'

'It is. By the way—your TV appearance this morning was most impressive.'

'Thanks,' I said, bemused by the rare nugget of praise. I waited for the punchline.

'Just as a minor point, because I'm all for people using their initiative, that interview wasn't properly authorised, was it?'

'How do you know?'

'Because Media Relations was closed and you didn't speak to me.'

'I tried to call—left a message on your mobile.'

'Didn't get it—these voicemails are so unreliable.'

'And I called you at home—didn't your wife mention it?'

'Oh dear—it may have slipped her mind. Look, I'm tolerably relaxed, but Eric Bailey won't be if he finds out. He hates partners acting like loose cannons with the media.'

'But what I said was totally innocuous.'

'Completely,' he agreed. 'And I *do* sympathise.'

'I guess it's the principle.'

'Egg–zackly. But don't you worry—I'll do my utmost to stand up for you.'

It occurred to me that the only way Bailey would discover about the incident was if Smithies told him, but I thanked him like a moron nonetheless.

'Oh, and, Amy,' came his parting shot. 'Do try and relax a bit. You've been so tense recently, and everyone's asking why.'

Who was everyone? I wondered.

'I'm perfectly OK,' I replied curtly. 'And I'll keep you updated on Ryan.'

The water-skiers grinned in gleeful relish at my predicament. To fire my ex's kid brother within days of shagging him would be challenging under the best of circumstances. And meanwhile, Smithies had set me up for a bollocking from the CEO. Because the more I thought about it, it had plainly been slimy Smithies rather than Carmody who'd given my name to the press. With his usual cunning, he'd boxed me into a corner, driving me to break the rules or be slated for not using my judgement. He could have played it either way.

Back in my office, the menacing blink of the voicemail light on my phone greeted me.

Bailey. I prepared myself for the torrent of invective.

It never came.

'Just a quick message to say congrats on your TV appearance—you came across as very human and caring. Ed Smithies is rather agitated that you didn't jump through all the hoops, but don't take any notice. It's good to see that some partners in this firm aren't afraid to step up to the plate and use their initiative when it's needed. Thanks.'

I hadn't expected Smithies' treachery to backfire quite so spectacularly. But perhaps I shouldn't have been surprised. It detracted from our CEO's authority if his minions were able to predict his actions with complete accuracy all of the time.

Amy one—Smithies nil.

***

Despite that stroke of luck, I'd still plenty to cope with.

Lisa sensed my gloom, and suggested a morale-lifting trip to the Savoy for cocktails after work. I hesitated—the apprehension plaguing me stretched far beyond what a few drinks could fix, and I was still loath to confess my idiocy to her. But my half-hearted excuses failed to convince her.

I've always had a weakness for hotels. As a child, holidays had been a welcome respite. Then, the most basic guesthouse had seemed luxurious. But even now, plush hotels represented a life of glamour and grandeur that still, although money was no object, remained tantalisingly out of my reach.

I especially loved the Art Deco charm of the Savoy's American Bar, with its live pianist and splendid array of bottles above the bar. And because the place evoked a bygone era, it was acceptable, even appropriate, to feel a little wistful for what might have been.

'So—come on—what's eating you?' asked Lisa, as we contemplated the extensive cocktail list. A creature of habit, I always plumped for a gin martini with an olive. By contrast, Lisa chose a different drink every time.

I'd share some of my difficulties with her, I decided, but not all.

'I've been told to fire Ryan. Smithies has his orders.'

She raised her eyebrows.

'Talk about kicking a guy when he's down.'

'I know.'

'And typical of bloody Smithies to delegate the hatchet job to you.'

'Agreed.'

'It won't be a popular move—there's no way anyone thinks Ryan's got anything to do with this.'

Surprisingly, that was true. Despite his creepy performance on TV, and his demonisation in the press, nobody truly believed Ryan might be a murderer, except for Smithies and possibly me.

'That's irrelevant, according to Smithies. Harsh as it sounds, Ryan's forever tainted by this.'

'Oh well, best get it over with and move on,' she advised. 'It's not the first time you've had to fire someone you didn't want to.'

'It's easier said than done,' I replied, as the waitress took our order. 'Ryan's disappeared as well. He's not answering his phone or responding to emails.'

'That's hardly surprising. He sees you coming a mile off.'

'I even called his mother to try to track him down.'

'Wow—your ex mother-in-law,' said Lisa, stunned. 'How did *that* go?'

'Chilly.'

Chilly was an understatement—she'd told me I was the last person in the world Ryan wanted to speak to before hanging up on me.

'You sure nothing else is worrying you?'

She scrutinised me with the discernment of someone who understood me too completely for comfort.

'Totally.'

'There's something, I can tell. And Smithies knows it too,' she added darkly.

'What—did he actually say so?'

'Well, he's aware we're friends, obviously. He asked if you were OK. I said yes, as you'd expect.' She paused. 'I lied though, didn't I?'

Shame pricked at my conscience. Lisa, who never lied, had put aside her principles and defended me to Smithies. I guessed I owed it to her to come clean.

The waitress set out the drinks, along with an eclectic assortment of nibbles.

'The thing is,' I said when she'd gone, 'firing Ryan is a bit trickier than you imagine.'

'Go on.'

She took a long swig of a strange pinkish confection known as a 'Blushing Monarch.'

After a fortifying glug of my own drink, I poured out the whole story, omitting only how rough he'd been.

'Wow,' she said, when I'd finished. 'These people skills courses don't seem to cover firing someone you've just shagged.'

And you couldn't help feeling there must be a reason for that.

'I never even knew you fancied him… I mean, when I said he was cute…'

'I didn't fancy him, except in the moment.'

'You were in a bit of state, saying shadows were watching you…'

'Yes,' I agreed, clutching at the easy defence. 'It was a stupid drunken lapse.'

'Have you told anyone else about this?' Her drink had gone in an instant, and with an imperious click of her fingers, she summoned the waitress to order another.

'No.'

'But the police must be aware he was at yours on Friday night?'

'No—they're not. He told them he stayed the whole weekend at Greg's.'

'He lied to the police,' she said, shocked. 'You've got to ask what he's hiding.'

'You said he was innocent just a moment ago.'

'This changes things. An innocent man would be keen to establish an alibi. Anyway, I guess you'll set them straight.'

I blushed. And she stared at me aghast.

'Seriously? You must be crazy…'

'Ryan wants me to back him up and it'll look bad if I give a story that's not consistent with his.'

'That's his problem, not yours.'

'But I feel…'

'Never mind how you feel. Suppose he's charged with murder and you're caught out in a lie—that's not a great place to be. It'll come out whether you lie or not, probably in court.'

I hadn't yet considered the possibility that this silly episode would be aired in a public courtroom. But now Lisa had pointed it out in her trenchant way, a strange queasiness came over me.

12

Thursday dawned—still no sign of Isabelle. The gloomy assumption that she must be dead gradually gained credence and hung like a pall of gloom over the team. In the afternoon, I watched a second press conference live on my computer. This time her parents spoke of her in the past tense and Ryan was conspicuous by his absence, forcing Carmody to deny that he was a suspect.

Detective Sergeant Holland came to interview me—a moon-faced guy who beamed engagingly through our meeting while showing remarkably little interest in what I had to say.

I answered him truthfully when he asked about my movements on Friday evening. At no point did he ask if I'd received a visitor and I saw no reason to volunteer the information. Lisa's advice would have been sound enough if Ryan had been a suspect, but he was not. In that case, what did Ryan's whereabouts matter?

He passed me a list of telephone numbers.

'Do you recognise any of these?' he asked. 'It might save us some time.'

I assumed they'd come from Isabelle's phone. There was no indication of when the calls had taken place, whether they'd been made or received, or how many of them there were—just a list without names.

'Yes—a few of them. That's Ryan's, and Greg's mobile, and Lisa's and Ed Smithies.'

Isabelle had a reason to be in contact with all those, except maybe Smithies. I speculated again about an affair, or worse.

'Did you interview Smithies?' I asked him.

'Oh yes, we found him most helpful.'

I pictured Smithies fawning around the police team, while giving away nothing.

'Did he say why he'd been talking to Isabelle?'

'Client matter.'

'Oh—I didn't think they worked on any clients together.'

This was untrue, but the temptation to subtly insinuate that Smithies might be in some way involved proved irresistible.

'He said they did,' replied DS Holland, leafing back over his notes. 'But we'll double-check. Are any other numbers familiar to you?'

'No—none.'

'Is there anything else you wish to add to your statement?'

I faltered. Surely this was the moment to explain? But instead I found myself expressing my bemusement at Isabelle's lack of pleasure in her promotion.

'Perhaps she found it a bit awkward, with the boyfriend, or her peers?' he suggested.

'Yes—that's possible.'

Or if she'd come by it dishonestly, I thought.

'Anything else?'

'No,' I said quickly.

'Well, do get in touch if anything springs to mind.'

'Yes,' I promised, avoiding his gaze. 'I will.'

At around seven pm DCI Carmody arrived at my office and greeted me with a firm but not bone-grappling handshake.

He was perceptibly relieved to have another press briefing behind him. This one had seemed tougher than the first—he'd dealt with some aggressive questions from the assembled throng of journalists, particularly about Ryan. In the flesh, Carmody showed no hint of the stilted hesitancy he'd displayed on screen—he stood taller and sounded more authoritative. With enquiring eyes and an aquiline nose, he resembled an intelligent budgerigar. His on-trend suit—most likely M&S upper end—was set off with a pink button-down collar shirt and coordinating tie. The whole ensemble screamed 'I am not a boring policeman' a tad too loudly, but I could forgive him that.

'Just dropping by to say thanks for letting us interview everyone. It's saved us a huge amount of time.'

'No worries.'

'Do you fancy going somewhere for a glass of wine?' he asked, out of the blue.

'What, now? Surely policemen aren't allowed to drink on duty?' I replied inanely, fearful of a hidden agenda.

'There's a whole team running this enquiry you know. I'm entitled to some time off.'

'OK then—how does Daly's wine bar sound—it's only round the corner?'

***

'You're much prettier in real life than on television,' he observed, as we moved into a booth vacated by another couple.

I relaxed. Maybe there was no hidden agenda. The experience with Ryan had left my confidence in tatters, so the idea Carmody might find me attractive cheered me more than the first sip of wine.

'Strange—I was thinking the same about you. Mind you, seven am isn't my best time.'

'I don't much enjoy these press conferences. I guess it shows.'

'Perhaps you need more practice.'

'Believe it or not I've been on the media training course—twice—they failed me the first time.'

'If I'd taken a course I'd have failed too.'

'I doubt it. You're very poised.'

It always amazed me how everyone bought into the myth of my supreme self-assurance—Smithies alone intuited the insecure confused mess lurking beneath the façade. Public speaking never troubled me at all. But then again, why should it, when putting on an act was second nature to me?

'Thanks—but it's a hell of a lot easier to do a short pre-prepared piece than deal with all those reporters firing questions at you. Some of them were positively hostile.'

'Yes, but I've got to get to grips with it—don't want to give them another reason to block my promotion.'

'What reason have they given so far?' I asked, hoping for some new weasel words to fob my people off with.

'Lack of operational experience.'

'That one isn't in the Pearson Malone lexicon yet—at the moment "the current economic climate" is the favourite excuse.'

'Another familiar sounding phrase,' he replied, smiling at the memory.

'But this case must help you?'

'Without a doubt. But it's terrible, isn't it? This poor girl is almost certainly dead and I can't help thinking what a great opportunity it is for me.'

'At least you're being honest, though.'

There were plenty who'd claim they hadn't given their promotion a second thought. Pearson Malone was stuffed to the gills with such altruistic liars.

The conversation flowed so naturally that when we hit choppy waters, he caught me off guard.

First my mother.

He casually mentioned how he'd been found abandoned as a baby and had no clue who his parents were. What a hideously personal disclosure for a first meeting, I thought—we weren't even on a proper date. But all the same I admired him being so upfront.

'Does it upset you?'

'No, not at all—it frees me to be myself. Although it can get a bit freaky when doctors ask me for family medical history. I mean, suppose I have a horrible inherited illness that's destined to catch up with me, or some mutant gene waiting to be triggered?'

'I can't see that's worse than *knowing* some crazy genes are lurking in there somewhere.'

'Why—do you have crazy genes?' he asked, with a laugh.

I batted away his question with the vaguest allusion to my mother's deficiencies. I'm sure he would have probed further, had an acquaintance of his not approached our table. The newcomer looked to be mid-forties, although his beard made it hard to be precise. He wore a classy leather jacket, Rolex watch and jeans too tight for incipient middle age.

'Darren,' Carmody said, standing up and shaking his companion's hand with unnatural enthusiasm. 'How the devil are you?'

'Pretty good. And I see you're at the forefront of the media these days—a bit more poised than on that course we attended.'

'Can't complain. What are you up to at the moment?'

'Oh—this and that,' Darren replied. His body language appeared defensive, as if he was keen to terminate the conversation.

'Like what?'

'A few different business ventures, but you don't want to hear about that now. I can see you're busy, so best leave you be—catch you around sometime.'

'For sure.'

And before Carmody could even say goodbye, Darren was gone.

'Who was he?' I asked.

'Someone I used to work with. I wonder what line he's in now—he's clearly prospering.'

Somehow I doubted if he would ever find out.

The distraction had allowed the discussion about my mother to be conveniently dropped, but the topic that replaced it proved to be even trickier.

'Isabelle's boyfriend, Ryan Kelly, he's your ex-husband's brother isn't he?'

'You're well informed.'

The first pinprick of discomfort punctured my positive mood.

'What's he like?'

It was a difficult question in view of recent developments. I attempted to respond as I would have done a week before.

'Who—Ryan? He's cheeky, easy-going—bit of a buffoon. Youngest boy in a large family—spoilt—idolises his eldest brother, my ex.'

'Pretty much what we've heard,' said Carmody, without revealing his sources. 'Are you particularly close to him?'

I tensed. What had prompted him to ask?

'Not particularly.'

'But you wouldn't say he has an unpleasant streak to him?'

'I wouldn't say so—no,' I replied, choosing my words with care.

'I don't suppose you could tell me where he is?'

'Why? Don't you know?'

'No.'

My niggling doubts gathered pace.

'I'm sorry. I wish I could help you—I've been searching for him myself to set up a meeting with HR.'

'Firing him, are you?' said Carmody, instantly grasping the point.

My cheeks flushed.

'I don't agree with it,' I explained hurriedly. 'But they're jumpy as hell in case he's implicated.'

'And in your opinion, is he implicated?'

Before last Friday, I'd have defended him without question, but now I paused before answering.

'I would have said not. Anyway, why are you asking me? You just told everyone he wasn't a suspect.'

He appraised me with those cold grey eyes, evaluating my judiciously worded responses.

'As a matter of fact, I didn't want to share my thoughts with the press at this stage, but we're rapidly rethinking our views on Ryan.'

'Oh.'

Bugger—that changed everything. And why was he sharing that information with me?

'Tell me—do you work on a client called JJ Resources?'

'Yes,' I said, bewildered by the apparent switch in subject.

'And recently you had a glitch on the account?'

'Yes, but nothing serious.'

'Not a fraud?'

'No—absolutely not.'

Only now did I cotton on. This was no friendly drink or quasi date, but an opportunity for Carmody to pump me for information. Ryan had told them about Isabelle's phone calls, perhaps in an attempt to deflect attention from himself. Now Carmody was cross-checking with me. But fraud? How had that idea popped into Ryan's head since last Friday?

I drained the last of my wine, bitterly regretting my earlier caginess with the detective sergeant. I'd answered his questions—no more and no less—in retrospect, a breathtakingly idiotic tactic. He may even have picked up on my shiftiness and mentioned it to Carmody, giving him another reason to quiz me.

'There's something I ought to have mentioned earlier,' I began, bowing to the inevitable.

'What?'

A torrent of words gushed out from my mouth, words having no connection with the thoughts swirling round inside my mind. Carmody listened, poker-faced, having dropped any social pretence for the meeting with indecent haste.

I left nothing out, apart from the bruising, not because it painted Ryan in a bad light, but because it defined me as a victim.

'Why didn't you tell DS Holland this?' asked Carmody, perplexed.

'Um, I'm sorry,' I mumbled. 'He didn't ask. It is rather embarrassing and it didn't seem relevant.'

'But it's relevant now you know Mr Kelly is a suspect, isn't it?'

'Well, yes, I suppose it you could say it's now germane to the enquiry.'

'It always was,' Carmody replied.

'I see that now—I'm sorry.'

'Would you be prepared to come into the station tomorrow to make a formal statement?'

'Sure. What time?'

'Say one pm?'

'OK.'

I glanced at my watch—nine-ten pm.

'I must go,' I said. 'Thank you for the wine, and it's been nice chatting to you.'

'Likewise,' said Carmody, in a lukewarm tone.

I rushed out of Daly's towards the Tube station. Only the knowledge I'd done the right thing, if rather late in the day, saved me from complete humiliation.

Yet in a curious way it had come as a relief to discover Carmody had no romantic agenda. It would have been like Greg revisited, the constant building pressure to explain, the stress of hoping he didn't spot my weirdness, of masquerading as someone else. It was tough enough to sustain a convincing front throughout the working day, but keeping up the pretence twenty-four-seven was impossible.

As I reached The Strand I heard footsteps behind me. There was no logical reason for anxiety, but I quickened my pace. My pursuer speeded up too.

I glanced behind me.

***

'Bloody hell—Ryan—you nearly frightened me to death, jumping out at me like that. Where did you spring from anyway?'

Fact was, I didn't feel much calmer now I knew who'd been in pursuit.

'I was in the coffee shop next door to Daly's waiting for you to come out.'

His breath stank of something much stronger than coffee and his voice held a threatening undertone.

'You were following me?'

'Need to talk to you.'

'No—*I* need to talk to *you*—I've been trying to get hold of you, in case you hadn't noticed.'

'Who'd want to answer those shit-formal messages CCD in to HR? I'm not dumb—it's obvious you want to fire me.'

'But where the hell have you been?'

'What did you tell him?' Ryan demanded, not answering my question.

I was wary of hanging around on the street. Carmody would be out of Daly's as soon as he'd paid the bill and would surely see us together.

'If we can go and sit down somewhere I'll explain. You hungry?'

'Not much, but I guess I should eat.'

With a sense of purpose, I steered him in the direction of Pizza Express.

Once inside, Ryan scanned the restaurant nervously, as if anxious about being recognised. But everyone was far too wrapped up in the minutiae of their own lives.

'What did you say to Carmody?' he asked again, after we'd ordered pizza and beer.

'The truth—everything.'

His face fell.

'Oh great. So I've just been caught out in another lie, when they're gunning for me anyway. Can't you see how disastrous that is for me?'

'But surely it helps you, it's an alibi.'

'I don't need a bloody alibi, because I didn't do anything. This is a total nightmare. My girlfriend's dead, which is bad enough. I can't go home because the place is crawling with forensics experts and every bloody TV station from Sky News to Al Jazeera. The media have condemned me, judge, jury and executioner. Her parents think the worst—they never liked me anyway. Hell—even my own family suspect me.'

'There's no proof that she's dead,' I reminded him.

'So you keep saying.'

Tears coursed down his cheeks, and he wiped them away with his sleeve, without regard for appearance.

'Everyone's got it in for me,' he sobbed. 'Whatever I do proves I'm guilty. I didn't cry at the press conference—I didn't look the family in the eye. Ha—he's dodgy—he did it. And if I had cried, they would have called them crocodile tears—wrong either way. How do you think I feel?'

'Dreadful.'

'Do you honestly believe I would harm a living soul?'

A week ago I'd have answered no without hesitation—but my yellowing bruises told a different story.

'Got to say, you were a bit rough with me the other night.'

'Jesus Christ, will you shut up about that,' he shouted, banging his fist on the table. 'It meant nothing—OK? I wouldn't have done it with you if I'd known it was such a biggie for you. When you came onto me like that, I thought there must be a different guy in your knickers every night.'

'You came on to me, and remember, I tried to stop you.'

'Nah—you were up for it. You *said* no, but you were gagging for it—a guy can tell. And now you're guilty because you were so dirty, and that's where all this is coming from.

Fair enough, we shouldn't have done it, but we did, and we can't change the past.'

And nor could we change his perception of it.

'So you say you were caught out in a lie,' I said, keen to switch subject.

'Bloody Greg. You'd expect your own brother to cover for you, wouldn't you? He could easily have told them that I spent all night Friday with him.'

'But it wouldn't have been true.'

'Who would have known any different? I had to change my story because of him.'

'To what? Apparently not the truth.'

'I told them I slept in the car overnight.'

'It was crazy to lie again. Why didn't you just tell them you stayed with me?'

'I don't want Greg to find out.'

'Neither do I. Believe me, I don't want *anyone* to know.'

'I guess it would have been easier to come clean in the first place,' he admitted, as our beers arrived. 'Now they think I'm covering up something terrible, and there's no way out.'

'Not necessarily,' I said, slurping at my beer as though it was the first drink of the evening. 'If you go to the police now and tell the truth, everything will be fine. You can say I asked you to lie to save my reputation, if you like.'

I omitted to mention what Carmody had told me about Ryan being a suspect—I sensed it might have tipped him over the edge. But I honestly did believe he could still put everything right.

'Seems to me like no one cares what's true and what isn't,' he said gloomily.

'What do you mean by that?'

'I'm convinced whatever happened to Issy is connected with JJ—those phone calls. I did tell them, but they're not interested. That's what I need to discuss with you.'

'There's nothing worth discussing. Like I said before, the business with the tax losses wasn't important.'

And in any case how could it be linked with Isabelle's disappearance? If indeed she knew of Goodchild's mistake, she'd already demonstrated she had no plans to disclose it. She posed no threat to anyone.

'But I've been thinking about the rest of it—the stuff I couldn't quite hear. There were lots of calls, and I'm sure Issy mentioned some kind of dodgy business at the slate mine, something about debtors. I'm thinking maybe she found something and that's why they killed her.'

Now Carmody's line of questioning made sense, but Ryan's story sounded weak and implausible. An affair between Isabelle and Smithies seemed a much more reasonable explanation for the secret calls.

'You didn't say anything about this on Friday.'

'I'd forgotten. But I've been racking my brains since Issy disappeared and it kind of came back to me.'

'If Issy had suspicions, why didn't she speak to me about them?'

'Perhaps she didn't trust you,' said Ryan sharply.

'So why didn't she tell you?' I retorted.

'You reckon I'm making this up, don't you?' he said as the pizza arrived.

'Frankly, yes.'

'But suppose I'm right?'

'Then it'll emerge in the investigation.'

'That's just where you're wrong, because no one gives a shit.'

'Have you spoken to Greg?'

Greg was, after all, advising on the disposal of JJ.

'He's the least interested out of anyone. The last few years have been tough for mergers and acquisitions. He's maxed out on his borrowings to buy his new fancy house and they're shedding Corporate Finance partners like there's no tomorrow. He *needs* the Megabuilders deal to go ahead.'

No doubt he did, but in all the time I'd been with him, I'd never known Greg to compromise on ethics.

'I'm sure that wouldn't affect his judgement. More likely he reckons there's nothing in it.'

'Or he's shutting it out.'

'I don't get why you're telling me all this,' I said.

'Don't you? Really?'

'No.'

'Well, I'd like you to help me.'

'With what?'

'Can you have a dig around the client papers, give me your honest opinion?'

What a cheek. I mean, he'd practically raped me, tried to hold me responsible, and now here he was asking for a mega favour.

I laid down my knife and fork—my appetite had disappeared. Digging round would benefit no one, least of all me. If I did identify any irregularities, Greg would be livid, and Eric Bailey had a terrible habit of shooting the messenger. At best, I would be forever marked as the one who derailed the JJ sale. At worst I would be 'counselled out'.

Yet as Ryan sat there, anxious and defeated, I pitied him despite everything. My gut instinct still told me he was innocent, and it was a bizarre story for him to make up. So I quashed my doubts and agreed.

'OK, but on one condition.'

'Name it.'

'You contact the police first thing tomorrow and tell them the whole story.'

'Consider it done,' he said.

It occurred to me after we'd parted that I hadn't progressed the meeting with HR. Still, perhaps there would be no need for it once Ryan had established his innocence.

13

But overnight, the game changed.

At five forty-five am, a dog-walker found the fully-clothed body of a young woman floating in the Grand Union Canal, near a quiet cul-de-sac in Southall. A fresh media base was speedily set up outside the cordoned off area—with all the TV stations competing to bring a novel twist to the breaking news. Uniformed police searched the surrounding grassy banks with wooden poles, although what they sought remained unclear.

Carmody made a brief statement, explaining how it was much too early to comment on the cause or circumstances of death. Although a pathologist was attending the scene, the post mortem would take place the following day. He also added that CCTV footage from the Uxbridge Road was already being studied. He confirmed that Isabelle's parents had been informed of the developments—they were naturally extremely distressed and everyone's thoughts were with them at this trying time.

Cut to the front of the Pearson Malone offices. An oily-faced Smithies stood, petrified, as if facing a firing squad rather than a camera. Like a goldfish out of water, he gulped his way through a stilted pre-prepared statement. His hands shook as he read from the piece of paper, his voice rendered even shriller by nerves.

The enjoyment of seeing him making a complete tit of himself was short-lived. When I checked my iPhone, which had been on silent overnight, I saw nine missed calls (five from Smithies) and four voice messages, in chronological order.

1. A journalist from Sky asking me to do a sound bite
2. A pleasingly anxious 'where the hell are you?' from Smithies
3. Danielle from the BBC hoping for a statement (PM had offered her the guy who'd been on Sky, she said, but they'd much prefer me)
4. Smithies asking if I'd heard the news

They could all wait. First I called Ryan—no reply. So I texted him.

Terrible news – thinking of u. Did u speak to police as agreed?

Seconds after I'd pressed the send button, as though on cue, a breaking news item flashed up. Police had arrested a twenty-five-year-old man at a hotel in central London. He hadn't been named, but I knew it was Ryan.

My phone rang.

Smithies.

'Where the bloody hell are you?' he barked. 'I've been trying to contact you for the past hour.'

I wasn't obliged to justify myself. The clock showed seven forty-five, and those bastards didn't own me twenty-four-seven.

'Sorry—had my phone on silent.'

'I suppose you've heard by now.'

'Yes—dreadful, I don't know what to say.'

'Well, say nothing then,' snapped Smithies. 'I do wish you'd been more accessible this morning. Eric Bailey is hopping mad that you weren't available for media comment.'

Doubtless Bailey's annoyance stemmed from Smithies' ham-fisted performance, but it didn't seem wise to say so.

'Yes, I'm sorry. I'm available now if you need me...'

'I don't. In fact, Bailey has said he'll be handling the media personally going forward and if you get any requests you are to ignore them. Is that understood?'

'Crystal clear.'

'This is a delicate situation and we can't risk making it any worse.'

'Of course not—I understand.'

Relief trumped my irritation at being censured for Smithies disastrous performance. I had enough stress in my life without having to psych myself up for the TV cameras.

***

An air of suppressed hysteria pervaded the office. Many people were scrutinising the BBC and other news websites, but quickly flicked them off their screens when they saw me approaching. The earlier excitement had evaporated in the sober face of a death and the arrest of one of their own. For although Ryan's name had not been officially announced, the internet buzzed with rumours.

How, people asked themselves, could a murderer have mingled among them without them realising? And whereas earlier in the week the prevailing mood had been in Ryan's favour, now no one gave him the benefit of the doubt—least of all Lisa.

'So the alibi you provided for Friday night didn't cut the mustard.'

Her 'nudge-nudge, wink-wink' attitude chafed, but it was only a foretaste of what I'd be compelled to endure when the exact nature of Ryan's alibi became public knowledge.

'Do you really think he did it, Lisa?'

She wore a lovely dusky blue skirt suit and silk blouse that screamed out 'job interview'. See, she could dress properly when she needed to. I felt a pang of guilt that despite my promise, I'd done nothing to get her promotion back on track—I should rectify that.

'I reckon he did. Lost his rag and killed her in the heat of the moment.'

Lisa's instincts were normally sound, but I had my doubts—the modus operandi simply didn't fit with my understanding of Ryan's personality. It was difficult to visualise him calmly bundling a body into his car and driving to Southall, before calling on me, and everything else. He would have rung for an ambulance in a total funk, claiming there'd been a terrible accident. Even if he had dumped Isabelle in the canal, he would certainly have cracked before the weekend was out. And his panic-stricken performance on Monday morning surely couldn't have been anything other than genuine.

Lisa didn't agree.

'For all we know, he may have confessed.'

'I shouldn't think so, based on what he told me last night.'

'You saw him last night? Really?' she said, wide-eyed in amazement and no doubt hoping for further salacious details.

'Only to discuss the HR meeting.'

'Too late for that now.'

I ignored this statement of the obvious.

'Actually, Ryan said something strange.'

'What?'

'This may sound odd, but did Isabelle mention anything about a fraud at the JJ slate division?'

She wrinkled her nose.

'A *fraud*? No—we had the disappearing tax losses, but nothing else. Why?'

'Ryan thinks Isabelle may have discovered something dodgy at JJ a few days before she went missing.'

'Isabelle never said a word,' Lisa replied quickly. 'It has to be a smokescreen.'

On balance I agreed, and Lisa had reinforced my decision not to overexert myself honouring my promise to Ryan. But Fate intervened, as she often does.

A cluttered office disturbed me, and I'd slipped behind in my efforts to keep on top in the past few days. Now I was seized with an overwhelming urge to restore order, and I set to the task with determination. For a start, the stack of JJ files could be replaced in storage now I'd signed out the revised computations.

But as I made to place them on the trolley outside my office, I noticed Isabelle had included the old reorganisation file in the bundle. Which seemed odd, because it wasn't directly relevant. But that was her, wasn't it—thorough to a fault.

A yellow Post-it label protruded from the top. My curiosity piqued, I flipped the file open to see what she had flagged.

It was an implementation checklist, prepared by Pearson Malone. The then junior on the client team had painstakingly reviewed each item. He'd concluded that the client had implemented the reorganisation precisely in line with our recommendations.

In other words, the tax losses had been available all along.

On the Post-it, in Isabelle's rounded girlish writing were the words, 'No client error.' I checked the log to see when she'd taken the file out.

Tuesday—three days before she'd died.

14

I felt reasonably relaxed about the trip to the police station to formalise my statement. With nothing to hide, I had nothing to fear. Or so I thought.

But the unfriendly vibes hit me the moment I stepped through the door to the interview room.

Carmody sat stony-faced on the other side of the desk, and DS Holland, sitting alongside him, bore little resemblance to the jovial character I'd met the day before.

'Ah, Ms Robinson,' Carmody began. 'I do appreciate you giving us your time. DS Holland will go through some of the procedural stuff with you.'

He explained I was attending on a voluntary basis, for them to formally record my version of events. He asked me to sign a declaration.

'Purely a formality,' he said when he saw me skimming over it.

'Give me a minute—I never sign anything before reading.'

They glanced at each other as though they regarded my request as unusual, perhaps indicating an inappropriate level of anxiety.

On the surface the document seemed innocuous enough—in particular the paragraph stating I was free to terminate the interview at any time. I wondered if I was allowed a solicitor. But why should I need one? I was a witness—a wholly innocent bystander, who planned to tell the truth. Yet I couldn't shake my sense of foreboding.

'OK,' he said after I'd signed. 'Now, in fairness… it's procedural, you understand… I have to caution you that you're not bound to answer any of these questions we put to you today. But if you do, your answers will be recorded, may be noted, and may be used in evidence.'

This statement disturbed me. Naturally I understood my answers might be used in evidence—that's what I'd been afraid of—my stupid little fling with Ryan being paraded in open court. But at the same time his words sounded worryingly familiar. The phrase "May be used in evidence against you" sprang instantly to mind. Maybe I shouldn't have signed the declaration so readily.

'We'd just like you to clear a few things up for us,' the sergeant replied. 'Following on from your earlier statement and your subsequent informal discussion with DCI Carmody.'

'Happy to help,' I replied, managing a weak smile.

'So tell us again about last Friday evening.'

'Starting from when?'

'From the beginning of the drinks party.'

'OK.'

Apart from some awkward probing into how much alcohol I'd drunk, it all went swimmingly until we got to the part where Ryan rang my doorbell.

'What time did Mr Kelly arrive?'

'I'm not sure,' I confessed.

'Surely you have some idea…'

'Somewhere between ten-thirty and eleven-thirty, at a guess.'

'Did he visit you regularly?' asked Carmody.

'No,' I said indignantly. 'He did not.'

'Why did he call on you that night?'

I thought carefully.

'He'd said he'd gone to see his brother, but Greg was out, so he popped into see me instead.'

'Greg being your ex-husband,' Carmody cut in.

'Yes.'

'Had Ryan ever called on you before?'

'Occasionally—when Greg and I were married.'

'Were you surprised to see him?'

'Yes, I was.'

'And what did you talk about?'

I gave a full account of our conversation, and how we'd ended up in bed.

'Had you been to bed with him before?' asked the sergeant.

'No,' I said, unsure about the relevance of this intrusive question. 'It was a one-off.'

'And when did he leave?' asked Carmody.

'About eight in the morning. I heard the front door go.'

'And he stayed with you all night?'

'Yes.'

'Are you certain?'

'As sure as I can be. And Ryan will tell you the same.'

He'd promised me he'd tell the truth. And with a murder charge hanging over him, he had every incentive to do so.

'Oh yes,' said Carmody. 'He's given us an account fully consistent with yours. But that means nothing, does it?'

'Oh?'

'Because you might both be lying.'

The accusation floored me. After psyching myself up to confess all, they suspected me of making things up—how ironic was that?

'But we're not—it's the honest to God truth. I...'

'Before you go any further, I should point out we have a few concerns about this new testimony.'

'Like what?'

'Am I correct in thinking you met Mr Kelly last night after our discussion?'

That wrong-footed me for a moment, until I realised that they must have kept Ryan under surveillance.

'Yes—he was outside Daly's—it wasn't prearranged.'

'It hardly could be, if you didn't know Mr Kelly's whereabouts.'

The clear insinuation that I might be lying hung unspoken in the air.

'I *didn't* know.'

'Why did he want to see you?'

'He wanted me to look into a potential racket at JJ Resources.'

Carmody had sensed an inconsistency.

'But last night, when I asked you about JJ, you assured me everything was above board.'

'Well I'm not so certain now.'

Carmody, drew himself up to his full height, and exchanged a spooky little glance with DS Holland.

'Funny how since you two met yesterday evening, your stories marry up so closely. Kelly only told us about your night of passion when we arrested him this morning, and now you open up to us on this so-called fraud.'

'But I already explained. The reason he lied to begin with was because he felt embarrassed.'

'Oh, I'm sorry,' said Carmody, zooming in on another perceived anomaly. 'I understood that *you* were embarrassed.'

'We both were,' I mumbled. 'And it was only this morning I discovered the tax losses were available after all. So you see they might have disclaimed them because they were scared of a scam coming to light if they answered HMRC's questions.'

My attempt at clarification did not cut any ice with Carmody. Nor, I suspected, did it make much sense to him.

'There is an alternative interpretation,' he said, leaning back in his seat, and with a hint of menace in his voice. 'Perhaps the reason for Mr Kelly's earlier reticence is that his visit to you never happened.'

I shook my head.

'Which may also be the reason you omitted to mention it to DS Holland.'

'DS Holland never asked me. And as I said, it was embarrassing.'

'But not so embarrassing that you couldn't tell me, after I'd made it clear we were onto Mr Kelly.'

I was staggered—he seriously doubted my new testimony. And amazingly, my reluctance to disclose that I was an alcoholic slut seemed to baffle them.

'Afterwards you went hoofing straight off to meet your lover and tell him you were alibiing him,' he continued. 'And he filled you in on the cock and bull story he'd been spreading about this client.'

'My lover.'

'Now be honest, Ms Robinson. Were you two having an affair?'

I stood up.

'You're kidding. What would a lad like that want with me?'

'You were available—you had money—you might advance his career. What are the usual reasons? Why even your boss Ed Smithies noticed you've got a soft spot for Ryan. Said you tried to promote him when he didn't merit it, and he had to intervene.'

Good old Smithies, sticking the knife in at every opportunity.

'Smithies is lying,' I shouted. 'In fact, there's some evidence *he* had an inappropriate relationship with Isabelle. He's trying to divert suspicion from himself.'

'He doesn't need to divert suspicion,' said Carmody coldly. He leant forward across the desk; close enough for me to smell his aftershave. I sensed he was moving in for the kill.

'Even if I accept for the moment that Ryan stayed over with you, we have some discrepancies.'

'Yes?'

'We had a report two days ago from a member of the public about the driver of a yellow TR7 acting suspiciously around the canal early Saturday morning. CCTV records show the car in the vicinity. What car does Mr Kelly drive?'

My heart skipped a beat.

'A yellow TR7.'

'How many yellow TR7s would you estimate there are still on the road?'

'Not many.'

'Indeed not, Ms Robinson. Less than a thousand TR7s of any colour are currently licensed in the UK.'

Carmody had me cornered. Either I'd invented the story about Ryan staying the night, or else I'd lied about him not leaving till eight. And yet, if Ryan had gone out, surely I would have heard him. I hadn't been so very drunk... or had I?

'Now, you're an intelligent woman. If you wish to avoid being charged with perverting the course of justice, I'd advise you to stick to the truth. So let's forget everything you've told us so far and start over. You're covering for Ryan Kelly aren't you?'

'No—no I'm not. Why would I?'

'Because he's your lover.'

'But he's not. We just...'

'Tell me the truth, Ms Robinson.'

'I am telling the truth. Ryan stayed with me all night. And anyway, you can't have it both ways. You can't simultaneously claim that I'm lying about Ryan being at my place, and lying about him not going out. It's one or the other.'

'You're a clever lady, Ms Robinson. I expect you have to be to run rings round the Inland Revenue.'

I didn't much care for the suggestion that I habitually lied in my professional life, but Carmody had the upper hand here.

'So let's suppose Mr Kelly spent the night with you on Friday. I'll ask you again—can you be absolutely certain he didn't leave in the night and then return?'

'How would he have let himself back in?'

'You tell me, Ms Robinson...'

'But...'

'Think carefully.'

'But where would he...?'

I swallowed. Could I say for certain that Ryan hadn't gone out? I'd been deeply asleep—I'd pretty much passed out the moment Ryan had come...

And tightened his grip round my neck...

'The fact is,' Carmody said, 'both you and Ryan lied.'

'I *didn't* lie.'

'OK—let's just say you omitted to tell us the whole truth to begin with. But when a witness is dishonest, it raises some interesting questions—such as how can we be sure there isn't a bigger deception? For all we know, Ryan confessed to you that he'd killed Isabelle on Friday night and you've been aware all along she was dead. Why, we might be considering a charge as an accessory.'

I stared at him, horrified. If he'd been trying to scare me, he'd succeeded. I'd been drunk, hadn't I? Anything could have happened.

'But that's complete nonsense…'

'So you say. And there's the text message you sent Kelly this morning—further evidence you cooked up the story between you.'

'No it isn't,' I said firmly. 'I wasn't comfortable with Ryan lying about Friday night, or the way he was avoiding everyone—I thought it made him look guilty. So I advised him to come forward and tell the whole story. Then I texted him to check he'd done it. That's all.'

Carmody ignored this.

'So—once more. Is it possible that Mr Kelly went out during the night?'

It was plain what answer he wanted. I pretended to think long and hard, then back-pedaled furiously.

'I can't be *absolutely* sure,' I said. 'If I was asleep…'

'Or drunk?'

'Or drunk. And I suppose he could have taken the spare keys from the hall table…'

I sounded weak and feeble—as if I'd been protecting Ryan only to retreat when I'd realised the stakes were higher than I'd thought.

Carmody nodded at DS Holland—satisfied they'd broken me.

'Thank you,' said Carmody. 'That's all for now. Interview terminated one twenty-five pm.'

I seethed as I stomped out of the police station towards the taxi rank on the corner. Carmody had been much too quick in assuming the worst. How I loathed that lying shit Smithies, stooping low to incriminate me, maybe for his own sinister reasons. And Ryan too, even if innocent, had dropped me in it. But most of my anger was directed inwards. I hadn't stood up robustly to Carmody's bully-boy tactics. At best, I'd left them with doubts as to my credibility as a witness, and at worst the sense that I'd been in it up to my neck. Never mind if my private life was exposed in court—now, through my own stupidity, I might end up in the dock myself.

15

Whichever way I looked at it, the JJ situation smelt odd.

Why would JJ disclaim available tax losses? Could they be worried that answering the HMRC queries might bring some wrongdoing to light? As I'd already observed, the fraud was a strange story for Ryan to make up, strange enough perhaps to be true.

Superficially, the case against Ryan seemed compelling, but what if he was right? Suppose Isabelle had stumbled across a crime, and had unburdened herself to someone seized with a need to eliminate the threat? Just because Ryan's car had been spotted didn't mean he'd been at the wheel. Someone could have set him up.

With my own guilt or innocence now potentially at stake, I opened up the electronic HMRC enquiry file.

As Isabelle had said, HMRC's questions mainly centred on the allocation of administrative expenses between the different businesses. The client had apportioned costs according to turnover. This didn't seem unreasonable to me, although HMRC preferred an apportionment pro rata to employee numbers, presumably because it gave a lower profit for the slate division. But none of this suggested dishonesty. At first sight, it seemed to me that JJ Slate had become profitable for a very simple reason—they were selling more slate. The gross margin appeared reasonable, and a cursory examination of the detailed divisional profit and loss account showed increased haulage and electricity expenditure. All of this stacked up.

HMRC's enquiries on the debtors' ledger were, as Isabelle knew, plain silly. The inspector suspected the client had boosted profits by failing to write off irrecoverable debts, but this manoeuvre would only change the timing of profits and not the amount. The debts would have to be written off sometime in the future. Yet the basis for his question seemed clear—debtors were unusually high as a percentage of sales. And that was a red flag.

Years back, I'd been the junior on the audit of an advertising agency where the client had been raising false invoices to puff up sales and increase staff bonuses. As part of an audit, a company's customers are asked to confirm the amount they owe. The client's accounts team had tried to hoodwink us by manipulating the "responses" from the "debtors", but to no avail. All the old debts had roused our suspicions. You see—fictitious debtors never pay.

Was it possible that the same was happening at JJ?

If anything had been amiss, you might expect the Pearson Malone auditors to have spotted it. But the slate division was a small part of a sizeable company, so how closely would they examine its books? I could ask the audit partner, of course, but I was loath to draw attention to my enquiries. It would be safest to speak to Greg, although that prospect didn't thrill me either.

I jumped—Lisa had sneaked into my office without me noticing.

'Hi—how did you get on?'

'With what?'

'Your police interview. I'm assuming you're the thirty-eight-year-old woman mentioned on the BBC website, who's been "helping police with their enquiries".'

This news alarmed me. I hadn't anticipated being the focus of office gossip quite so soon.

'Would have been nice if you'd told me beforehand,' she said.

'Well, you didn't tell me you were at a job interview.'

'How did you guess?'

'It's obvious—foxy suit, silk shirt, hair in a neat little chignon.'

'I'm leaving—people who plan to leave go to job interviews.'

'And witnesses go to police interviews.'

'Was it about last Friday?'

'Sort of.'

'So how did you get on?' she repeated.

'Oh, fine.'

'There's no way you're fine. Come on—tell all—you can trust me.'

It wasn't a question of trust, simply that I didn't want to rehash all the ghastly details.

'OK—if you must know—it was a complete disaster,' I told her. 'They think I'm inventing a story to alibi Ryan. Between us, the outlook's a bit bleak for him. His car was caught on CCTV early Saturday morning near where the body turned up.'

'But wasn't Ryan with you all Friday night?' As ever, Lisa had homed in on the key point.

'They're saying he went out.'

'And did he?'

'I can't be certain—I was so drunk, Lisa.'

'But I guess he *must* have, if they traced the car.'

'Not necessarily. Suppose Isabelle had found something dodgy at JJ? She gets killed and someone sets Ryan up by driving his car.'

'But we discussed this earlier,' said Lisa. 'And you agreed that Ryan made up the story to throw the police off the scent.'

'Ah, but that was before I found out about the tax losses.'

'Found out what?'

I had seldom known Lisa to display such a lack of interest in what seemed to me an important matter. She sounded bored before she'd even understood the essence of my argument.

'Those losses were available—neither we nor the client screwed up. And Isabelle was aware of that, because she'd checked the file. Now why would the client disclaim available losses unless they were afraid of what the HMRC enquiries might bring to light?'

'Didn't we suspect Jim Jupp of using this to wangle the Pearson Malone Entrepreneur of the Year award?'

I shook my head.

'You said he wouldn't sacrifice actual losses just for that—remember?'

'I'm not so sure now. I mean, what does it matter to him? The guy's trousering five hundred mill in the next few weeks.'

'But HMRC was asking questions about debtors, and they look pretty dodgy to me.'

'Dodgy—how?'

'High—as a percentage of sales.'

'You're jumping to conclusions based on incredibly slender evidence.'

'Maybe, but just suppose for a minute there was some kind of swindle and Isabelle discovered it. Someone other than Ryan would have a motive for killing her, wouldn't they?'

'I guess so,' she agreed. 'But it's none of your business, is it?'

As a suspected accessory to murder, I felt it was my business, but said nothing. It was plain that Lisa had no interest in opening up a hornets' nest when she was on the verge of leaving the firm.

'How did your interview go?' I asked, instead of arguing back.

'Oh, pretty smoothly,' she said. 'It was only a preliminary discussion.'

'With?'

'Brown & Taylor.'

Pearson Malone's biggest rivals and my previous firm.

'Potential partnership?'

'We'll see. You didn't go through the assessment process there, did you?'

I'd never confessed to Lisa that I'd failed Brown & Taylor's partnership assessment all those years ago. A whole three days of them probing into my psyche had freaked me out. In a superhuman effort to stop them sniffing out what I urgently wished to conceal, I'd come across as bland and weak. Pearson Malone didn't use an assessment centre for partners hired externally from another firm, but a series of discussions and interviews instead. It was much less demanding to hold the fiction together for an hour at a time and I'd passed all ten meetings decisively.

'No,' I lied.

She peered at me strangely, like she knew I'd fibbed, and a little piece of me shrivelled and died inside.

***

By late afternoon, the police had charged Ryan with Isabelle's murder. Until then, all Carmody's rhetoric about perverting the course of justice and being charged as an accessory had been nothing but hot air. Now I worried I might be unable to extricate myself from this absurd situation. I considered calling a lawyer but, fearful of over-reacting, I decided to sit tight for a while and see how it played out.

Inevitably, the news of me "helping the police with their enquiries" had spread. The BBC's low-key anonymous disclosure had now mushroomed into a major story, including my name, across all the major media channels.

The first person to quiz me on this was Jim Jupp, ostensibly calling to ask who would attend the slate mine tour in place of Isabelle. The little bitch would have been proud to be hailed as such a key player on one of her clients.

'I'll go myself,' I said without hesitating, hoping the trip might give me some further insight into any potential irregularities.

'Excellent,' he said, with insincerity. Then he moved on to the real purpose for his call.

'By the way, what's all this about you helping police with their enquiries? It's everywhere in the news.'

'Beats me why it's such a hot story,' I said with a nervous laugh. 'I was resolving some loose ends, that's all.'

'I'm pleased it isn't anything more serious,' he replied. He sounded unmistakeably sceptical.

Smithies was also agog to hear the details.

'Everyone's saying you've been interviewed under caution,' he announced cheerily. 'What on earth's been going on?'

He'd evidently tuned into the highly exaggerated rumours doing the rounds, rather than checking the news himself. I told him the same as JJ, but Smithies was less easily fobbed off.

'*What* loose ends egg-zackly were you resolving?'

'I'm not allowed to say. The police investigation is confidential.'

Smithies was astute enough to realise that direct questioning wouldn't elicit any further information. Instead he resorted to his usual tactics of unsettling me in the hope of garnering more clues.

'How odd. There must be a reason they latched onto you…'

His gaze seemed knowing, but I held firm. I was painfully aware that he had new ammunition to use against me, even without any details. Sly allusions to my possible connection with Isabelle's murder would be dropped into conversations at the appropriate point, along with suggestions that I'd been covering up for Ryan. Hell, he could make up whatever he wanted, no matter how bad it sounded.

'I can't think what the reason might be,' I said confidently.

It occurred to me that if Smithies was Isabelle's killer, playing up my involvement might be driven by more than plain spite. If a crime was being committed at JJ—if they were sleeping together—if Isabelle had unwittingly revealed her discovery, then he had a motive—to protect his creepy brother-in-law. And if he'd framed Ryan, dragging me into the net would further obscure the truth. But much as I loathed the man, this train of logic still contained far too many ifs to be compelling.

'I should mention,' he went on, aware that he hadn't hit home yet, 'Bailey is disappointed you didn't find the time to compromise Ryan out.'

'It was a tough ask. He was on the run, and now events have overtaken us…'

'Oh, *I* understand completely. We can't always respond to fast-paced developments. I told Bailey you'd tried your best, but he's not the most tolerant of men.'

His tone was at best condescending, at worst malevolent.

'No.'

'Well, let's hope events don't move on any further,' he said, cryptically.

But events would move on further, because somehow they'd developed a momentum all of their own.

***

'Is this about Ryan?' Greg asked straight away when I called him.

I hesitated. How much did he know?

'Indirectly, yes.'

'Come over now.'

I'd expected him to feign busyness, to assert his importance over mine. But either he'd mellowed or was so disturbed by Ryan's situation that the corporate mask had slipped.

This was the first meaningful contact I'd had with Greg since our divorce. We felt no great animosity towards each other—that would have required a greater passion in the first place—but the sheer size of the building limited our encounters. Someone once calculated that if you stepped into an elevator at random with someone in the Pearson Malone London office, it was fifty-fifty you'd never see the person again. True or not, avoiding a member of a different department involved little to no effort.

Greg was on the telephone as I arrived. He leant back, hands clasped behind his head as he engaged in empty chitchat with a crony. His brash, assertive demeanour didn't surprise me—Greg had always found it easy to compartmentalise his life.

His secretary, seated outside his office, scarcely acknowledged me as I hovered outside the door. She was a bare-faced dragon with hair scraped back in a tight bun, grey pleated skirt and a grubby cream nylon blouse. Perhaps they'd thought it unwise to let him loose with another dolly bird after what had happened the last time—or perhaps Greg didn't trust himself.

Always one to play it safe sartorially, Greg wore a subtly pin-striped navy suit, a pristine white shirt, and what could have passed for an old school tie. He quickly cut short his conversation when he saw me waiting. For a few seconds, we eyed each other with a shared incredulity that our lives had ever been linked.

'Amy. How are you?' he asked. He gave me a bitter little smile, exposing new veneers on his front teeth.

'OK, thanks. More to the point, how are you?'

No aspect of his appearance betrayed the strain he was under, but I understood enough of him to realise his macho posturing did not reflect his true emotions. And equally, he recognised that pretence was useless.

'Been better,' he said, shaking his head sadly. 'Not good news about little bro.'

'I know. But everyone's certain he's innocent.'

'I wish I shared their optimism. You've heard all the evidence stacked up against him, I suppose?'

'Yes,' I agreed, still unsure to what extent he knew about my involvement.

'Did he really stay at yours that night?'

'Yes.'

'Ah—I suspected he might be making it up, along with a load of other stuff.'

'No. It was only a one-night stand. We were drunk…'

Sensing my discomfort, he said, 'Look, it's OK—none of my business. You don't have to explain. Shame you couldn't give him an alibi though…'

My cheeks reddened. He had much more information about my police interview than I felt comfortable with. How had he come by this so soon after the event? I wondered.

'I'm sorry. But his car…'

He cut my apologies short with a dismissive wave of his hand.

'Don't stress yourself—we're getting together the best legal representation money can buy—they'll find an angle.'

I hoped, probably in vain, that the angle wouldn't involve me. For I could imagine, all too vividly, how Ryan's shit-hot defence team would tear a flaky prosecution witness like me to shreds.

'I may have an angle. That's why I came to see you.'

'And what's that?'

'Now I know Ryan mentioned it to you already—but what if JJ Slate *is* running some sort of racket? As I see it, the main evidence against Ryan is the car. There's no reason for anyone else to have been driving it with Isabelle in the boot, unless it was to set Ryan up. If JJ Slate has something to hide, they would have a motive to frame Ryan.'

He leaned forward in a way which I chose not to interpret as patronising.

'Believe me, Amy, there is no racket.'

'So everyone keeps telling me. But have you seen the divisional accounts?'

'Yes.'

His answer took me by surprise.

'Then you'll have spotted what I did—there are far too many receivables. I thought some of the debtors might be fictitious.'

'Really.' He sounded weary, as if I was retracing a well-ploughed furrow.

'I know you don't wish to hear this, how desperately you need this deal…'

'Oh Amy, for Christ's sake. I'm not *that* desperate,' he yelled. 'If I could find *any* way to save Ryan, I would grab at it—even if it meant the deal falling through. You must realise that. What kind of person do you think I am?'

I blushed, wishing now that I'd spoken with more tact.

'I'm sorry,' I said.

'When Ryan brought this up,' Greg explained, 'I checked out those accounts and yes—the receivables are high. So I contacted the partner in charge of the audit. He told me they did a full debtors' circularisation, and also that the vast majority of the debts owed were repaid between the year-end and the audit. Plus, as he was at pains to point out, the slate division is so small it's doubtful if an adjustment material at group level could arise.'

Which was precisely why they might not carry out much work on it, I thought, but didn't say.

'And don't forget,' he added, 'the Megabuilders' due diligence team has picked through everything.'

'Yes, I suppose they have.'

'Besides,' he concluded. 'What's the point of artificially inflating the profits? Who benefits? No one has extracted any cash.'

'True,' I agreed. 'But I just wondered…'

'Amy, I appreciate your efforts to help Ryan, but the police have checked and discounted this as a line of enquiry.'

'But why would Ryan invent the story?'

'As I understand it, we had a dispute over some tax losses—you would be more up to speed on that than me. Perhaps he misunderstood the position.'

'Possibly. But you do realise they conceded those losses unnecessarily?'

'Not what I'd heard. I thought the client messed up, but we took the rap for some wacky political reason nobody except Bailey understands.'

'That's precisely the point—the client didn't mess up. On the file, I found a detailed implementation checklist…'

'Then you've missed something. Why would a client disclaim the losses if they were available?'

'If they were up to something dodgy and they were worried it might come out.'

He shook his head.

'That's just not possible. We've been into it to the nth degree of detail.'

Indeed, contrary to Ryan's perception, Greg did seem to have explored all the possibilities with great thoroughness.

I conceded defeat, pleased to avoid the inconvenience of raking up shit on a prestigious client in the run up to a trade sale. I'd done what Ryan had asked, and must now lay the whole matter to rest.

'OK—I give in. Sorry to put you through the wringer. But I had to ask, for Ryan's sake.'

'I understand,' he said.

'One other point,' I said as I was leaving. 'Did Ryan suggest that Isabelle might be having an affair with Ed Smithies?'

Despite everything, Greg roared with laughter.

'Yes, last weekend, but the idea's ridiculous. I would be careful who you say that to if I were you—if it gets back to Ed he'll go loopy. He's already worried that you don't like him.'

'That *I don't like him*—you must be kidding.'

'No, seriously—he reckons you're out to stab him in the back.'

'That's the pot calling the kettle black—*he's out to get me*. And vile piece of shit that he is, he's trying to twist it all round.'

'You've got him all wrong, Amy. He's not a nasty person. Yes, he makes quick business judgements, which pisses everyone off, but—hey—he's usually spookily accurate. As a matter of fact, he's worried about you—feels you're under a lot of pressure.'

I found it infinitely depressing the way everyone bought into Smithies' lies without question, but it didn't seem worth arguing with Greg. He wouldn't change his mind.

'So no affair?'

'Absolutely not. Look, Amy, I hope you don't mind me saying, but I get the sense you're a bit lost since Ed took over.'

'I do mind you saying, because you're wrong.'

'OK, but I'm here, if you ever need to chat about work stuff.'

'Thanks—I'm alright.'

I had begun to suspect this wasn't entirely true. But hell, I still had my pride. And I wasn't yet reduced to using my ex-husband as a counsellor.

***

Seized with the urge to demonstrate just what excellent shape I was in, my next stop was Adrian Townsend, UK Head of Tax, and Smithies' boss.

Townsend was the polar opposite of Smithies. Reserved and owlishly intellectual, he led the tax practice with a benign benevolence almost extinct in Pearson Malone since Bailey and his bully-boy henchmen had seized control. Smithies and his ilk saw kindness only as a tool with which to leverage their own interests, and once Townsend had served his purpose he'd be out. But for now, he clung onto the vestiges of power and had agreed to meet me without hesitation.

Not that this meant much. He was quite capable of beaming affably throughout our meeting, making supportive noises while carefully avoiding any commitment to action.

But I had two strategic advantages. One—Townsend detested Smithies with a vengeance. Two—for once, Smithies the master tactician appeared to have goofed.

Townsend greeted me effusively.

'Ah, Amy—nice to see you. Very tricky times in your team at present, I imagine.'

If Smithies had made the same remark, I would have suspected a hidden meaning, but Townsend gave a credible imitation of genuinely caring. Too bad Smithies was jockeying to be elected as Townsend's successor, before he'd even formally announced his retirement.

'Yes, morale's taken a knock, but they'll get through this with some TLC.'

'Good—I imagined you'd have it all under control. And are *you* OK?'

Why did everyone keep asking me that? It had to be Smithies spreading his poison.

'It's a tough time,' I confessed, 'but I'm holding up.'

'Yes indeed. And I understand you've been helping the police with their enquiries.'

I tensed—Townsend might be more sympathetic than Smithies but in no way did that lessen my reticence on the subject.

'Frankly, I'm amazed it's had so much coverage,' I said blithely. 'I was only clearing up a few minor points.'

'So—Lisa Carter,' he said, moving swiftly to the matter in hand.

'Yes—I'm disappointed that you've pulled her from the partner assessment centre, despite passing the initial selection interview.'

'I sympathise,' he said, 'but in the current economic climate we had to review all the candidates objectively...'

'Yes, yes.' It irked me beyond belief to be palmed off with the same drivel as I dished out to others. 'But what was the review process?'

'Ed Smithies met with each of the section heads and discussed each case, and he based the decision on the results of those meetings. I reviewed the findings and signed off on them. I must say, the process seemed quite fair to me.'

I didn't agree—effectively Smithies had made the decisions and Townsend had rubber-stamped them. I suspected too that Smithies had nobbled Townsend before our meeting, but wasn't unduly troubled. I had yet to play my ace.

'You may have a big problem,' I told him bluntly.

'Why's that?'

'Six people in the tax practice had their partnership applications cancelled as a result of this "objective" review. You may not have noticed, but five are female and one is Asian.'

I watched his face for any trace of a reaction, but saw none.

'I see.'

'The potential for a discrimination claim is enormous,' I went on, ramming the point home with all the subtlety of a pile driver.

In truth, I didn't believe Smithies was a sexist or a racist. But that didn't mean he'd applied any objective criteria in deciding which of the candidates to eliminate.

'Ah, yes,' Townsend replied, fiddling with his cufflink. 'And are you suggesting that Lisa is planning to lodge such a claim?'

'Well—you know Lisa—feisty, outspoken, doesn't put up with unfairness.'

Had he noticed I'd avoided answering the question directly? I thought not—I fancied he was too busy weighing up how best to manoeuvre the situation to his advantage. Perhaps he wasn't so different from Smithies after all. And it wasn't exactly a lie—Lisa had alerted me to the situation.

'That would be unfortunate,' he said, with his usual flair for understatement. 'Especially so soon after we've publicly committed to increasing the proportion of female partners.'

Finally, he'd latched onto the key issue.

'Which is why I'm bringing the matter to your attention,' I replied.

I must admit it puzzled me that Smithies—normally so careful to ensure every action he took was "on message"—had made such a blatant gaffe. I could only conclude that power had gone to his head and made him reckless. Still, his loss was potentially Lisa's gain.

'Leave it with me,' said Townsend. 'And thanks.'

The key question now was how he might deal with the information.

As I walked back to my office, I congratulated myself. Even as my own harshest critic I knew I'd shone. The tough, cut-through-the crap Amy was back.

16

The weekend passed uneventfully. I didn't get drunk or laid and instead caught up with household tasks and shopping. By Sunday, I'd found the energy to enjoy a health-giving run in the park.

I marvelled at how capably I'd coped with the challenging circumstances of the past week. I'd appeared on live television, held the group together, fulfilled my promise to Ryan and tried to help Lisa. Even the interview with Carmody seemed less traumatic in retrospect—it wasn't everyone who could keep cool in the face of hostile police questioning. And while Carmody's threats about potential charges were worrying, what evidence did they have against me? If there'd been something concrete, surely he wouldn't have been so gung-ho in releasing my name to the media.

The future seemed less bleak now too. Although the night spent with Ryan would emerge in his trial, I would deal with it. After all, there were plenty of male partners in Pearson Malone with truly appalling records of inappropriate relationships. And I'd even chased away the horrible guilt that gripped me about the murder being my fault, because I'd failed to promote Ryan. Such ridiculous self-flagellation didn't deserve to occupy any space in my mind. Now that I was embarked on this positive thinking offensive, it also struck me that the weird Little Amy voice had been mercifully silent over the past few days. Yes—I was on the up.

Then on Sunday evening my landline rang.

'Hello—Amy?'

My precarious equilibrium toppled in an instant as I recognised the old and quavery voice.

'This is Cynthia Hope, your mother's next door neighbour.'

'Oh, hello,' I said. The brightness of my voice bore no correlation to the dread I felt inside.

'Your mother didn't want me to call you.'

No kidding.

'She said you were far too busy to be bothered.'

'Bothered with what?'

'She fell and broke her hip.'

'When?'

'The other day,' she said vaguely.

'Where?'

'Outside in the street.'

I clung to a pathetic optimism that the secret might still be safe.

'And where is she now?'

'In the hospital. But there's a problem.'

'What?'

'They won't let her come home.'

The optimism died.

'Why not?'

As if I didn't know.

'They came inside, to check it was safe for her to go back home. I gave them the key...'

My stomach tightened.

'Yes?'

'Have you any idea how your mother is living?'

'No,' I replied truthfully. 'It's been some time since I last saw her.'

Although I could make an educated guess.

'Squalid is the word for that house. Something must be done.'

Squalid was the word but believe me, if anything could have been done I'd have done it.

Here's the Big Secret—the one I kept from everyone, including my husband and my best friend.

My mother lives in clutter and filth because she likes it that way—she's a compulsive hoarder. You tidy it up and she trashes the place again in no time at all. Left to their own devices, hoarders fill their houses to the rafters with rubbish. For all I knew, she'd reached that stage now. After all, this had been going on for thirty years.

When I was eight years old, my father dropped down dead. My life changed irrevocably from that point on. I'll never know whether that was when the hoarding began or whether my father had kept it in check—it hardly matters. Masses of stuff came into the house but little left it, and it quickly became so chronically untidy and dirty that no outsider could be allowed to enter. I tried to clear it up, but it was no use—the house grew more and more chaotic, because I wasn't allowed to throw anything out. After a couple of years the plumbing broke, but repairmen couldn't be allowed to see the mess so they didn't get called.

And I was forbidden to tell anyone how we lived. Even as an adult I kept the Big Secret because somehow it must reflect badly on me to have grown up in a shit hole.

I left as soon as I could and got on with the business of pretending to be a successful professional leading a charmed existence. And no doubt my bravura performance had fooled them all, despite the quivering jelly underneath the façade. Not even Smithies would suspect I'd been raised in a trashcan. But the time for avoiding the truth had passed, as deep down I'd known it eventually would.

'Something *must* be done,' she repeated.

'What do you suggest?'

'I think you need to see it for yourself—it won't be a simple matter to resolve this…'

I didn't need to see, but in a moment of weakness brought on by shock I agreed to go over the following afternoon.

I put down the phone and poured myself a mega gin and tonic, breaking my alcohol-free weekend. But no amount of booze could assuage the feelings of panic and shame. People now knew, had properly seen, what a pigsty my mother lived in. And naturally they must all be asking themselves, *how can Amy let her mother live like that*?

Paradoxically though, I couldn't stop her.

'*What a muddle you're in*,' piped up a familiar little voice, full of self-righteous condemnation. '*I knew this would happen eventually.*'

Little Amy stood in front of the fireplace; in the same outfit she'd been wearing the night Isabelle had died. There could be no doubt now—the voice I'd been hearing for the past couple of weeks was hers.

I closed my eyes and opened them again. She was still there. And disbelief gave way to a grudging recognition that I must be less together in my head than I'd thought.

17

Voicemail message from Eric Bailey

Hello, this is Eric Bailey with a message to all our people.

As you may know, the police announced on Friday that Ryan Kelly, an employee of this firm, has been charged with the murder of Isabelle Edwards, another member of staff.

Naturally, we struggle to accept that one of our own people could be the perpetrator of such a terrible crime. Nevertheless, we are doing everything we can to cooperate with the police in their enquiries.

Now, it's important to remember that under the fundamental principles of UK justice, Ryan is to be regarded as innocent until proved guilty. But it's also worth pointing out that in this country the police do not generally bring charges without solid evidence.

In these challenging times, I would remind you all about our rules on speaking to the media. Any infringement of those instructions by staff or partners, however senior, will be viewed with the utmost seriousness. Likewise, you should refrain from making any comment on internet chat rooms or social networking sites.

I trust I can rely on your professional judgement and discretion in this matter.

Thank you all in advance for your cooperation.

Translation by Amy Robinson

Let's keep our dirt to ourselves.

Ironic or what?

18

With a heavy heart, I punched my mother's Croydon address into the sat nav of my sleek Mercedes CLK, and pulled out of the underground car park.

It was impossible to estimate how much rubbish she might have accumulated in the ten years since I'd last set foot in the house, but that didn't stop my imagination. If I pictured something truly dreadful, it might lessen the shock at what I actually found.

'*Nah*,' said Little Amy. '*It's always worse*.'

She knew as well as I did how our mother could surpass our worst expectations, and seemingly take pleasure in doing so.

My former childhood home was a three-bedroom inter-war semi in a leafy avenue, with pebbledash and bay windows. From the outside, superficially at least, it resembled the other houses on the street. The garden was neat and the exterior décor no worse than some of the neighbouring properties.

Cynthia Hope was hovering impatiently at the window, awaiting my arrival. The past decade had aged her. At one time she'd been a force to be reckoned with—a former headmistress. But she'd lost her vigour somewhere along the way—with a shrunken, fearful face, her tweed skirt and baggy sweater tired and pilled with age.

'It's good of you to spare the time,' she began. 'Your mother tells me you're quite the tycoon these days—far too grand to associate with the likes of her.'

How typical of my mother to blame me for our estrangement. And how typical of Cynthia to unquestioningly accept her version of events.

Cynthia scrutinised my car with suspicion—as if it corroborated the fiction my mother had woven to explain our alienation.

'Won't you come in for a cup of tea first?'

I refused, although I did step inside while she fetched the key. The house was neat but dated and shabby—as my mother's would have been if she hadn't succumbed to this terrible hoarding sickness.

'Would you like me to go in with you?' she asked, although understandably she didn't sound keen.

'There's no need.'

'You might find it easier to go round the back,' she said—I assumed because of the stiff lock. Maybe she didn't realise I had the knack of jiggling the key at precisely the right angle.

'No—front will be OK.'

'Please yourself,' she said.

As I made my way up the path, the illusion of a normal house began to unravel. Naturally the curtains were drawn, to ensure none of the neighbours saw the horrors within. But my mother never seemed to consider what they made of the dusty windows and the haphazard arrangement of flowerpots, replete with dead plants, on the inside window sill.

The lock had been stiff for as long as I could remember—a repair would have involved someone seeing inside the house. It now seemed reluctant to yield even to my much-practised nifty jiggling. But I persisted and eventually the key turned.

I'd scarcely opened the door a crack before the musty stale odour of my mother's wasted life hit my nostrils. A visceral terror swept over me as I fought for breath. Dread of the doorbell ringing—fear that my mother would die and abandon me in that squalid pit—the relentless ordeal of keeping friends and boyfriends at bay. My whole childhood was encapsulated in that foetid odour. I steadied myself against the doorpost before pushing open the door, or rather, attempting to push it open.

I now understood why Cynthia had suggested the back entrance—I could scarcely squeeze through the front. In the gloom I saw that apart from a tiny pathway, the hall was waist-deep in a jumbled mass of debris. I caught my breath as I took in the sheer scale of the squalor—worse than my worst imaginings.

How did my mother manage? She'd been a solidly-built woman the last time I'd seen her, whose lack of self-discipline embraced overeating as well as the senseless accumulation of crap. Either she'd slimmed down, or she no longer used the front entrance. That sounds ridiculous I know—I mean any normal person would clear the clutter once it obstructed their movements——but for hoarders, stuff outplays convenience every time.

Once I'd levered myself in, I picked my way along the narrow goat trail through the mountain of rubbish. I felt calmer now—brilliant in a crisis, as ever. Among the random debris, I spotted shopping bags (never unpacked), unopened mail, newspapers, suitcases, boxes of book-club purchases, mail order packages, hats, gloves, coats, garden chairs and casserole dishes. Despite my primeval response to the smell, the scale of the mess didn't shock me, at least not on an intellectual level. Unbridled over-acquisition combined with failure to discard led to one outcome. And the only limit to the depths plumbed (or more accurately the heights scaled) by a hoarder is the ceiling.

A chest of drawers stood in the centre of the hallway, heaped precariously with junk. As I inched round it, I must have disturbed the pile, for a huge avalanche of junk tumbled down, missing my head by inches and obliterating the small footpath.

I stumbled through to the lounge in the semi-darkness and flicked on the light. Nothing happened, but I edged past the piles to the standard lamp by the television, which gave more than enough light to see the worst.

The floor was heaped like a mountain range, with mini-crests created by landslides from the principal peaks. No part of the carpet was visible, but another barely navigable goat trail zigzagged through the room. A jumble of clothes—indoor, outdoor, and underwear teetered perilously on the sofa. Who could say if they were clean or dirty? Next to the sofa, my mother had erected a camp bed, presumably because upstairs had become uninhabitable.

The dining table, its original purpose long since abandoned, was buried beneath stacks of dirty dishes and other debris. A half-hearted attempt to disguise the chaos by throwing a tablecloth over the pile was both ineffective and misguided. The chairs had been requisitioned as additional repositories for magazines, catalogues and yellowing newspapers. I checked the date on one—shortly after my last visit.

Apart from the bed, the one item of furniture capable of use was my mother's favourite armchair—its headrest heavily soiled during many years of mindless television viewing.

Moving on to the kitchen, I marvelled at how she cooked anything. The counters were encrusted with ancient grime and stacked with expired packages of biscuits and cakes, boxes of pasta and discarded egg cartons. A Le Creuset casserole stood by the back door, full of an evil-smelling liquid of uncertain origin. Old food wrappers littered the floor, and the hob was thick with burnt-on food residues. Green slime covered the sink and more dirty dishes together with the pre-historic remains of meals covered the drainers. The ironing board had served as an additional table for many years, but the enormous cardboard box taking up most of the floor space was a new development. I checked, and found it to be empty.

On opening the fridge, the stench of death knocked me back. Gagging, I hastily shut the door but not in time to prevent a mass exodus of fruit flies. By the way, to cut a long story short, this is why I don't eat red meat.

I retreated to the hallway and then onwards and upwards. A mattress wrapped in brown paper partially blocked the stairs, apparently carelessly abandoned on its way up.

My scrutiny of the three bedrooms was limited by my inability to open the doors due to the junk behind them. I managed to reach round to the light switches, but when I clicked nothing happened. However, the silhouettes of more gigantic heaps of rubbish were plainly visible even in the gloom.

Her bathroom was the only semi-functional room. The tub, basin and toilet, though filthy, were potentially useable, although there wasn't much space to manoeuvre. She'd crammed the room to the ceiling with precarious towers of plastic storage boxes full of towels, sheets and multi-buy packs of toiletries. At least the plumbing worked now, since my last intervention. It hadn't for the previous eighteen years.

I jumped as my phone rang—Lisa.

My heart pounded as I answered it, as though she could see my secret shame across the ether.

'Where are you?' she demanded.

'At a meeting in Croydon.'

'Which client?'

'Prospective target,' I lied.

'I'm so pissed-off with you,' she began, launching into a rant without checking it was convenient to talk. 'I specifically asked you not to bother trying to get me reinstated on the partnership assessment, and what do you do? You go running to Townsend stirring up shitloads of trouble for everyone.'

'I was trying to help you.'

'I wish you'd kept me in the loop. And I can't *imagine* why you told them I'm lodging a claim.'

'I didn't say so in as many words…'

'But you obviously implied it. Anyway, the whole thing got escalated up to Bailey and he threw a real benny over the merest possibility of a lawsuit and gave Smithies a huge bollocking.'

'And what about you?'

'We're back on the assessment centre, all six of us.'

'So that's positive isn't it? I mean, perhaps "thank you Amy" might be called for.'

But no gratitude was forthcoming.

'You must be joking. Smithies and Bailey believe I'm a dangerous activist, and as we all know "perception is reality", so I don't give much for my chances, do you?'

'They might be too scared to fail you.'

'I don't plan to find out. I've made up my mind to leave.'

'That's up to you,' I said. 'But now you have the chance to give it a shot—you have a choice.'

My gut feel was she'd go for it, despite her protests.

'What bugs me is the fact you didn't tell me—it's becoming a habit with you. I had to practically drag it out of you that you shagged Ryan, then you keep quiet about the police being after you, and now this…'

'I'm sorry—I should have kept you informed. But it's all sorted now, and I do hope you give it a go.'

Even as I apologised, I was acutely conscious of the big hoarding secret I still hadn't shared. But this seemed a singularly inappropriate moment to blurt it all out.

'Not a chance,' came her curt reply. 'And if I were you, I'd keep a low profile. Smithies is gunning for you big time.'

'That's OK—I'm a big girl—I'll handle him,' I told her, almost convincing myself as I said it.

After Lisa rang off, I gazed around me in despair. The task ahead was gargantuan.

Little Amy sat in the armchair, legs crossed and smoking a cigarette.

'Oh great,' I said. 'What are you doing here?'

'*I live here, remember.*'

'You shouldn't be smoking.'

'*She lets me.*'

The poor kid had no idea it would take her another twenty years to kick the addiction.

'You do understand that she doesn't give a damn about you?'

'*What—because she allows me to smoke?*'

'No, because she makes you live in this shit hole.'

'*I don't care,*' she said nonchalantly. '*I get a heck of a lot more freedom than my friends in their dreary little bourgeois lives.*'

I gasped—had any part of me ever believed that the freedom neglect afforded compensated for living in such squalor? I had no memory whatsoever of such thoughts, only of a desperate longing for the normal life everyone else enjoyed, without knowing what normal was.

'You're rationalising it.'

'*And you sold out to the life I despised.*'

'Hang on,' I said, staggered by the sheer absurdity of her attitude. 'You can't criticise me for things I've done, because *you're* going to do them in the future.'

'*Whatever*,' she replied, coolly. '*Anyway, it's up to you to clean up the mess now.*'

'But if you hadn't been so lazy, it wouldn't be in this state.'

I'd deliberately aimed for a raw nerve there, but felt no guilt. Was it even possible to be cruel to a figment?

'*That's not fair. I try to tidy up, but she shouts at me. And I try to stop her buying stuff but she won't listen.*'

'Although you come out of the shopping OK, don't you? With plenty of clothes.'

With hindsight, I saw the deal in all its shabby clarity—complete freedom and nice clothes in exchange for colluding and denying the squalid truth. How had I been dumb enough to fall for it?

'*I look great don't I?*' she retorted, as though this justified everything.

Undeniably, the clothes had been a huge help in sustaining the illusion of normality. I'd been the envy of my school friends, and no one would have dreamt how we lived—but I'd paid dearly.

To be fair, Little Amy had tried on many occasions to clean up, each time hoping against hope that our mother would endeavour to keep the tidied parts nice. And each time she'd repaid those efforts by re-hoarding. Sometimes she'd talk of having the badly-needed repairs done and expect praise for the mere intention. But when she failed to deliver on these empty promises, she attacked Little Amy over the state of the house. Ultimately tidying became impossible anyway, because of the sheer volume of stuff.

In the end, a healthy regard for my own sanity had compelled me to walk away from this draining cycle of hope and despair. After I'd left for university, I visited the hoard house as little as possible.

But ten years ago, I'd given it one last shot. Struck by guilt, I'd taken three weeks of my annual leave to clear the downstairs, bathroom and landing. I'd ignored her protests and made trip after trip to the rubbish dump. Then I'd called the plumber to fix the hot water and the toilet. At the time I believed I'd achieved something useful. But within weeks, she'd junked it up, almost as bad as before, by moving stuff in from the garage. I realised then it wasn't my fault—all the self-reproach over the years had been needless. I pleaded with her to seek psychiatric help. She refused (how would these fools assist a towering intellectual like her?), and that was the end. We could have gone on, I suppose, chatting on the phone, meeting away from the house, and avoiding the subject, but it would have been meaningless. I've always possessed a sound instinct for self-preservation, and I sensed that my life would be immeasurably simpler uncoupled from hers.

'You don't tell her, do you, how you hate living here? I know you'd like to have hot water on tap, flush the toilet without using a bucket of water, and have a clear table for doing homework. And wouldn't it be nice to take a bath without transporting pans of boiling water upstairs? Yet you never complain. Why not?'

'*Because it would upset her*,' Little Amy replied.

As I criticised her, it sunk in properly, for the first time, that these were all fundamental rights for a middle-class child in Croydon. But my mother had chosen to ignore my rights to avoid the anxiety of dealing with the hoard and facing up to the perceived shame of being mentally ill. This was unacceptable behaviour by any standards.

Surely, on some level, she must have recognised something was wrong. But she had blanked it out, put on an elaborate pretence of normality, and inveigled me into her grubby concealment tactics. I'd lied to my friends about why they weren't able to come over and cowered behind curtains if any of them were sufficiently foolish to call round. I'd adopted "perception is reality" long before it became fashionable, hiding behind my fancy clothes and bubbly personality, all to keep her dirty secret. I'd been like an undercover agent, but with cover so deep that I daren't even admit the truth to myself. And for years she'd unscrupulously capitalised on the natural loyalty of her child, without any remorse. My thoughts and feelings were so unimportant that they could be denied, trivialised and subverted.

What, I asked myself, *would I say, if one of my team came in and told me this story*?

Faced with Little Amy, so vulnerable and deluded, the answer stared out at me. My poor muddled, inadequate mother, traumatised by the sudden death of her husband, did not fit any conventional image of a child abuser. But nonetheless, that's what she was—which made me a victim.

But I couldn't stomach the victim part. Here I was, a successful professional. The hoarding hadn't touched me, not really, not now. This was my mantra, and I said it often enough, it would become true.

'*You have to help her,*' said Little Amy, interrupting my internal dialogue. '*Everyone will criticize you if you don't.*'

I hesitated momentarily. After the crap job my mother had done in raising me, I owed the woman nothing. And did I care what Cynthia Hope and her coven thought?

No.

'I'm doing nothing,' I said. 'This is her house, not mine.'

'*What a bitch,*' pronounced Little Amy, and disappeared.

***

'Appalling, isn't it?' said Cynthia. 'I had no idea it was this bad…'

It would have been easy to agree that the state of the house was indeed shocking and surprising, but I declined to play along. Pretending the mess was a recent development represented another form of collusion with my mother, and from now on I was done with that.

Besides, as I considered the facts dispassionately, I realised it ought to have been abundantly obvious to the Hope woman long before now that something was wrong. And the same went for all those other po-faced bitches who called themselves my mother's friends. Many clues were there, right under their noses. They must have speculated as to why she never held coffee mornings, and the meaning of the drawn curtains and cluttered windowsills. Didn't they notice how quickly my mother closed the front door behind her when they came to collect her for outings? Maybe someone had asked to use the bathroom and been refused—didn't she wonder why? Had these women no curiosity whatsoever?

Truth was, they'd ignored the evidence, for fear of causing a scene. And in so doing, they'd let her get away with child abuse.

'So what do you plan to do?' she asked, undeterred by my silence.

I now realised I'd made a mistake in coming here. It had built up Cynthia's expectations to an unrealistic level.

'Nothing,' I said. 'It's not my problem.'

'But you can't let your own mother live in this filth, surely?'

'This is how she wants to live,' I said. 'And you know it. We can both lie to each other, or be straight. If she was a normal mother who raised me in decent surroundings, then arguably I would have some moral obligation towards her now. But she's surrounded herself by increasing squalor since my father died thirty years ago, with no regard to my needs or feelings. At least I'll be respecting her feelings by leaving all this alone.'

'But she did her best to bring you up. It can't have been easy on her own, and you were such an ungrateful child…'

That did it.

'Now see—you've lived next door to her all the time. You must have had a fair idea of the state the house was in and that it wasn't a suitable environment for a child. And you're telling me I should have been more appreciative of that. Oh come on—get real.'

'Honestly,' she persisted. 'I just didn't realise. I mean, we all knew your mum's a bit of a clutter bug, but she's such a sweet person…'

I cut her off.

'She was and is a mentally ill person, who didn't give a shit about her little girl. And, whether you care to admit it or not, I've got every right to disown her and all this. If you reckon it's so important, you can do something, since you're obviously so fond of her.'

'She always says you don't care to associate with her now you've come up in the world.'

'Bull. God knows the bar isn't set high, but she doesn't meet the minimum standard for a mother. That's why I've cut off contact.'

'But you must visit her in the hospital, surely? After all, she's the only mother you've got.'

Still she clung to illusion that I would preserve all the middle-class niceties.

'No chance.'

'But you have a duty...'

The simmering anger finally boiled over.

'And you had a duty to report a vulnerable child living in squalor but you shunned it. So don't you lecture me, you sanctimonious old bitch.'

I left her standing speechless and horrified in the doorway as I rushed to the car, floored the accelerator and set off screeching down the road.

19

I honestly still believed I was alright. Yes, it's odd to have a conversation with your fourteen-year-old self, but you can rationalise anything if you try hard enough—ask my mother. In my warped logic, Little Amy's role was to help me decide whether to offer assistance. For the last ten years I'd understood that I was blameless, but now Little Amy had helped me to see that my mother's treatment of me was abusive. This absolved me of any responsibility to help her. Little Amy's job was done, so surely she'd leave me in peace. And as for Cynthia Hope—well a hypocritical busybody like her deserved to hear a few home truths about herself.

I put away a quarter bottle of gin and was rewarded by the worst night's sleep ever. Seeing the hoard again had reawakened memories dormant for a decade, giving the rubbish dream a new vibrancy. Armed men pursued me through the hoard. I dived frantically into the mountains of crap to take refuge, but the bullets rained hard and fast. I woke, shaking with fear, and hurried to the bathroom to vomit.

Although I felt considerably better by the time I'd hit the office gym and arrived at my desk, the illusion of wellbeing was short-lived. Smithies had asked to see me.

He offered me tea—a bad sign. I hoped I wouldn't puke it straight up.

'Amy,' he said, flashing his hideous crocodile grin. 'How are you?'

The question freaked me out—or rather it destabilised me, to use Smithies' own terminology. And as I'd expected a swift and brutal reprisal for my intervention over Lisa, I found his syrupy pleasantness worrying.

'I'm good, thanks.'

The water-skiers looked down on me pityingly in the long pause that followed—a pause he hoped would be long enough to fracture the brittle façade of my composure. I steeled myself. Whatever he had in his arsenal, Smithies' tactics wouldn't work. I was tougher than he realised.

'I'm sorry to say Eric Bailey took a very disturbing telephone call yesterday afternoon.'

Bonus points to Smithies for a surprise opening gambit. I'd expected him to begin by mentioning Lisa, and couldn't imagine what lay behind this more oblique attack.

'Yes?' I said, trying to sound unconcerned.

I figured the call must somehow be connected with the murder investigation. Charges of perverting the course of justice or accessory to murder were hardly career-enhancing. And I remembered with a shudder how quickly they'd despatched Venner, Smithies' predecessor. Was this my firing meeting—Smithies' ultimate retribution?

Another lengthy pause intensified the suspense. Then he hit me with it.

'From your mother's neighbour—a Miss Cynthia Hope.'

Adrenalin surged through my veins, as though an invisible hand had injected a powerful narcotic. Bile rose in my throat. The game was over—he'd trapped me in the first few moves.

Clearly, the Hope woman was less frail than she'd appeared, and I'd been stupid enough to underestimate her. This man had been angling to discover my weakness ever since he'd taken charge. Now, through my own stupidity, I'd handed the dangerous knowledge to him on a plate.

'She claims you were extremely abusive to her yesterday afternoon,' he said. 'Now leaving aside the lie you told Lisa about being at a marketing meeting, Miss Hope's allegations are serious. Do you know what she told us?'

'No.'

I could imagine, though, and I cursed Lisa for grassing me up.

'She says she called you over when she discovered your mother was living in squalid conditions, which apparently you've been aware of for a while. And for this, you subjected her to a torrent of abuse, and told her you refuse to lift a finger to help.'

I said nothing.

'I notice you're not denying the allegations,' he said, misinterpreting my silence.

'I don't have to confirm or deny anything,' I said, when I'd summoned enough emotional strength to speak. 'This is a personal matter. Bailey shouldn't have been involved.'

'But, Amy, we are all ambassadors of the firm twenty-four-seven,' he said, trotting out the Pearson Malone cliché of the month.

'Yes, I know.'

'It would be open to Miss Hope to bring charges...'

'*For what—speaking your mind? The toffee-nosed cow.*'

'But fortunately she has no intention of doing so—she merely wanted to warn us you were under a considerable strain.'

How helpful, I thought acidly.

'Amy, I realise the shock and guilt when you found out about your mother's living conditions must have been terrible for you.'

He oozed with sympathy, but that didn't make him less dangerous—quite the reverse. My track record was strong, but in the final analysis this counted for nothing. Smithies had trashed the careers of dozens of people on a whim. And without a doubt his end game was firing me. Underneath all the treacly pseudo-empathy, he'd already worked out that the latest developments presented him with an unparalleled opportunity to destroy me.

'I'm so sorry we all failed to notice what strain you were under,' he burbled on. 'And it's such a shame you felt unable to confide in us about what's been happening in your life.'

I found it impossible to respond appropriately to this mawkish drivel, so I said nothing.

'You didn't have to lie about that client meeting yesterday. Every family has its challenges and absolutely no shame in it.'

I tried to imagine how Smithies would have fared if he'd grown up in a hoarded house. Would he still have the same ruthless arrogance and overweening sense of entitlement? Shit no—he'd be a wreck in a straitjacket in a padded cell in an institution.

'We've all lost our tempers at a time of stress—it's perfectly normal. And how are you to blame if the silly old woman complains to Eric Bailey? He doesn't hold it against you, honestly. He can seem harsh and unsympathetic, but he gets it, just as I do.'

I severely doubted if either Bailey or Smithies got even a fraction of it.

'And it must be especially trying for you, coming hot on the heels of your other worries.'

'What other worries?' I asked, prickling.

'The numbers for your operating unit are simply appalling,' he said, pointing gravely to the printout of the fortnightly profit and loss account.

I hadn't yet seen the figures, but wasn't surprised. In the last two weeks, the pay review, the murder of one team member and the arrest of another must have all reduced productivity. A blip in performance was wholly predictable.

'They were bang on budget last month,' I bleated. 'Surely they can't be so bad.'

'Well, I don't want to depress you,' he said, hastening to do so, 'but utilisation for the last two weeks is considerably below average. You're behind with billings and cash collection, and as for the recovery rate on what you did manage to bill—frankly, I've seldom seen such a low percentage.'

'Can't you cut us some slack? It's been hard for the team to concentrate, as I'm sure you appreciate.'

'Obviously there are mitigating circumstances, but you seem so stressed at the moment, it's unfair to burden you…'

'It's my job to be burdened,' I cut in. 'I'm touched by your thoughtfulness, but I'm honestly OK...'

He sipped at his tea and fixed me with his trademark reptilian gaze.

'You know, I admire your strength, but sometimes you need the insight to recognise that you require help.'

This was how it went. Once the gossip started about someone suffering from stress, the outcome was all but guaranteed. Smithies had started the rumours, but like a fool, I'd played right into their hands.

Smithies moved in for the kill.

'Now, I don't want you to take this the wrong way,' he went on, straining hard to convey his sorrow at the bad tidings about to follow. 'But Bailey, Townsend and I all agreed it would be advisable to relieve some of the pressure on you.'

'You did?'

'So we've decided that pro-tem, I should take over the running of your group.'

I should have anticipated this—not firing, but a demotion—the first step towards it. He'd lost no time in playing the new cards I'd dealt him to his maximum advantage. What a mug I'd been.

'What—you mean I'm not group leader anymore?'

'Egg-zackly—just for the time being, though.'

'But surely...' I began.

'Yes, yes, I know what you're going to say,' said Smithies, without giving me the opportunity to say it. 'And it's so brave of you to keep battling on against the odds.'

'It's two weeks' results,' I said, trying in vain to modulate the rising pitch of my voice. 'With extenuating factors...'

'Sure,' he said. 'There are always extenuating factors.'

'But I'm perfectly fine.'

'Amy, the way you're overreacting to this temporary change appears to validate my thought process.'

That was another tried and tested technique. They did something to upset you, and then cited your distress as justification for their action.

Temporary change—bollocks—he'd appoint one of his toadies and cut me out. And without a leadership role, I'd be a sitting duck in any downsizing of the partner team. Everything I'd fought so hard for over the years hung in the balance—all through my own stupidity and weakness.

'I felt sure you'd understand once you got used to the idea,' he said, interpreting my silence as acquiescence.

But I refused to give in without a fight.

'I'm only too familiar with your agenda,' I told him. 'Before long, you'll install one of your own guys as leader. That's been your game plan from the start.'

He shook his head sadly. However true the accusation, even uttering it evidenced paranoia.

'Look, you seem to have issues none of us were aware of,' he said, in his most avuncular tone. 'I've suspected something of the sort for a while now. I won't ask you how your mother came to be in such a terrible state...'

And I won't tell you.

'But what a pity you felt unable to open up to anybody here. We like to think of ourselves as an extended family as you know, and our employee-counselling programme is second to none. I would urge you to make use of it, by the way—it's strictly confidential. But in the meantime, please have faith in us while we make your life easier.'

'Seems like I don't have much choice,' I replied bitterly.

'And can I offer you some advice?'

I suspected the advice would be forthcoming even if I said no.

'I think you have a hard time trusting people. You should loosen up a bit. There's no reason you couldn't have told us about your mother's situation.'

Except there was a reason, and he was it.

'And in a similar vein, I felt hurt by the lack of trust you placed in me over Lisa's promotion. I'm at a loss to understand why you didn't discuss it with me before running to Townsend.'

I clamped my mouth firmly shut, afraid of what I might say.

'But rest assured, all this will remain strictly *entre nous* including, for the avoidance of doubt, your inappropriate relationship with Ryan, of which we'll say no more.'

It would have appalled me that he'd found out, but somehow the discovery of the hoarding had eclipsed the Ryan issue to the point where I simply felt numb. Bloody Greg must have spilled the beans—just when I'd begun to put the hurt of our divorce behind me and believe in him as a decent human being. It went to show, you couldn't rely on anyone.

I saw with appalling clarity how it would play out from here. Smithies had already broadcast my issues with alcohol and stress, and capitalised on my possible involvement in the murder. Now on top of that, he could allude to impropriety with Ryan, in addition to unspecified family problems adversely affecting my performance. What an overabundance of ammunition I'd provided him with. Even without making specific allegations, his snide insinuations would give the blackest possible impression. With every drip of his poison, people would lose faith in my ability and judgement, and I'd be powerless to arrest my descent on this downward spiral. No question about it—my career at Pearson Malone was over.

'Anyway, sermon finished,' he said in an artificially bright tone that I found immensely dispiriting. 'I do hope reducing your workload will give you an opportunity to sort your life out. And I'm always happy to chat if you feel the need.'

Hell would freeze over first.

'And in the meantime, I hope you don't mind me saying so but you might be happier if you helped your mum, even though you're not keen. Guilt is an insidious emotion—eats away at you.'

How would he know?

'Perhaps if you hired someone to have a little clean around.'

I restrained myself from laughing out loud as I grasped that he had no conception of the scale of the squalor. Like most normal people, he simply couldn't imagine it.

'After all,' he concluded. 'She's the only mother you've got.'

'*Yes*,' said Little Amy. '*And that's the whole fucking problem.*'

And for once, I agreed with her.

20

When Eric Bailey's number flashed up on my phone later in the day, I supposed he'd be following up on the Cynthia Hope incident. But instead, a different topic preyed on his mind.

'Amy, I've heard something disturbing.'

'Yes, Smithies spoke to me earlier. I'm sorry you were troubled.'

'No, no—not that idiotic old woman, I mean the stories you've been spreading about JJ.'

This caught me unawares.

'What stories?'

'About potential accounting irregularities.'

'I contacted the corporate finance partner, that's all.'

'Your ex,' said Bailey pointedly, as though my brief marriage to Greg defined me as a person.

'Surely I'm allowed to talk to another person in the client team if I have concerns? I thought we were trying to foster a "collaborative culture".'

Although I was not in the best frame of mind I still managed, in an aggressive gesture, to throw his words from a recent partners' conference back at him.

'Nobody is disputing your right to consult with the team, even if the issue you've raised is completely lacking in substance. But what you may not do is chatter to all and sundry on such a sensitive matter. Incredibly, I heard all this from Ed Smithies, who's the last person who should be privy to any information about the client, given his close family connection.'

Now it was clear. In addition to his disloyalty in telling Smithies about Ryan, Greg had mentioned the JJ business to him as well.

'I can't understand how Smithies came to be aware of it.'

There was no benefit in implicating Greg—it would only backfire, and already I was on the back foot.

'I can—you've been indiscreet—perhaps after a few glasses of wine?'

Oh my God—Smithies was unstoppable in his quest to ruin me.

'Certainly not,' I said.

'Greg thought you might be trying to exonerate his brother, for whatever reason, by bringing this up now.'

For whatever reason—loaded with meaning.

'But surely everyone would want Ryan exonerated if he's innocent?'

I didn't imagine for a moment that fighting back would help my cause, but I had my pride. These guys acted as if they had carte blanche to destroy me—how could I not retaliate?

'Naturally.'

I detected a slight caginess in Bailey's voice. We both knew a rogue employee murderer was vastly preferable to a criminal investigation affecting a major client.

'But that doesn't excuse a breach in confidentiality,' he said, recovering quickly. 'I hardly need remind you how disastrous any adverse market chatter about JJ would be at this critical time. If I hear a whiff of it, I'll know who's responsible. Ed didn't want you on this client, and frankly I'm now beginning to see why.'

I wondered fleetingly as to the real reason Smithies hadn't wanted me, but dismissed the thought.

'Now see, I'm not a total bastard. I realise you're going through a rough patch, Amy, but you should watch your step. You keep blipping up on my radar screen for the wrong reasons.'

I opened my mouth to reply, but he'd already hung up.

Afterwards as I reflected on our conversation, I marvelled at how a complete non-issue could have stirred up such a storm.

***

'Hoarding,' said Lisa incredulously, as we sat in Daly's after work. I'd finally got round to the Big Secret after a lengthy rant about my demotion, Greg's disloyalty and Smithies' vindictiveness.

Gulping at my wine as though it was a magic potion, I spilled out my story as if I was in a confessional, including the antics of the meddlesome Hope woman.

'But when you wouldn't share with me, I figured it was something terrible.'

'It *was* terrible.'

'What—growing up in a messy house?'

I sighed. The recent TV shows had helped people understand hoarding, but they didn't show the full horror. I would have to take Lisa to the house for her to experience the smell and the stifling oppression of all the stuff inside it. And I couldn't bring myself to mention the plumbing situation—the final taboo.

Moreover, that was just the physical discomfort. How could I begin to explain the humiliation that was indissolubly linked with the mess? What words could adequately convey the pervasive shame, the sensation of being different, and the ever-present fear of discovery? Would someone with her brash confidence ever understand the aftermath, the enduring sense of unworthiness, the fear that the higher I soared, the further I must fall?

'It's easier to talk about it now,' I explained. 'But growing up, I had no word to describe the chaos, no support groups on the internet, no TV shows. I honestly believed we were the only family in the world who lived like that. I felt so ashamed. I'm *still* so ashamed.'

'But why?'

'Imagine you'd grown up somewhere so squalid you can't ask your friends in. Suppose you had to invent excuses for why they can't come over.'

'I wouldn't have made excuses—the mess was down to your mum, not you.'

'True, but she always told me it was my fault, that I was such a bad daughter she gave up all hope. And I believed her. It's not so easy as a kid when the person who's supposed to love you unconditionally tries to manipulate you like that. And those stuck-up bitches at school would have been appalled—I couldn't have faced them.'

'That's a posh school for you,' said Lisa, as ever losing no opportunity to ridicule my middle-class background.

'The fact is, hoarding is a form of child abuse.'

'That's a bit strong, isn't it?'

'No—it's not. Kids have a right to a clean and safe environment and parents have a duty to provide it.'

'But you've grown up alright, so it can't have been too bad.'

In that one disparaging sentence, Lisa had cut to the heart of the matter. Yes, I'd been desperate to have "grown up alright"—in itself a form of denial. Yet if I was honest, the hoarding had affected every aspect of my life.

Sharing my insecurities with Lisa had never been easy, because I needed her to admire and respect me. But without explaining in more detail, she would continue to belittle my suffering, incapable of comprehending how fundamental my upbringing had been to the person I'd become. And how could I criticise her, when I'd scarcely begun to realise it myself?

'Is this why you cut her out of your life?'

'Yes.'

'But if that's how she likes to live…?'

'I can't forgive her for forcing me to endure it.'

'But you've left now.'

'I don't care to be associated with anyone who lives in a pigsty, particularly someone in denial about their illness.'

'Well you are something of a neat freak,' said Lisa, as if the fault lay with me for being too intolerant and judgmental.

'Now you know why.'

'I still don't get it though. Why was it so difficult to tell me the truth?'

She had stumped me there. Over thirty years, a routine of secrecy becomes ingrained and the reasons for it buried in the mists of time. Moreover, shame doesn't disappear overnight.

'I don't know,' I confessed. 'It seemed… impossible…'

'I wish you hadn't lied to me yesterday about being in a meeting. I mean, even as I was having a go at you for keeping secrets you were up to your old tricks. It's starting to annoy me.'

'It annoyed me that you grassed me up to Smithies.'

'He asked where you were—how was I to know you were lying about it?'

Fair enough, I supposed.

'I'm sorry,' I said.

'You keep saying sorry—I just wish you'd change.'

'I'll try.'

'Anyway, if you want my advice about the hoarding, you need to sort out your strategy. That woman expects action.'

'I don't care what she expects—I don't have to do anything.'

'You'll feel guilty if you don't,' she said, unwittingly echoing Smithies.

'Not in the slightest,' I said, although in truth my conscience still troubled me.

'Even so, why don't you draw a line under this once and for all—hire a firm to have it all cleared out while she's in hospital?'

'There are firms to do that?'

'Sure,' she said, as though I was a cretin. 'Something needs doing. You have money, someone will be happy to take it and sort it out.'

What a great idea. During the previous clean-up, my mother had been at home, and I'd been obliged to pussyfoot around her, picking through the crap item by item. I'd endured three weeks of histrionics and resistance. This time, I would decide what to chuck out—in fact, I'd pretty much decided already—almost all of it must go. And I could hire someone to do the legwork, an idea I hadn't considered previously. It sounded so easy, and yet it was impossible.

'She'd never agree to it.'

'So don't ask her.'

Was that really an option? I asked myself.

'I'll think about it.'

'No—don't think—do it. You'll feel better afterwards and who knows—once the place is tidy she may keep it in order.'

Little Amy would cling to that hope, I knew, but the adult Amy didn't believe in miracles anymore.

'I'd be surprised.'

'But won't you visit her in the hospital?'

'Absolutely not.'

'Not as an expression of hope in the future?'

'Especially not as that.'

'But she's the only mother you've got.'

'Yes,' I said through gritted teeth.

There was little more to be said about the hoarding, but Lisa wasn't done with dispensing her advice.

'I hope you don't mind me mentioning,' she said. 'But I do think you're being a bit paranoid about Smithies.'

I did mind, because she'd obviously miscalculated the strength of the man's will to bring me down.

'Paranoid? Not a chance. First, he leaves me to deal single-handedly with the media. Then he gossips about me and Ryan. After that, he drops me in it with Bailey, demotes me, and spreads snide rumours about my drinking. I'm convinced he's trying to destroy me.'

'Hm,' she said.

'And don't forget, he tried to block your promotion.'

'Well, he is a total scumbag,' Lisa agreed. 'But you've done yourself no favours. If you hadn't slept with Ryan there wouldn't be anything to gossip about. If you hadn't mouthed off at your mum's neighbour, she wouldn't have called Bailey. And let's face it, you do drink a bit too much.'

'You're supposed to be my friend.'

'A friend tells you the truth, hon, even if it's not always what you want to hear.'

'Yeah—sure. And you'd never tell a lie, would you?'

It was a standing joke between us. She'd written the exact phrase "I never tell a lie" in her partnership application papers. I'd tried to exercise my editorial control and change it to “I have a refreshingly honest approach”, because to claim never to lie subtly suggested that others did. But she’d batted away my suggestion—this was *her* submission and she’d word it *her* way.

‘Fact is,’ she told me sternly, ‘you’d be better off getting Smithies on side than making an enemy of him.’

‘What, like you are?’ I said in sarcastic tones.

‘Point taken, but seriously…’

‘I can’t—he’s not just a scumbag. He’s a truly evil person.’

‘What?’

‘I think he killed Isabelle.’

She was so astounded at this, that she knocked over her wine glass.

‘In the name of God, why?’ she asked, mopping at the spillage dripping from the table.

‘Because she found evidence of fraud at the slate mine, he murdered her to save his brother-in-law’s skin.’

She eyed me sternly as she grabbed another wad of napkins.

‘Now you have to admit that is nuts.’

‘It isn’t. Why did Smithies go to Bailey and tell him I was spreading rumours?’

‘Because he thought you were?’

‘No—he expected Bailey to blow up and scare me off delving into this any further.’

‘There is nothing to delve into though—you spoke to Greg and there’s nothing in it. Let it go, Amy—believing your boss is a murderer reeks of paranoia.’

After completing the clean-up, she refilled her glass with the remnants of the wine, then held up the empty bottle.

‘Another one?’

‘No thanks,’ I said. ‘Like you said, I’m drinking too much.’

As we walked in silence to the Tube station, I found it impossible to suppress a growing conviction that Smithies' poison had spread to Lisa. But didn't that reek of paranoia too?

***

There's a good reason everyone advises you to delete your ex's number from your phone.

Far from making me more chilled about the day's events, the wine had stoked my anger. And as I strolled home from the Underground I found myself dialling Greg's number.

He amazed me by answering. He was no Einstein, but even so he ought to have anticipated a furious outburst.

'Yes, Amy.'

I caught an edge of weary resignation in his voice.

'What possessed you to tell Smithies about Ryan?' I demanded.

'He sensed something was up—said you'd been hopping around like a cat on a hot griddle every time he mentioned Ryan's name. He actually thought it was much worse than a one-night stand, so I helped you out by setting him straight.'

'Yeah—I'm so fucking grateful.'

'Amy—are you drunk?'

'No, I'm stone cold bloody sober. Why does everyone think I'm a complete soak?'

The silence at the other end of the line answered that question as eloquently as anything he might have said.

'And why mention what we discussed on JJ? Smithies shouldn't have any involvement on that client. Plus, he got onto Bailey pronto and I've had a severe bollocking, which I totally didn't need right now.'

Despite my efforts to stay calm, the pitch of my voice had risen by an octave or so.

'Amy, I hope you don't mind me saying, but you seem a bit overwrought.'

'Unlike you—cool as a cucumber. Your brother's being held on a murder charge—no sweat. Isabelle's killed because she finds some dodgy stuff on one of your clients—what the heck? You and that audit guy with the intellect of an ape agree that it's easier all round to ignore any problems. Easy to see where your priorities lie, Greg.'

'That's simply not true. Can you imagine how hurtful it is when you suggest I'd let my own brother go to the wall? Amy, I promise you there's nothing untoward going on at JJ. Now, if you'll excuse me we have guests.'

'We—yes—Tiffany—that stupid little tart of a secretary you married.'

'Well, it's a damned sight better than being married to all your secrets. Why the hell didn't you ever tell me about your mother?'

'Smithies shouldn't have told you. He promised he'd keep it confidential.'

'*Dammit, he assumed I knew*,' Greg replied. 'Jesus—we were together for three years—what sort of marriage did we have with *that* coming between us?'

'You were always such a judgmental prick—perhaps that's why I kept quiet.'

'Amy,' he said, 'listening to the way you're talking, I'm feeling you might benefit from some professional help. Would you like me to...?'

'No,' I said. 'Piss off.'

As I hung up, I spotted Little Amy lurking in a shop doorway. She said nothing, but smirked triumphantly.

21

I hadn't yet hauled myself out of bed and into the shower when my phone rang. It had been another uncomfortable night in the hoard house, this time trapped with a fire raging and no means of escape. Now I lay dozing quietly in an attempt to regain my equilibrium.

I came to with a jump. Shit—Smithies—at 7.02. Didn't he realise how these early morning calls unsettled me? On second thoughts, maybe that was his intention.

'Hi there,' I said as brightly as I could manage.

'Just calling to check how you're holding up after the shocking news.'

'What news?' I asked, my stomach tightening.

'You mean you haven't heard?' He paused for dramatic effect. 'Ryan Kelly's committed suicide—hanged himself. It's breaking on Sky.'

'Oh God—no.'

I sank back into the pillows, shaken to the core. I hadn't seen this coming at all.

'I thought you'd be shocked,' he said, sounding pleased.

Shocked didn't even come close to describing it.

'Why yes. Aren't you?'

'Obviously,' he said breezily. 'Although, I must admit this does bring the whole episode to a nice tidy conclusion, doesn't it?'

The most loathsome aspect of this statement was its accuracy, and it applied to me even more than Smithies. Ryan's death meant I wouldn't have to regale the court with an account of my drunken one-night stand. Even better, any potential charge as an accessory had surely died along with him.

'Yes, I suppose it does,' I agreed.

'I'm heading into the office now and I'll do what I can to calm the troops. No need for you to rush in though—I expect you'd like some time to compose yourself, given how close you were to Ryan.'

'Thank you for thinking of me,' I said tartly.

I flicked on the television. The media gloves were off. No trial meant no contempt of court, and you cannot libel the dead. They enjoyed complete freedom to say what they liked about poor Ryan, and they made the most of it.

The consensus was that he'd been guilty and unable to live with the crime he'd committed. Nobody suggested that following a wrongful arrest he'd had zero faith that justice would be done. I sat on the arm of the sofa, mesmerised by the commentary, and weighed down with guilt.

I should have done more to defend him—should have promoted him. Hell, if he'd been given his promotion he would have been with Isabelle that night and she would have been safe. Instead, he'd spent the night with me and then I'd betrayed him too. In my heart, I knew he hadn't left my house at the critical time, yet I'd capitulated quickly under pressure to save my own skin.

There were no tears though, because I don't do grief. The sudden death of a parent leaves you with few illusions as to the transient nature of life. Grief is a silly, selfish emotion. The dead person has gone and is indifferent to your feelings, so your misery is wholly centred round your own inability to adjust to the loss. Me—I can adjust to anything.

In truth, if I was able to stomach the guilt, Ryan's death brought an opportunity for closure and rebalancing my life. I would clear out my mother's squalor then move on, and I would stand up to Smithies instead of allowing him to bully me. Finally, I would forget any ideas of uncovering any double-dealing at JJ—better to let it lie, whatever the truth. It would be a neat and tidy end to everything, just as Smithies had suggested.

But as you must realise by now, life is never neat and tidy for me.

22

Pearson Malone sent a sympathy card and a wreath—Smithies' doing, of course. Although Ryan hadn't quite been posthumously transformed into Employee of the Year, he'd graduated from being public enemy number one. His death had erased most of the complications preceding it, not least the need to fire him.

Smithies suggested I should attend the funeral on behalf of the firm 'as you'll presumably be going anyway'. Purely because I couldn't think how to refuse, I agreed.

I was determined not to let the depressing corporate hypocrisy around Ryan's death drag me down. I had much to do.

First came 'Project Mother'.

As Lisa had suggested, if you have the money, there's no task that can't be delegated. I was stunned by the number of clearance outfits in the London area, offering comprehensive solutions to an obviously widespread issue.

Clearall described themselves as "hoard clearance specialists" on their website, with particular expertise in trauma situations and council properties. Why a council house should be any different from any other property mystified me—maybe I should ask them. They claimed, somewhat brazenly, to provide a solution to any situation. That remained to be seen, but agreeing to meet me the same evening was a promising start.

Unquestionably, my main motivation was to fulfil other people's expectations. I felt more comfortable with my subsidiary motive, which was to capitalise on a unique opportunity for action, and to ensure I never found myself in the same position again. This time I would foot the bill, but if my mother re-hoarded, she'd have to face the consequences on her own—there would be no repeat performance. And if she didn't—perhaps our relationship might be salvaged. But I didn't hold out much hope.

My cheeks flushed as Andy, Clearall's managing director, coldly appraised the level of squalor. Alongside my lingering embarrassment, I wrestled with a sense of inadequacy. Even as a child, my failure to keep the house presentable shamed me, and the blame my mother heaped upon me did nothing to allay my distress. Little Amy could be exonerated, but grown-up Amy found it tougher to disclaim responsibility. I wasn't even an average adult, but a high-flier who cut a swathe through complex challenges every day. It seemed ridiculous to have allowed matters to reach this stage. But as Andy bluntly pointed out, if the families could sort their hoarding relatives, he wouldn't make a living.

'I've seen worse,' came his verdict. 'Two days' work for a team of five—four large skips—assuming you're keeping the furniture.'

Although it was mainly obscured by junk, I guessed the furniture was worn and tatty but still functional. I could easily afford it, but buying new stuff for her was far above and beyond the call of duty. Let her buy her own if she wanted—she hadn't ended up in this hole through poverty.

'Pretty much.'

'And anything else goes?'

'Yep.'

'Just to be clear, if we find any valuables we'll put them aside.'

They wouldn't. Despite the apparent impossibility of the task, I was positive I'd locate every item of importance before they started work.

'OK. So how much?'

His eyes lighted on my gold watch and diamond earrings.

'Five thousand plus skip hire. Half in advance. Card payment or bank transfer.'

'Can you work at the weekend? I need it done while my mother's away.'

'Ten grand,' he said without hesitation. 'We don't normally do weekends.'

I produced my premier Mastercard. It was a rip off but the price was irrelevant.

'Will you be able to supervise the clearance?'

'Yes.'

'And will your mother sign a consent? We've had some tricky situations in the past, you see, with hoarders claiming they never authorised the clean-out.'

I wavered. Obviously my mother couldn't provide a signature without becoming aware of the plan. And once aware, she wouldn't sign anyway.

'Send me the paperwork and I'll sort it out,' I said with confidence. Forging a signature offended my ethical senses, but needs must.

'*I knew you'd do it in the end*,' said Little Amy after he'd gone.

'I do wish you'd go away,' I snapped. 'You make me worry that something's wrong with me.'

'*Well, something is wrong with you*,' she retorted, and promptly disappeared.

I stared at the empty chair in disbelief. I'd have gladly paid ten grand to clear out the junk in my head.

***

Later that evening, my phone showed "number withheld" as it rang.

There was no reason not to answer.

'Hi—Amy.'

A male voice, which I didn't immediately recognise.

'Who is this?'

'Dave Carmody.'

Unbelievable.

'Oh—not DCI Carmody today then.'

'No—not today.'

'Why are you calling?'

'To find out how you're doing.'

'You think I want to tell you?'

'I owe you an apology.'

'Too right.'

'And I totally get how angry you must be—looking back, we may have handled things a tad insensitively.'

'*A tad insensitively—he must be joking*.'

'If that's your idea of an apology, it doesn't cut it.'

'OK, I apologise unreservedly and I'm asking you out for dinner.'

'Why?'

'Because you're an interesting, attractive woman.'

'*Believe me, you're not*.'

I sort of agreed with Little Amy. What was interesting or attractive about a drunken slut who could be easily intimidated? Unless he was one of those weird guys who got off on weak women. Or maybe he wanted something else from me, under the pretence of asking me for a date. Two weeks ago I might have been tempted to give him the benefit of the doubt, but the new Amy didn't take any crap from anyone.

And Little Amy certainly didn't.

'The answer's no.'

'I guess I'm not surprised. Anyway, it was worth a try.'

He sounded genuinely downcast and I vacillated for a few seconds, but held firm. My guts told me DCI Carmody would be a disastrous influence on my life.

'Well, I don't suppose our paths will cross again, so all the best for the future.'

I couldn't bring myself to reciprocate the good wishes.

'OK, bye,' I said, and hung up.

'*And good riddance*!'

23

I would have gladly ducked out of the trip to JJ Slate, but felt it unfair to dump the assignment on anybody else at such short notice. Although Lisa had suggested a Friday meeting, Isabelle had insisted Thursday would be better, to allow her a long weekend at home.

As I set off in the car, it struck me how death is always lurking round the corner, even when we least expect it. The last time Isabelle drove this same route she would quite reasonably have expected to be making the journey many times in the future. Ryan must also have anticipated a long and healthy life ahead. And in a few years I would be older than my own father, dropped down dead at forty-two, always assuming I didn't succumb to the same fate before then.

Despite these gloomy thoughts, my spirits grew lighter as the suburbs gave way to the motorway, and then to the leafy winding roads of Wales. I'd left my problems far behind in London.

According to Wikipedia, the JJ Slate mine's history extended back far beyond its current ownership. It had first been developed towards the end of the eighteenth century and a hundred years later had grown to one of the world's largest, employing over three thousand men. To call it a mine was, I discovered, something of a misnomer, since the majority of its grey slate was excavated by quarrying. However, a vein of highly prized and more exotic green slate lay beneath a heritage site of outstanding natural beauty. It therefore had to be extracted via underground workings—the last working slate mine in Wales. As a result of technological advances, the workforce now stood at a mere two hundred.

A fine drizzle fell as I drew up at the security barrier, and with dismay I noticed the muddy ground. How stupid of me to have worn my black patent stilettos. Every time I thought I'd regained control, I did something utterly dumb as if to prove what an idiot I was. I could only hope that alternative footwear would be provided for the site tour.

A red Porsche 911 with a personalized JJ registration plate took pride of place in the car park. Surely we weren't to be graced by the presence of Jupp himself? I pulled up alongside it and tried to navigate a path to reception through the murky puddles.

Neil Waterhouse, the managing director of the slate operation, was a pompous little nerd, with a sweaty handshake and a fancy job title that meant bugger all. A visit from the Pearson Malone tax partner had swelled his ego and he swaggered around, puffed up by his perceived importance. Just the type to be on the fiddle, I reckoned—arrogant enough to assume he wouldn't be discovered, and stupid enough not to cover his tracks properly.

Not that any of that mattered now.

'I've been reading up on the history of the mine,' I said, to make polite conversation as we waited for Rob, the capital allowances specialist. 'Incredible how few workers there are here compared to a hundred or so years ago, isn't it?'

'Not really—times move on,' he said, leaving me in no doubt as to the futility of continued attempts at communication.

'Does JJ come out here often?' I asked.

'No, very seldom,' said Neil quickly.

I detected a trace of nervousness in his response, which deterred me from asking if he was here today. I remembered JJ demurring when I'd proposed the tour, and wondered if he might be on site to ensure no one inadvertently gave anything away. But how could a mine tour reveal a white-collar crime? Quickly, I reined in my imagination—I'd resolved not to think about it anymore.

JJ didn't show and Rob arrived a couple of minutes later, saving me from any further exchange of pleasantries with Waterhouse. Rob was based in our Manchester office—a balding guy with sandy coloured hair and gold-rimmed glasses. I recognised him straight away—he'd been another of Greg's cohort who'd been a guest our wedding. From memory, most of the guests had been connected with Greg. Rob gave no acknowledgement of this tenuous connection—most likely he'd forgotten.

The quarry foreman kitted us out with ruthless efficiency—hard hats, boots and waterproof outer clothing.

'What shoe size do you take?' he asked.

'Three and a half.'

'We don't have any *quite* as small as that,' he said, exchanging a condescending smirk with the other men. 'Still you can't wear those, can you?' He observed my mud-splattered Jimmy Choos with disdain. 'Here's a six. If you put on a few pairs of these thick socks they shouldn't be so big on you.'

I resembled Charlie Chaplin as I trotted out to the waiting buggy. First stop would be the quarry, then the slate crushing plant, and lastly the mine itself.

All went smoothly to begin with. I stayed in the background as Rob asked technical questions on quarrying methods and equipment used, interjecting only to demonstrate that I was adding value. I inferred from Rob's copious note-taking that there was plenty of scope for tax claims, especially in the crushing plant.

Our final destination was the underground workings. We boarded a narrow gauge train which sped back through the quarry before beginning its dizzying descent to the mine. I thought of Isabelle's grandfather, making this trip daily and not seeing sunlight all day. Even at its worst, Pearson Malone couldn't top that for unpleasantness.

According to my online research, only one of three mine-shafts was currently being mined. The small train whizzed over the points past a short branch line to shaft number one en route to shaft three. A heavy metal door, which looked as though it hadn't been opened for years, sealed off the disused area. And yet the railway tracks leading to it were gleaming. Without fully registering the thought, I questioned why.

I'd expected freezing temperatures down the mine, but according to the foreman they maintained the temperature at a constant fifty-four degrees Fahrenheit, or twelve degrees Centigrade. I learned that a significant amount of energy was used to extract the heat generated by all the machinery. In addition, pumping out the water that threatened to engulf the mine periodically required considerable effort. Which explained the humongous electricity bill I'd seen when I'd checked the accounts. We stood around admiring the mechanical diggers and ventilation units, and Rob rattled off another series of technical questions, many of which sailed over my head.

In the gloom, there was something about the looming heaps of scrap slate awaiting removal which reminded me of the hoard house. The miners lived my childhood life in reverse—

working in horrible conditions and returning to clean homes. But they didn't have to lie, or pretend their workplace was pristine, because everyone expected mines to be dirty. I saw now that the deceit had harmed me more than the mess, together with the shame and the guilt my mother laid on me.

As I focussed in the gloom, I picked out more detail in the piles. I peered more closely, and wished I hadn't.

Because these weren't piles of slate at all, but towering heaps of junk, piled up to the roof.

No—they couldn't be, surely... Wouldn't somebody have noticed? I watched, transfixed, as the others chatted away, oblivious to the unfolding apparition. The piles shifted, closing in on me—menacing and predatory. My dream had come to life.

An unfamiliar tightness gripped my chest and squeezed the breath from my lungs. My head spun—my hands tingled. Surely they had lured me here and poisoned me with some hallucinogenic drug. Seized by a force more powerful than my own free will, I coughed and spluttered as the tsunami of dread swept to a crescendo.

'*Run, run, or they'll kill you.*'

But if I ran, they would surely catch me—I could have moved faster in my stilettos than those damned stupid clown's boots. I fought the impulse to bolt, took one step away, and then another, and another, slowly and steadily. Before anyone noticed, I'd slipped away.

Once out of sight, I broke into a trot, back along the railway track, my lungs and limbs screaming for air. Finally my legs buckled and I slumped, opposite the door to Shaft 1—a gasping, shivering wreck drenched in cold sweat, like an addict in withdrawal.

Then the door slid open and as my eyes adjusted to the dazzling white light I understood everything.

***

Through the door, I saw row after row of plants under powerful lights. An overwhelming musky sweetness transported me back to my university days.

Cannabis—they were growing dope—here in the slate mine.

'*Get moving—you can't be found here*,' Little Amy exhorted.

Quite right. Whatever else happened—they mustn't discover I'd seen the plants. With the last dregs of strength, I dragged myself around the corner, where the foreman discovered me seconds later.

'What do you think you're doing?' he asked. 'You can't go wandering off—health and safety.'

'I'm ill,' I gasped and promptly vomited, involuntarily adding a touch of authenticity to the story.

Puking had triggered a miraculous recovery, at least physically. My poisoning panic had proved baseless, but anxiety still gnawed at me. Why did I keep hallucinating? What was real and what was not?

As the little train chugged back to the surface, my repetitious apologies were met with half-hearted reassurances. Everyone appeared to accept my claustrophobia at face value. Who knew—it might even be true. I fielded their asinine questions about whether I'd ever had anything similar happen before, and swore to them I was OK.

But was I?

I shunned their offer to put me on a train from Llandudno. The prospect of other passengers eying and judging alarmed me far more than concentrating on a lengthy drive. Besides, I'd have to work out how to retrieve the car if I left it at the mine.

As I reversed the journey I'd made in such a spirit of optimism that morning, there was plenty of time for reflection. If perception was reality, then everything was real, which was palpably false. That gave the lie to Smithies' favourite mantra, unless I truly was insane and my perception counted for nothing. Common sense told me neither the hoard in the mine nor Little Amy existed. But the rest? I'd not seen a cannabis farm before—how could my imagination conjure one up in such plausible detail? Other evidence pointed to the existence of the drugs. For one thing, the slate mine was an ideal location for growing dope. It must be immune from heat-detecting helicopters and used so much energy already that the powerful lights might not add significantly to the cost.

Suppose the drug farm existed. The local JJ team must be in on it, fraudulently boosting profits to keep head office happy while they all got on with the real, far more lucrative, business. An apparently pointless deception now had a purpose. JJ must be involved too, otherwise why would his car be parked there? But if JJ was implicated, why the cover-up? So maybe I'd imagined the cannabis farm too.

There's a limit to how long you can swirl around the same unanswerable questions. Once home, and anaesthetised by several large gin and tonics, my brain obligingly shut down for the night.

24

The next morning found me slightly shaky from lack of food, but otherwise unscathed.

There was no logical reason for the events of the previous day to affect my decision not to pursue my investigations, especially given my unreliable perception. And yet this rational analysis didn't sit comfortably on an emotional level—I felt a tremendous urge to validate my discovery.

I parked the urge somewhere in my subconscious, lest it should distract me from the busy day I had planned. I'd booked a day's leave to pick through that gargantuan storage unit—my mother's house—before the Clearall team came at the weekend. Fortified by a McDonald's sausage and egg McMuffin, I set off in a determined frame of mind to Croydon.

As I shoved open the door, the foetid odour hit me afresh. For a moment I tensed, preparing myself for another attack of the vapours. But it never came. I breathed deeply and took in the squalor, as a sense of calm washed over me. I was back to normal, or rather normal for me.

By Monday, the rubbish would be nothing more than an unhappy memory. Three decades to create a monster hoard—three days to clear—it seemed impossible. But Clearall had signed up to that challenge.

Despite everything, the corner of my soul belonging to Little Amy still hoped a fresh start would cure my mother. But hope only set me up for disappointment. I would never have the mother I wanted—she didn't exist anymore. Just as the house had been buried under piles of debris, so any goodness in her was trapped within the bubble of denial and delusion she inhabited.

Before starting, I took pictures—the first interior photographs of the house for more than thirty years. I needed to capture the level of squalor forever, both to prevent me kidding myself it hadn't been so terrible, and to document my efforts.

Now for the tricky part. My mother had always claimed to keep her valuables in a bureau in the lounge, but I was sceptical. As I unlocked it, a welter of old, mainly junk mail fell out.

If my mother opened letters at all, she invariably replaced them in their envelopes and then noted the contents on the envelope. I'd always found this practice absurd—after all, if you throw away the envelope you can *see* what the letter is. Amid all the crap, two communications from HMRC remained firmly sealed—her phobia of tax demands second only to her phobia of throwing anything out. I ripped them open and laughed—each contained a repayment cheque for several hundred pounds, long out of date.

The valuable stuff was, as I'd suspected, scattered randomly around the house—but that didn't worry me too much. There's an instinct to finding items in a hoard. Strictly, locating a particular object might seem impossible given the volume of stuff, but rarely did anything become irretrievably subsumed in the trash heap. Sometimes belongings were damaged beyond repair, but they seldom sank without a trace. That didn't mean the search would be easy, though.

I can't explain the subliminal logic that led me to the passport hidden in a plastic storage container in the bathroom, or the jewellery in the piano stool. Nor can I say what prompted me to check inside that old kettle in the kitchen, stuffed with share certificates and the deeds to the house. Anyway, irrespective of the thought process, within an hour, I'd stashed all these items in my handbag. They were probably all that was worth saving—she would have her bank cards and cheque book in her own bag, I guessed.

If you're concerned about childhood photographs, forget it. They'd all been ruined when the garage roof had developed a leak ten years before. Fortunately I'd already salvaged a precious few from my grandmother's house—the only evidence that I hadn't sprung into the world as a fully formed adult. I did discover a college graduation picture while searching though, stained beyond salvation. My mother had used it as an impromptu stand for the teapot. These quasi-accidental acts of malevolence hardened my heart. Yes, she was ill, but it doesn't take much effort to keep a picture of your daughter's special day safe.

Next, I dug a canyon through my old bedroom, where crumbling posters of forgotten pop idols clung to the faded kids' wallpaper my father had hung weeks before he died. After I'd left, my mother had commandeered the room as yet another repository for her rapidly burgeoning wardrobe. Her clothes were now heaped high, the summits of some mounds reaching almost to the ceiling—a remarkable feat for a five-foot-tall woman.

From the piles, I picked out an assortment of clothes for her to wear afterwards. I had no idea if they were the best ones or the most appropriate, and didn't much care. I marvelled at the collection of exotic outfits she'd managed to accumulate—plenty to see a member of the Royal Family through a year's engagements. Her obvious yearning for a better life triggered a strange sadness, but I choked it off—this woman wasn't worthy of my pity.

My old wardrobe was stuffed full of clothes I'd worn at school, including the pale blue batwing jumper, pilled and moth-eaten.

'*That looks horrible now.*' Little Amy peered over my shoulder as I examined the sweater.

'Well it is nearly twenty-five years old,' I said. 'Clothes aren't meant to last such a long time.'

'*They're not?*' she said dubiously.

And then I remembered, Little Amy didn't realise people threw out clothes. Only several years later at university did she make that discovery.

'*And I hate those—they're vile.*'

She pointed to a pair of Doc Martens I'd worn in the sixth form.

'Don't worry—you'll like them in a year or two.'

The sight of Little Amy reminded me painfully of what I was struggling to blank out—what I might or might not have witnessed underground. I knew I should ignore her and bring myself back on track. But the kid was stubbornly persistent.

At lunchtime, I checked my phone and found a missed call from Lisa.

'Hey,' she said, when I called her back. 'Just checking you're OK.'

Why wouldn't I be?

'I'm at the hoard house, picking out the wheat from the chaff, but apart from that I'm fine.'

I deliberately omitted to mention the previous day's hallucinations, but Lisa had already heard her own version of the story, prompting her call.

'Are you sure? They say you had a funny turn yesterday.'

Who said, I wondered?

'I felt a bit giddy and then lost my way, that's all.'

'You've done it again,' she moaned. 'I'm supposed to be your best friend and you never tell me anything.'

This was my moment to explain what I'd stumbled across in Wales, but I ducked it. It sounded so incredible—she surely wouldn't believe me.

'And that's all it was?'

'Absolutely. Would I lie to you?'

'I guess not—are you alright now?'

'Yes, of course—just getting ready for the big hoard clear-out tomorrow.'

'So you took my advice.'

She sounded surprised.

'You bet—I even faked her signature on the agreement…'

'It's the right answer,' she said, without hesitation. 'And best of luck.'

In its own way, the conversation had been useful. Any suspicion that a client was involved in a crime had to be reported to Pearson Malone's MLRO (Money Laundering Reporting Officer). He would decide what action to take and whether to pass the information on to law enforcement. I'd been considering reporting the cannabis farm, even though I wasn't one hundred percent convinced I'd truly seen it. I now realised I couldn't do it. If I hesitated to tell my closest friend for fear of being disbelieved or thought crazy, how realistically would I summon up the courage to confide in anyone else, especially after Bailey had warned me off rocking the boat? So, either I gathered more evidence, or let it go.

By mid-afternoon I'd achieved my objectives in the house, although you'd never have thought it. The fundamental law of hoard clearance says when piles of stuff are disturbed their volume increases, being less densely compacted. Consequently, the mounds often appear larger even after removing a considerable amount. And all I'd done was to redistribute the crap.

Nevertheless, a square metre of the lounge carpet was now visible and I bent down to pick up a newspaper that had fallen to obscure it.

I read the headline with a rush of vindication.

TYCOON'S SON JAILED FOR DRUGS FACTORY

Jason Jupp, prodigal son of Jim Jupp, had been busted for running his own LSD factory while studying chemistry at Cambridge and jailed for eight years. That had to be why his father had fallen out with him, why they'd had that massive row when I'd attended JJ's headquarters.

Now everything fell into place. It was *Jason*, not Jim, growing cannabis—*his* Porsche with the personalized number plate. I was not a crazy woman suffering from weird hallucinations—I was a sane, rational person who'd uncovered a major drug farm at a client. Now surely I *had* to do something.

Little Amy sat in my mother's chair, eying me curiously.

'*See—there's some point to keeping newspapers, isn't there?*'

Oh, the irony. My mother would be jubilant—the slightest usefulness of one item in the hoard would justify filling the house to the rafters.

Yet a niggling doubt punctured my elation. Was it possible that I'd glanced at this newspaper before and unconsciously taken in its contents? Instead of the article confirming what I'd seen, had it merely provided the material for my hallucination?

'Oh, come off it. You saw what you saw.'

But that was the trouble—I'd begun to doubt my own senses. Little Amy wasn't real, yet she insisted the cannabis farm existed. Logically it didn't stack up.

'Are you real?' I asked her.

'Of course,' she replied.

What was I to do?

***

Either 'nothing' or 'seek psychiatric help' would have been sensible answers to that question, but I was trapped like a fly in a spider's web. Each time I attempted to disentangle myself, another connecting thread ensnared me—but who was the spider? That question spurred me on.

I still lacked hard evidence of the cannabis farm's existence, without which Pearson Malone's MLRO would be reluctant to act. A repeat visit to the slate mine to confirm what I'd seen was out of the question. I could only hope to gather more evidence from the paper trail. And if nothing else, I owed it to Ryan's memory to examine JJ Slate's books again.

So far I'd seen an analysis of debtors broken down by the age of the debts. But the audit team must surely be able to provide a more detailed ledger with customers' names. And since re-invoicing old debts to make them appear more recent was a classic fraudster's ruse, I would also ask them for a list of credit notes. A breakdown of debts cleared after the year-end would be useful too.

To avoid arousing suspicion, I directed my information request through the most junior members of the audit and tax teams. Despite the circuitous route, five minutes after I'd arrived home, the data pinged into my inbox. I printed off the documents and poured myself a generous glass of Chardonnay. Now down to business.

It took me all of thirty seconds to spot a suspiciously hefty balance on the debtors' ledger—owed by a company called Parallax Projects Ltd. The sums involved were disproportionately large and quite a few credit notes had been issued on the account. Fresh invoices, in subtly different amounts, had been raised at the same time, so the "debts" appeared younger than their true age. I suspected too, but couldn't prove, that they'd reissued some invoices in the names of other customers and allocated those other companies' payments against them.

Again I wondered why the audit team hadn't spotted anything. But the fact that they hadn't didn't automatically mean they'd been negligent. Contrary to public opinion, an auditor is not necessarily expected to spot a fraud—it's possible to plan and carry out a competent audit and still miss it. When you think about it, this isn't so surprising, because a criminal will go to elaborate lengths to throw everyone off the scent. But auditors should exercise "professional scepticism" when considering the possibility of fraud. And without delving too deeply, there was plenty here to arouse suspicion.

But that was the point—they probably hadn't checked the numbers at all, let alone subjected them to the same scrutiny as I was now. As Greg had pointed out, the slate mine was a tiny division of JJ. With around two percent of turnover and four percent of employees the auditors wouldn't have regarded it as a key area. I called up an online company search on Parallax, cynically doubting its existence.

I was wrong. Parallax was a privately owned property development company, too small to require an audit, although apparently large enough to be purchasing a colossal amount of slate.

Greg had also said that loads of debts had been cleared after the year-end. Frankly, I doubted if the audit partner had even checked and fully expected to find the balances still outstanding. Wrong again. Three months after the balance sheet date, just before or during the audit, Parallax had paid everything it owed to JJ and (pardon the pun) wiped the slate clean.

Which was odd, because fictitious debtors never pay.

And if the debtors weren't fictitious then how could there be a fraud?

I had reached a dead end and to be honest, that suited me down to the ground.

25

By late Saturday afternoon the piles of rubbish had diminished appreciably in size.

The fundamental law of hoard clearance was unknown to the Clearall team, who were palpably dispirited to see their early efforts yield few visible results. I questioned whether they were as experienced as they claimed. But they kept at it, and finally their hard work paid off.

No further vital valuables came to light, but Clearall extracted other items of potential value. There were clothes still in their wrappings, new dinner services, three vacuum cleaners (despite the lack of visible floor space), an ice-cream maker, and four sets of kitchen scales.

'Give them all to charity,' I said.

'Any particular one?'

'The NSPCC.'

Finally, they produced a school photograph from one of the clothes piles. It showed angelic Little Amy, aged thirteen, beaming broadly in a skilful masquerade. Even I could almost believe this girl lived in an immaculate home with state of the art plumbing. Little Amy irritated me immensely, but you had to hand it to her—the poor kid could put on a damned convincing front. I would take the picture home and frame it, or perhaps have a mega-enlargement in my office, Smithies-style.

By Sunday evening and six skips later, they were done, and the carpets cleaned. The eerie emptiness of the house unsettled me, and I could scarcely believe how easily the noxious smell had been eliminated. I asked Cynthia Hope around to see the results. I detested the meddling old busybody, but after all the trouble she'd caused I wanted her to bear witness to my achievements.

'Just think,' she said, 'all these years she wouldn't allow me in here—so unnecessary. I'm so glad you helped her. After all, she's the only mother you've got.'

I said nothing.

26

A fine mist shrouded the churchyard, symbolising the suffocating sadness we all felt at Ryan's passing. His promising life had been cut short in the most tragic of circumstances and the suspicion clouding his final weeks made it impossible even to mourn his lost future.

My black Armani trouser suit and peach silk shirt gave the impression of someone en route to a job interview rather than a funeral. But whoever buys a new outfit for such a grim occasion? People grab whatever vaguely suitable garments they have to hand.

Despite the hostility of our last conversation, Greg greeted me with a warm hug outside the church, much to the disgust of his mother and a heavily pregnant Tiffany. A malicious pleasure swept over me as I took in her puffy face, swollen ankles and shapeless body. For someone who had invested all her effort in physical appearance, it must be hell to lose control—and with luck her belly would be flabby forever.

'Thanks for coming,' he said, ignoring the women's hostile glances. 'It means a lot to me.'

'Look—I'm sorry for being out of order last time we spoke.'

There was nothing to be lost in apologising, despite the residual anger that I felt. I'd implied that he didn't give a shit about his brother, and that now that sentiment seemed singularly inappropriate.

'It doesn't matter. I'd give anything to turn the clock back and have Ryan with us. I feel so terrible we none of us recognised how traumatised he'd been…'

'Don't. It wasn't your fault.'

The fault lay with me. Now that I'd convinced myself that all was well at JJ, I also had to accept that nobody except Ryan had any reason to kill Isabelle. And what reason for him to kill her except for a stupid argument about a promotion? Two lives wasted for nothing—my responsibility.

Unlike Tiffany, Greg's mother did not hold back in voicing her displeasure. She'd never cared for me anyway, as she'd hoped Greg would marry the daughter of a furniture shop owner in Cork. Theresa had aged significantly in the time since I'd last seen her, her nervous, haunted air more exaggerated than ever, with thinner lips and baggier eyes.

'Dear God, you've got a nerve showing up here after everything. Have you no shame?'

'Ma,' said Greg. 'Please leave it. This is not the time or the place…'

'Take no notice,' said Mr Kelly senior, who'd been standing silently at his wife's side. His breath stank of whiskey, though it was not yet eleven am. 'She's a wee bit upset—we all are. Thanks for coming, Amy.'

I'd always liked Greg's father—he was someone you could have a laugh and a drink with—a bit like Ryan on a good day. And though Greg had sometimes hinted at a darker side to him, I'd not seen any evidence of it.

As I walked into the church, the censorious stares bored into me, as though everyone held me responsible for the whole sorry business. The Kelly sisters and assorted spouses, in particular, gave me the evil eye as I passed.

I tried not to speculate about who knew I'd slept with Ryan, and whether Greg had shared the news of my mother the garbage lady with his family. I carried on walking with my head held high. None of this mattered—today wasn't about me, and I was here not for them but for Ryan. Surely for his sake I could hold it together for one lousy day.

As you'd expect, Greg gave a composed and professional tribute to Ryan. Delivering his speech in measured tones he urged us all to remember the fun times with Ryan. He reminded us that Ryan hadn't been convicted of any crime and that his family and friends were utterly convinced of his innocence. Ryan would now be judged, he added, by the final arbiter. A nice touch, considering his upbringing in the Catholic faith had hardened Greg into a resolute atheist.

***

For obvious reasons, I hoped to avoid joining the family at the local pub. I made to slink away, but Greg's father caught me.

'Come on, girl—a wake's not a wake without a few drinks.'

'Only if I'm welcome,' I said carefully, glancing at Theresa.

'I say you are, and what I say goes.'

He took me by the arm, perhaps for support, as we walked along the lane.

'Don't understand why he left you for the other one,' he said, with engaging candour, in Tiffany's earshot. 'No fun at all, her.'

He had no clue how little fun I'd been for Greg, how the strain of being the perfect wife had proved too much. But why dash his illusions? And it struck me now that the fault had lain equally with Greg. There'd been no room for either of us to be anything less than flawless.

I dreaded interacting with the rest of the family, so when a girl around Ryan's age intercepted me outside the pub, it seemed like a gift from heaven.

But not for long.

'You're Ryan and Issy's boss, aren't you?' she said in a haughty voice. She was immaculately made up and dressed rather showily in black velvet.

I had been, I thought bitterly, until Smithies had pulled the rug from under my feet.

'Yes.'

'I need to talk to you.'

I waited for an impassioned tirade—another stab at my conscience—but Kelly senior interrupted.

'C'mon, have a drink, both you lovely girls.'

Mrs Kelly was plainly disturbed that her husband had now cornered two women. She came to reclaim him, glowering at us both.

'Who are you?' I asked the girl, certain I'd not met her before.

'Oh—sorry—I should have introduced myself. I'm Chloe Fenton, Isabelle's friend.'

I didn't warm to her. She had that same smug, self-congratulatory aura as Isabelle, and I feared she might be about to launch an attack that I lacked the strength to withstand.

But when she offered me a cigarette I realised she had no intention of arguing. I'd given up smoking five years before, but there's nothing like an untimely death to highlight the folly of trying to prolong life. She lit my ciggie with a classy vintage lighter.

'I'm amazed you're here,' I said, 'as Isabelle's friend...'

'Ah yes, I see what you mean, but Ryan's best friend is my boyfriend—we met through Issy…'

She broke off, unsure of how to express the nuances of her moral dilemma.

'No—it's OK, you don't have to explain. I understand—this is tough on everyone.'

She exhaled a long jet of smoke.

'Anyway, I'm certain Ryan didn't have any involvement in Issy's death.'

My ears pricked up.

'Why do you say that?'

'There was stuff happening—unconnected with Ryan.'

'Such as what?'

'It was him—Smithies.'

'*Smithies*?'

Good God—I'd known it all along.

'You mean an affair?'

She tossed back her blonde mane in a contemptuous gesture.

'Oh *poor Issy*—she would be appalled to hear you say that—isn't he totally repulsive?'

'Totally,' I agreed, puzzled as to why Isabelle would have even discussed Smithies' sex appeal or lack of it with her friend if they weren't having an affair.

'Well, why suggest it then?'

'Sorry. Go on.'

'It was the promotion. Smithies promised her the promotion if she kept quiet.'

'About what?'

'OK, I guess I can trust you,' she said, lowering her voice, 'and I really *need* to tell someone, in confidence.'

'Go on,' I said gently.

'It was all to do with her client—JJ Slate.'

The nicotine rushed to my head.

'Tell me,' I said.

'The client accused Pearson Malone of making an error, but Issy discovered that wasn't true, and was keen to defend the firm.'

'Yes—I know.'

'But then, this Smithies guy tells her to drop it, that the client had screwed up but everyone had agreed to keep it under wraps. He told her a key competency for a senior manager is discretion when required. He didn't say explicitly that the promotion depended on her keeping quiet, but you get the general drift.'

Smithies would have phrased things sufficiently ambiguously as to render the whole conversation deniable, for sure, but the intention was clear.

'But there wasn't an error,' I said.

She stared at me, astonished.

'How did you guess?'

'I didn't guess. It's my client, and I checked.'

'So did Issy. You know her style—mad keen to find the client's mistake, to ensure it didn't recur on a future project.'

Why else? It was somehow fitting and faintly amusing that Isabelle's death might have resulted from her painstaking thoroughness. I mean, whoever would take the time to review someone else's cock-up?

'And did she tell Smithies what she'd found?'

'God, no. He'd lied to her, and she didn't want to lose her promotion. But she obviously asked herself *why* he'd lied…'

'And?'

'She said she thought there was a problem with the accounts.'

Just as I had.

'When she tell you this?'

'It was the Tuesday before she died—we went for a drink. She told me that after she'd checked the file, she realised there might be a problem with the debtors, and she asked my advice.'

'And what did you say?'

'I advised her to leave well alone, particularly as Issy thought that Smithies might be aware of whatever was going on. But she was horrified at the thought that she might have covered up a crime to get a promotion, and she was determined to find proof.'

'Why didn't you tell the police about this?' I'd tired of the cigarette and chucked the remainder of it into the flowerbed.

'I didn't see any connection with Issy's disappearance,' she said.

That didn't stack up. How could she *not* see a connection?

'That's not the real reason, is it?'

She flushed visibly.

'I couldn't tell,' she said. 'I'd lose my job.'

'Why?'

'I work at head office at a major bank,' she said, grinding the stub of her cigarette into the ground with the toe of her black patent shoe. 'Issy said she believed JJ were churning out false invoices to a customer. The company banked with us and well, it was all totally improper, but Issy asked me to get hold of the bank statements.'

'What was the name of the customer?' I asked, ninety-nine point nine percent sure of the answer.

'Parallax Projects.'

I nodded in a non-committed kind of way.

'And did you give her the statements?'

She shifted uneasily from foot to foot.

'It wasn't easy, I can tell you. Everyone thinks banks run amok, but in fact we have strong internal controls. Anyway yes, I did get them for her—I gave them to her the next morning.'

'And where are they now?'

'That's just it—I have no idea. Which worries me, because someone might work out where she got hold of them.'

I wasn't clear if she was worried for her safety or her job—perhaps both.

'So in your view, what happened to Isabelle?' I asked.

'Well, I'm not too sure what she found, but she said it wasn't what she'd originally thought, but something was wrong. She told me she was going to speak to someone she trusted about it before deciding what to do.'

'Who?'

'Not a clue.'

'Pity.'

'But somehow, either before or after she spoke to this person, I think the JJ lot cottoned on to what she'd found out and murdered her. Which really upsets me.'

I must say, she didn't sound upset at all. And what could Isabelle have found? I wondered. The debts had been cleared, so there was definitely more to all this than a simple inflation of profits.

'So man up and come forward.'

'What good would it do? Nothing can bring Issy back.'

'No—but it may help them catch her killer.'

'Don't get me wrong,' she said, touching my arm. 'I feel rotten about Ryan dying too, absolutely rotten, but I can't bring him back either, can I?'

No, I thought, *but you could have prevented him from being arrested.* She was as cowardly as me, worse even.

'And now he's gone, no one's interested anymore are they?'

She was right on the money there.

'Why are you telling me all this?'

'Because it seems so unfair. Ryan was charged with a murder he didn't commit and nobody cares.'

'So report your suspicions.'

'I've told you why I can't do that,' she retorted. 'But I was thinking—it might be better if you checked it out—see if there's anything in it.'

First Ryan, now Chloe. Why, oh why, did everyone ask me to act as an unofficial investigator into something undoubtedly best left alone?

'There isn't.'

'You can't be certain of that—you're curious—I can tell. And you're not surprised by what I've just said either, are you?'

'Maybe not, but with those papers gone we'll never know what Isabelle uncovered. Unless you'd care to provide another copy of the statements.'

I'd expected her to balk at the prospect, but I'd read the situation wrongly.

'I have copies of everything,' she said. 'Issy was worried someone might try to steal the originals and she mailed me copies the day before she died. If you promise not to tell where you got them, I can let you have them.'

Isabelle's efficiency was relentless. I tussled with my conscience, inquisitiveness and reluctance to get involved. Curiosity won.

'OK—bring them to my office tomorrow.'

'Actually,' she said, producing an A4 envelope with a flourish from her handbag, 'I have them here.'

***

Game set and bloody match to Chloe Fenton—another "butter wouldn't melt" ice maiden with a flair for manipulation. I'd sleepwalked into her ambush and was now back on the hook, while she'd neatly wriggled out of all responsibility.

Isabelle's antics had been equally annoying. Fancy checking out someone else's mistake, and keeping copies of incriminating evidence. If she hadn't checked, she'd still be alive. And if she hadn't kept copies, I wouldn't be in this predicament.

As I poured out the meagre contents of my miniature gin bottle on the Heathrow flight from Cork that evening, I pondered on what to do.

Of course, I'd be perfectly justified in ignoring the latest developments—the Fenton girl was in no position to complain. I hadn't yet opened the envelope—a deliberate decision. Once aware of its contents, I might be obliged to take action. So the obvious answer was to dispose of it intact—chuck it in a litter bin at Heathrow, or shred it at home. I flagged the stewardess down as she passed and asked for two more gins. She regarded me with thinly disguised contempt, although I was nowhere near being drunk.

The funeral should have marked a turning point, allowing me to process the whole sorry sequence of events and move on. But each time I tried to extricate myself, I was sucked back in. It felt as if some divine force was driving me forward, but to where?

As the second and third drinks slipped down, my hostility towards Chloe Fenton mellowed. She'd bent the rules to help her friend, and how could she have foreseen how disastrously it would all end? And which of us would have the moral courage to disclose a wrongful act that would cost us our jobs?

In fact, how was I any better, sitting here contemplating the destruction of whatever information I now possessed?

I was convinced it all came back to Smithies. He'd instigated the lie about the tax losses, presumably to protect his brother-in-law. He might genuinely believe that Goodchild had made an error, or he might know more. And while Chloe seemed certain Isabelle hadn't discussed her suspicions with Smithies, he had an uncanny knack of finding things out, as I knew to my cost.

Could I imagine Smithies killing in cold blood? Yes—if he felt he'd get away with it, and it would best further his own interests. Ever since, and even before, all this started, Smithies had set out systematically to wreck my career. For him, other people were mere pawns to be sacrificed. Wasn't murdering someone a natural next step?

I ought to have been frightened, but I was stronger than he knew. And if that bastard had murdered Isabelle, I would bring him down.

27

Faced with diverse reflections of Smithies loitering in my doorway the next morning, my newfound boldness wavered.

'Can we have a quick catch up?' he asked, closing the door behind him.

Taken at face value, the request wasn't unreasonable—but I feared what lay behind it. His X-Ray vision seemed to home in on the unopened envelope on my desk.

'How did the funeral go?'

'Oh, pretty grim,' I said. 'But what can you expect?'

'Well, I certainly appreciate you attending, in all the circumstances.'

Only Smithies had the ability to make such a superficially innocuous thank-you so heavy with meaning.

'So Lisa's off to the partnership assessment centre next week.'

'Yes.'

'I hope you've helped her prep for it—so many candidates fall down because of poor preparation, sad to say. Such a shame when it happens.'

He sighed theatrically; presumably aware I'd done nothing.

'All in hand,' I lied.

'And how are you, Amy, in yourself? Are you any better?'

Up until a few minutes before, I could honestly have said yes. But the paranoid sense of foreboding that had defined all our meetings to date now resurfaced.

'*Don't let him wind you up*,' counselled Little Amy.

Don't worry; I won't, although I wished she'd piss off.

'Much better, thanks,' I mumbled.

'I heard you had a funny turn last week—in the slate mine.'

I noticed he used the same words as Lisa.

'Yes—a kind of claustrophobia.'

'Odd,' he said. 'Let's hope Eric Bailey doesn't find out about this—you know how he hates weakness…'

Naturally, Smithies would find a plausible reason to tell him.

'Have you seen a doctor?'

'No—that's not necessary.'

'And how is your mother doing?'

'As far as I know, OK.'

'What—you haven't seen her?'

'No.'

'Did you take my advice and organise a little spring clean round the house?'

Either he was trying to belittle the issue for his own ends or hadn't grasped the scale of it. I honestly couldn't tell which.

'I did.'

'She must be very grateful.'

'I guess so.'

I wondered how my efforts had in fact been received. Gratitude was the least probable reaction. A meltdown was possible, but surely Cynthia would have told me. Most likely my mother would play the martyr and enjoy complaining to her so-called friends about how her busybody daughter had chucked out all her precious things. And even those who now realised she was a hoarder would indulge her in the fiction, because they were all too polite to challenge her. And then she'd start to hoard up once more.

'If you need time off…'

'Thank you, but no.'

'Strange,' he said, taking in the surroundings. 'Your office is unnaturally empty—must be a form of rebellion against your mother.'

'I'm complying with the clear desk policy,' I said acidly, peeved by his amateur psychology.

'Still, moving out will be a doddle.'

He said this with the hint of a threat—he seldom missed a trick in the mind games.

'I don't plan to move out anytime soon,' I replied in a deadpan fashion.

'Well, I'm glad to hear you tell me you're flourishing. And remember, we're all here to comfort you in your time of need.'

I asked myself what the purpose of the meeting had been. Smithies would claim that concern for my welfare had prompted him to see me, but I knew different—he'd been continuing in his efforts to psych me out.

That settled it—the instant he'd gone I did what I could put off no longer, and ripped open the envelope.

***

In addition to the bank statements, there were debtors' schedules, identical to the ones I'd blagged from our audit department. Isabelle had traced the payments from the bank through to the post year-end receipts. The client had evidently undertaken a big tidying up exercise just before the auditors arrived, suspicious in itself.

I now saw clearly that my assumption that debts paid off equals no racket, had been an oversimplification to justify me abandoning my enquiries.

Next—a copy of an interesting calculation in Isabelle's handwriting. The slate quarry and mine were valued on the balance sheet based on the estimated reserves of slate left in them. Each year, the value was written down. From this, and information on JJ's website, she'd approximated the tonnage of slate extracted during the year. But dividing the slate mine's sales by the market price of slate yielded a much larger amount. Even when stock movements between the beginning and the end of the year were taken into account, there was still an anomaly. In broad terms, they'd apparently sold far more slate than they'd mined.

Finally, came a bunch of invoices addressed to JJ Slate from a company called Evans Haulage. I speculated on how Isabelle might have obtained them—not from the audit team for sure, as the entire haulage cost would have been immaterial from an audit perspective. Maybe the client had unwittingly handed them over on some pretext. The invoices related to various customers of JJ, but two referred to Parallax Projects. She'd ringed round the numbers of both invoices, which were way out of sequence with other invoices raised in the same month.

Conclusion—those two invoices were bogus. Someone had photocopied old invoices and changed the other details, while overlooking the serial number.

For all her hard work though, brainy Isabelle had nowhere near finished the job—she'd flagged up questions rather than answers. Conspicuous by its absence was any information on the drugs, but the best part of two million pounds had come into Parallax's bank account every quarter. She'd put question marks by the deposits, but I had my own ideas.

The only problem was that my ideas didn't make sense. Nobody paid for drugs by bank transfer—banks were fussy about where cash came from, shit-scared of money laundering. And anyway, if drug money had been routed into JJ via

Parallax, where was it coming out again? What was the point of having the money tied up in the JJ group?

I called Greg, but he didn't answer his mobile. When I tried the landline, his dragon of a secretary told me, with obvious pleasure, that he'd gone away with his wife to chill out after the funeral. He would be out of contact until Thursday week. This was a great pity, since strictly it left me no option but to follow the Pearson Malone procedures and report this to the firm's MLRO.

Making a report was easy in principle, but considerably harder in practice. James Potter, our MLRO, was another big buddy of Smithies and I didn't trust him an inch. Also Greg would be livid to find I'd gone behind his back, and Bailey had already warned me off. The temptation for all these people to minimise, rationalise and dismiss my claims as crazy would be irresistible, particularly if I mentioned the cannabis farm. For I still had no direct evidence of its existence. In summary, I didn't fancy it a bit.

'*So*,' demanded Little Amy. '*What do you plan to do?*'

'Bin the bloody lot.'

'*You can't do that. It's ducking the issue. I've got to grow up into you. And I have no desire to end up like Mum, avoiding everything.*'

Jesus Christ, the little cow knew which buttons to press, but I couldn't be manipulated so easily.

'What do you expect me to do?'

'*Call that shitbag Carmody*,' she said. '*Let him deal with it.*'

That was it—I'd had it listening to her crap.

'No way.'

28

Following my conversation with Smithies that morning, I couldn't stop thinking about my mother's response to the enforced clean-out. The uncertainty niggled away in the background, popping occasionally into the forefront of my mind. I shrank from calling her, but the silence was puzzling. Was it remotely possible she'd accepted the need for action and was pleased with the results?

I'd just concluded that a call to the loathsome Hope woman might be the best way forward, when she beat me to it.

'Your mother got home yesterday and she's not happy at all,' she said gleefully.

I should have known. It never paid to have any expectations of my mother—it merely gave her the power to disappoint.

'No?'

'She says you've thrown out all her valuable possessions.'

'Not true—I went to a great deal of trouble to salvage them.'

I wished I hadn't bothered—the backlash would have been the same irrespective of what I'd chucked out.

'But you have got rid of a *huge* amount. I had *no idea* you'd be disposing of things. I promised her you wouldn't.'

As a former English teacher, Miss Hope's mathematical ability was doubtless limited, but surely she understood basic volume calculations.

'Now listen,' I told her firmly. 'You saw all the stuff in there and the space it took up. Tell me—how exactly did you expect me to tidy it all away *without throwing anything out*?'

'But you could have used your intelligence,' she said, ducking my question in a stern headmistress–like tones. 'Your mum is terribly upset, she's thinking of calling the police, especially as you forged her signature on the agreement with the cleaning company.'

I supposed it had been inevitable that she'd find out about that.

'It's all hot air—she'd never report me. Taking control of events would violate the habits of a lifetime. She'd much prefer to be the victim.'

'You shouldn't underestimate how angry she is.'

'Oh, I'm not. And you shouldn't underestimate the pleasure she gets out of playing the martyr.'

'Well,' she said in pained tones, 'I thought if I told you what was brewing you might try to defuse the situation.'

Her lack of insight into my mother's personality astounded me. After some three decades living next door, she saw nothing beyond the image my mother, the master illusionist, chose to project. Even the "discovery" of the hoarding hadn't shaken her certainty.

'From where I'm standing there's nothing brewing. And just so we're clear, I have no intention of ever helping my mother again. And you, you interfering old busybody, you can go and fuck yourself.'

29

There were too many egos round the table at the JJ all-parties meeting that afternoon—lawyers, brokers, grey suits from Megabuilders, plus Jupp and the slimeball Goodchild. Only Greg was missing—his number two in the corporate finance advisory team stood in for him.

Oh yes, and Little Amy sat in a chair in the corner, wearing her school uniform and smoking again—hers the biggest ego of the bloody lot. This was a disturbing development—normally she kept her visual appearances for when I was alone.

The sparring began early, as each of the participants vied with the others to determine who was the toughest, most macho tiger in the jungle.

'Now I think it's fair to say I have some concerns,' began the lead partner from Megabuilders' legal team, a chippy little Scouse guy called Kevin.

'Yeah—like what's going to happen to the drug dealing division none of you guys know about yet.'

'We're less than two weeks away from completion and there's still some major issues to be resolved. And your lead advisor can't even be bothered to attend our final catch-up.'

The "major issues", or at least the ones he was aware of, were probably easily manageable points of detail, of the type you'd expect this late on in the process. But attempting to unnerve the guy off the subs bench made for good entertainment in an otherwise dull meeting.

'I'm sure you all appreciate the tragic circumstances,' pitched in JJ.

'Shit happens,' Kevin replied, with a shrug. 'You deal with it.'

'*Or avoid it, in the case of some people.*' Little Amy looked pointedly at me.

'In any case, the guy's suicide is tidier all round,' he added with breathtaking obnoxiousness.

'Yes, the brother was obviously guilty,' Goodchild opined, in a clumsy attempt to build rapport.

I watched him intently for signs of complicity, but he showed no sign of discomfort. I wondered—if Smithies had killed Isabelle to save Goodchild, would he have even told his brother-in-law what he'd done?

'*Ryan wasn't guilty. Isabelle was killed to cover up for these arseholes. And you're allowing it to happen.*'

'Let's try and stick to the point,' said JJ, glaring at Kevin. 'Since there's so much to be done.'

It was unclear to me whether he was uncomfortable with the direction of the discussion, or merely displaying his well-known aversion to wasting professionals' time.

'*Him and Goodchild must be up to their necks in it,*' said Little Amy, reading my thoughts. '*And you're letting them get away with it.*'

But what could I do? I could hardly blurt out my perception of the truth, here in the meeting. And I was loath to make an internal money laundering report, especially when I still had no proof.

'*I told you—ring that prick Carmody.*'

Which wouldn't be happening either.

As I'd predicted, the open issues were all relatively trivial, but the Megabuilders' contingent seemed entrenched in their aggressive mind-sets. They were so nasty that I concluded they deserved to buy a company riddled with fraud.

Greg's sidekick handled the assault with aplomb. He'd either been comprehensively briefed by Greg or had effectively been in control of the whole project from the outset. I suspected the latter.

The tax position was left to me to resolve. Rob, the capital allowances specialist, had told me there should be ample claims to cover the hole left by the losses, but Megabuilders were doubtful. Rather than attempt to convince them, I suggested the sum in dispute be held in an escrow account and released when the claim had been agreed. Perhaps because they'd all been worn down by constant wrangling, everyone agreed.

'You can't allow them to get away with this—why should Ryan take the rap? You're just playing along with their game.'

She had a point. Ryan's "guilt" was far too convenient for everyone. Intentionally or not, all of them were helping to cover up some kind of swindle, and possibly a murder. And by taking the easy path, I was colluding with them.

I was done with colluding—I'd kept my mother's illness hidden for years, through shame and ignorance. I'd allowed her to avoid the consequences of facing it, and helped her to weave a fiction with her friends. And see where that had got me.

Little Amy needed to know she wouldn't always be stuck in the same rut, and the only person able to prove it to her was big Amy. She'd come into my life, I reasoned, to show me a different way, and when I'd finished she'd give up bugging me.

OK, you win, kid, I thought.

'Anyone else got any points to raise?' asked Kevin, when he'd been through his own exhaustive list.

'Not at the moment,' I said.

'But just you wait.'

30

'So what made you change your mind and take me up on my dinner offer?' Dave asked as we sat the next evening in an absurdly pricy Mayfair restaurant. When I say pricy, I mean relative to Dave's salary, not mine—yet he'd chosen the venue. It crossed my mind he might be on expenses.

'I decided you deserved another chance,' I lied. Happily, Little Amy had slithered off somewhere, so I wasn't forced to endure her sarcastic comments.

I'd dithered for ages over what to wear. If it had been a proper date, I would have known precisely how to dress. But I had a purely business agenda for the evening and so, I strongly suspected, did Dave. I settled on a forties-style tea dress, with a turquoise bolero jacket to go on top—demure but businesslike.

'I'm not convinced I do,' he said with a hangdog expression, 'but thanks anyway.'

No expense spared, he ordered a bottle of Bollinger Special Cuvée at a hundred and five pounds.

'What are we celebrating?' I asked.

'My prospective promotion. They've signed me off for the superintendent assessment process.'

The disclosure took me by surprise. Could this after all be a genuine celebratory dinner, to which he'd invited me because he fancied me? I remembered that night in Daly's when his sole purpose had been to pump me for information. I'd be careful not to delude myself again, although for now I had little option but to play along with the fiction.

'Congratulations,' I said inanely. 'But aren't you counting your chickens a bit soon?'

'No—I've been told I've every prospect of being successful. And besides, I've been waiting long enough to be put forward. That in itself is enough reason to be cheerful. We can always have another celebration when I've got the title.'

I refrained from commenting on the multiple assumptions contained in that final sentence, as the waiter returned with the champagne and poured out two glasses.

'To us,' said Dave.

'And to the prospective promotion.'

'That too,' he said.

We chatted about nothing in particular until the arrival of the tiniest smoked salmon roulades I'd ever seen—little more than canapés. It's one of those peculiar economic paradoxes that the more expensive a London restaurant is, the less food they provide. The bread rolls were equally miniscule, but the four carb-phobic designer stick-insect women at an adjacent table nevertheless waved them aside.

'Before we get too far, I have a confession,' Dave said.

'Go on.'

'We'd verified that Ryan Kelly visited your house before we interviewed you. One of your neighbours confirmed she'd seen him arriving.'

It worried me that my neighbours kept such close tabs on me so late at night, but not as much as Dave's earlier lack of transparency.

'So why suggest I was lying?'

'Tactics. We needed you to admit that Kelly could have gone out in the night.'

'With hindsight, I don't see how that helped you anyway. You never had any definite proof that Ryan was driving the car—a serious weakness in the case.'

'Not such a weakness as you might imagine,' Dave replied. 'To create reasonable doubt the defence would have to establish a realistic possibility that someone else was behind the wheel. Kelly always claimed that he'd been set up, but we found both sets of car keys in his possession, and then there was the bigger question. Why the hell would anyone want to set him up anyway?'

Unwittingly, he'd led the discussion exactly where I wanted it to go.

'But suppose there was a plausible motive for someone other than Ryan to kill her, and to put Ryan in the frame.'

Dave's face fell.

'Oh dear,' he said, before I had a chance to expand on my theory. 'I suppose you're still on about this fraud business. Ed did warn me that you might bend my ear about it.'

'*Ed Smithies*?' I sounded incredulous, but truthfully it came as no surprise to me that Smithies had wheedled his way so far into Carmody's trust.

'Yes—nice guy—invited me to the Pearson Malone box at Wimbledon a few days ago when his client pulled out unexpectedly. As a thank-you for the sensitive way we'd handled the enquiries.'

How on earth could it be appropriate for Carmody to accept a freebie on this basis? Surely the police had rules forbidding it?

'Oh, I see.'

'We had a great time,' he went on, oblivious to the frosty tone in my voice. 'And Ed mentioned in passing that you had a bee in your bonnet about some alleged racket at JJ. He thought maybe you felt guilty about what happened to Ryan.'

A bee in my bonnet. Why did everyone feel they had free rein to trivialise my thoughts and experiences, and attribute non-existent motives to me? Smithies had potentially sinister reasons for playing down my unease, but he had Dave Carmody wrapped round his little finger, so must have figured he'd get away with it.

'Oh yes,' I said, rapidly backtracking as I questioned the wisdom of confiding in Carmody. 'At one point I did give some credence to Ryan's idea, but not now. I was just speaking hypothetically.'

'Oh, Ed will be relieved. And so am I.'

He put his hand on mine. I managed a weak smile, but Smithies thwarting my plan had sent my spirits into a tailspin. Mortified, I found tears coursing down my cheeks.

'Hey,' he said. 'What's wrong?'

'Sorry—there's stuff happening on top of this Isabelle and Ryan business—and I'm so stressed out.'

He handed me his handkerchief.

'Yes, Ed did say you'd been tense lately.'

And what right did Smithies have to trumpet his opinions on my state of mind?

'You can't believe everything he says,' I said, dabbing at my cheek.

'But he's not wrong on this though, is he?'

'I guess not,' I reluctantly agreed.

'You're not a big fan of his, are you?'

'Why do you say that?'

'It's been obvious from the off. I even asked him about it. He said that inexplicably you had a real down on him. He seemed mystified, and genuinely hurt.'

The odious man had covered every base with his Oscar-winning portrayal of the decent boss trying to fathom the irrational hatred of an unstable subordinate. Yes—he'd spread his poison far and wide—first Greg and now Dave. But convincing anyone of it was another matter altogether.

'Hurt—unlikely—Ed has no feelings. And he's trying to make everyone believe I've gone crazy.'

As soon as the words were out, I regretted saying them.

'Why would he do that?' Dave asked gently, in tones suggesting he'd completely bought into Smithies' lies.

'I don't know,' I snapped.

I never had understood Smithies' rationale for selecting me as a victim, before even any suggestion of deception or murder. Had he merely scented weakness and gone for it? If so, his judgement had been impeccable. I cut a pathetic figure sitting here sobbing, while the anorexic bitches at the next table gazed at me in mock pity.

'Frankly, I think you're overreacting a bit, Amy. Ed's anxious about your welfare and so am I. I hoped tonight might cheer you up. Heck, if I'd realised you were under so much strain I wouldn't have given you the third degree in the interview. But I thought you were a real tough cookie...'

'I am a real tough cookie,' I sobbed unconvincingly. 'Which is why he needs to break me.'

Dave shook his head.

'That makes no sense at all.'

I quickly evaluated my options. Surely Dave wasn't so much in cahoots with his new best buddy Ed that he wouldn't listen to reason. I had to confide in someone not embroiled in the toxic Pearson Malone establishment, and could ill afford to throw my one lifeline away. Besides, I'd never hear the last of it from my teenage alter ego.

'It does make sense if Smithies killed Isabelle.'

After an unnervingly long silence, he spoke.

'Do you seriously believe that's possible?'

Dave's tone of voice and facial expression were professionally neutral and non-judgmental—but somehow I could tell he gave no credence to the suggestion.

'Yes—based on what I know.'

'That's bonkers,' he said, quickly ditching his tolerant façade now he saw I was serious. 'He may not be your favourite person but…'

'Are you aware that the finance director at JJ is Ed Smithies' brother-in-law?' I cut in.

'I must confess I wasn't.' A puzzled expression clouded his features. 'But I don't see how that's relevant.'

'Isn't it obvious? If Isabelle did discover dodgy dealings at JJ, then Smithies would have a motive for killing her—to protect his brother-in-law.'

'But you just told me that Ryan's suspicions were wrong.'

'I lied, because I was afraid that you might alert Smithies. But then I thought better of it. I have to trust you, because apart from you there's no one.'

Dave switched back to his open-minded mode, having decided that humouring me was his best option.

'I promise I won't say a word. Tell me more.'

'Goodchild stands to lose millions in share options if the company sale falls through. I think Isabelle discovered something wrong and Smithies killed her to protect his family.'

'That sounds a bit fanciful to me. What evidence do you have?'

'I have evidence—some dodgy invoices and other stuff. I can show them to you if you want.' I held off mentioning the cannabis farm—if he thought what I'd said so far sounded fanciful, it might strain his credulity too far.

'But nothing to tie Smithies into the murder, apart from a potential motive?'

'Not directly, no.'

Dave sipped at his champagne as he contemplated the best way to handle me. I regretted now having suggested that Smithies might be the culprit—which appeared to undermine the integrity of the rest of my allegations.

'I'm sorry to pop your balloon, but Ed Smithies has a cast iron alibi for the night in question.'

'Well he would have, wouldn't he?' I retorted.

'It's been verified. And besides, I've come across plenty of murderers in my time and in my opinion, Ed isn't one of them. He's a typical City type, streetwise and politically astute, and though some of those guys would do all sorts to advance or protect their own position...'

'That's just it,' I said. 'He'd do *anything* to protect his position, or rather his sister's.'

Dave shook his head.

'Guys like him don't tend to kill. They have much more effective ways of neutralising a threat.'

'But that's what he's doing with me—neutralising the threat. He can't take the risk of killing another person, but he can demolish my credibility.'

'I have to say, this sounds so flaky that if you don't watch it you'll demolish your own credibility.'

As if I wasn't painfully aware of that already.

'But what about the fraud? Aren't you interested even in that?'

'I might be, but what do you expect me to do?'

For a deluded moment, I believed he might actually help me.

'Investigate it, of course.'

'Amy, if you truly suspect any criminal activity, I'd advise you to follow your firm's procedures and contact your Money Laundering Reporting Officer.'

If I'd thought clearly, it should have been obvious all along what the answer would be.

'Ha,' I snorted. 'Do you realise how impossible that is?'

'Why?'

'Because everybody's got such a vested interest in JJ. Apart from the Smithies connection, our CEO Eric Bailey is Jim Jupp's best friend. Pearson Malone has a multi-million pound fee resting on a successful completion of the company sale and the Corporate Finance Partner is my ex-husband. So for one reason or another they're all desperate for JJ's books to balance. Nobody will listen to me, because everyone's perfectly happy that Ryan's taken the rap.'

'But the MLRO is independent,' Dave protested. 'That's the whole point.'

'No—he's not—you don't get how it is with him. He's another one who's a big buddy of Smithies.'

'Buddy or not, ignoring your report if he thinks there's any substance to it would be a criminal offence. Pearson Malone is a highly reputable firm. He wouldn't take the risk.'

'So you're refusing to help me.'

'No, no—I *am* helping you. If you give me the evidence I have to disclose where I got it. If your firm find out you haven't been through the proper channels they'll go nuts. Does that make sense?'

'I suppose so,' I said grudgingly, wondering if he was really obliged to reveal his sources. For I was acutely mindful of Dave's possible motives. If I handed the documents to him, he'd be compelled to act. The revelation that he'd arrested the wrong man would hardly aid his promotion. Whereas if, as I expected, Pearson Malone buried my report, who would be any the wiser?

'But I have to say, you've got Ed Smithies all wrong,' Dave went on. 'He *is* concerned. Why—he called me up specifically to ask me not put you under undue strain. He told me your mother was unwell, that she had a hoarding problem which you were sorting out.'

So much for Smithies' assurances about absolute discretion. I could just about forgive him mentioning the hoarding to Greg, but this was unforgivable.

'He had no business to mention that.'

'But it might help you to talk about it.'

'I severely doubt it,' I said. 'And you don't care anyway. You believe I'm barking mad too.'

'That's not true,' he protested. 'But I wish you'd open up a bit.'

'I can't open up—it's not in my nature—I'm not the same as you. In Daly's, you explained how you'd been found as a baby. That's an incredibly personal matter to bring up in a first meeting. I simply wouldn't do it.'

'But it's my unique selling point—I tell everybody about it—people are interested. Perhaps you should regard the hoarding in the same light.'

'But the hoarding's over—it's not part of who I am now.'

'I beg to differ. It's a huge part of you and much better to recognise that and integrate it into the rest of your life.'

Perhaps, but could I bear to announce to the world that I grew up in a trashcan? No—I'd shrunk from telling Dave, and wouldn't have voluntarily confided in Smithies even if he'd pulled out my fingernails one by one with pliers. Bad enough that I'd confessed all to Lisa.

My Dover sole arrived, but I had little appetite. Now I'd established that Dave wouldn't assist me, only politeness kept me there. And politeness didn't stretch to sitting meekly listening to impractical advice on how to live my life.

'Sorry,' I said. 'I have to leave—I can't talk about this stuff.'

'What's eating you? Are you scared that if you reveal too much of yourself, I'll go off you?'

'No,' I lied, 'but I've had my fill of people who drag me down and belittle my feelings. I'm sure you had an ulterior motive in asking me here. I have no idea what it is, but I suspect you're using me.'

'Who are you to talk?' he said. 'Looks to me like your only purpose in meeting me was to avoid making an internal report of this hare-brained conspiracy theory of yours.'

'Yes—you're right, as it happens—and since you've refused to help, the meeting is pointless.'

I stood up and walked out of the restaurant, ignoring both his pleas to come back and the supercilious stares of the other diners. And I vowed I would never, ever see him again.

31

Flouncing off had been immensely satisfying, but I was no further forward.

Despite my anger I recognised the sense in Carmody's advice. I should follow the correct procedure and make a disclosure to James Potter, the firm's MLRO. If he blabbed to Smithies or Bailey, or chose to ignore my report, too bad. And if anyone criticised me for daring to report, ditto.

I had plenty of choices if they screwed me over. It beat me why I'd suffered for so long. Lisa's foray into the job market suggested that our rivals Brown & Taylor were seeking new partners. While I'd no desire to go back there, other firms must be hiring too. I'd spent too long in this poisonous environment and it was time to fill my lungs with fresh air.

'*So—go and see Potter.*'

The next morning, that's exactly what I did.

Potter was a bespectacled highbrow, who'd found that the cut and thrust of client work aggravated his dyspepsia. Consequently he'd gravitated towards one of the few jobs in Pearson Malone which required a purely intellectual judgement on a set of facts. But would the web of allegiances in this case allow him to use his intellect to the full? I still had my doubts, particularly given his friendship with Smithies.

It was a surprising alliance, as superficially the two men had little in common. But I'd heard that Potter had helped Smithies out of the poo at least once, and that Smithies had been instrumental in Potter's move into his current role. The bond was built on mutual benefit and respect, but would Potter have the guts to stand up to pressure from his friend, or from Bailey? That wasn't my problem—it was Potter's judgement call to make a report to the authorities. For me, it would be like confessing to a priest and absolving myself of all responsibility.

All psyched up to go, I sat in the waiting room outside Potter's office, proud that I'd been able to conquer my fears to follow the correct path.

Then disaster struck.

Bailey walked in, knocked on Potter's door and entered without being bidden. Two minutes later he emerged, minus the piece of paper he'd been holding. In the intervening time, I'd held myself together by dint of a superhuman effort, but my resolve was rapidly unravelling.

'Hello, Amy—here to see Potter, are we?'

'Dumb question—why else would you be waiting outside Potter's office?'

'Hopefully not about our friends at JJ,' he quipped.

'No, no absolutely not,' I replied with a tinkling laugh, as my newfound daring melted away like ice in a heatwave.

And I established, in a moment of frightening mental clarity, that I couldn't do this, wouldn't have done it even if Bailey hadn't put in an appearance. Once again, I'd been deluding myself.

It was a simple matter to analyse my reluctance. I could live with the consequences if everyone accepted my story—they wouldn't be pretty but I'd take that on the chin. But the point was that nobody would believe me—they would all band together to mock and discredit me to avoid the truth. And that would be unendurable.

Potter beckoned me in through the glass door. I knew I couldn't just cut and run without making an excuse, so I pleaded an urgent conference call I'd just been summoned to join.

'I'll contact you later to make another appointment,' I lied.

'*Cowardy custard*,' said Little Amy.

Lisa was in my office when I arrived back, armed with several reports for me to sign off.

I'd been trying to reach her for more than a day to discuss prepping for her partnership assessment, and I suspected she'd been avoiding my calls.

'Where've you been?' she asked. 'Had you forgotten we were meeting for a catch up?'

'No,' I fibbed. And then, staring at the pile of papers, 'Jeepers—that's a whole morning's work by the look of it.'

'Shouldn't take a mo,' she said briskly, as though determined to be in and out as quickly as possible.

I worked my way through what she'd brought. None of it needed reviewing—Lisa was a better technician than I would ever be. Normally, I liked to whizz through and make the odd salient comment to show I'd added value. Today though, I signed without raising any questions.

I sensed that my failure to confide in her about the hoarding and other matters still rankled with her. But surely it would be possible for me to make amends…

'I've been trying to contact you—to ask if I could help you prep for the assessment centre?'

'Bit late for that now. I mean you've known for nearly two weeks that I'm attending.'

'Not too late at all. Why don't we sit down over the weekend and…'

'No thanks,' she said. 'I have all the help I need.'

Something stopped me from asking her where from.

'Well then, fancy a drink after work?'

'Um, sorry, I've something else on.'

'Another time?'

'Sure. How's your mum by the way?'

'OK, I guess.'

'You *still* haven't seen her?'

Her voice conveyed more than a hint of rebuke. Like everyone else, she judged the relationship by conventional standards and found me lacking. She'd been prepared to make allowances when there'd been "something terrible" lurking in my background. But the hoarding was no big deal to her—she neither understood the secrecy surrounding it nor why it had driven a wedge between my mother and me.

'No.'

Did anyone seriously imagine I'd found it easy to cut off contact with my own mother? That I was callous enough to take this draconian action on the trivial grounds of her failure to meet up to my standards of tidiness?

'Shouldn't you get in touch with her?'

'No.'

'Up to you,' she said. 'You might find the relationship more fulfilling if you tried harder. But then, being close to people doesn't come naturally to you.'

Her barb stung. It also irked me that without having met my mother, Lisa appeared to be taking her side. My feelings never seemed to matter to anyone.

'Perhaps not,' I agreed. 'But you and me, are we OK? Lately you've been a bit off with me. Can't we clear the air?'

Lisa didn't hesitate before replying.

'I'll be honest with you—it's grim being your friend at the moment. You never tell me anything—you're really paranoid about everyone. And if I'm brave enough to suggest there's something wrong you become angry and defensive. What am I supposed to do?'

What was I supposed to do, throw myself at her mercy, and beg for another chance? Not likely—it takes two to break a friendship. I suspected she'd somehow manipulated me to get on the assessment centre, but I daren't say so. She'd pounce on any such thoughts as further evidence of my paranoia.

'I'm sorry you feel that way,' I said lamely, instead. 'And fingers crossed for next week.'

'Thanks—I'll be fine.'

'And call me when you're through.'

'Sure, yes.'

She left without a backward glance.

'*She won't call you—she's not your friend anymore*,' whispered Little Amy.

Which was a shame, because I'd been contemplating asking Lisa's advice on JJ. But that was impossible now, with the permafrost between us.

Scarily, apart from an imaginary version of my fourteen-year-old self, I was entirely alone in the world.

***

Fact was, as I'd warned Carmody, no one at Pearson Malone would ever accept there was any irregularity at JJ Slate. Too many links and personal agendas clouded people's judgement. And without any definitive proof, discrediting and belittling me was a much easier option than facing the truth. Eric Bailey had probably been joking around, but there'd been a menacing edge to his comments—*don't you dare rock the boat, Amy Robinson.*

The answer was obvious. Possession of suspicious documents, which could always be explained away, was not enough. I needed proof. Then they would have to sit up and take notice, like it or not.

I took a mental inventory of what I had.

Debtors ledger—bank statements—haulage invoices—calculations.

Out of all the bundle of papers, the invoices intrigued me the most. They were all for deliveries to Parallax Projects at an industrial estate in East Grinstead, Sussex. But as I'd spotted before, the serial numbers of two of them were out of sequence, meaning they might be forged. Fake transport invoices for non-existent consignments of slate.

I'd quickly established that the East Grinstead address was the registered office of Parallax, which was not wholly surprising. But I'd made little progress otherwise, and hadn't unearthed any links between Parallax and Jason Jupp—quite the reverse. A Companies House search showed he was neither a director nor a shareholder.

Questions swirled round my mind. Where had the two million paid into Parallax every quarter come from? Why was everyone pretending to sell slate? Was there a secret JJ drug-dealing division of which the auditors, central management, and Megabuilders were all unaware? Why hadn't Parallax paid off the JJ invoices on a timely basis and avoided arousing anyone's suspicion? Why pay the money into JJ anyway—why not just to Jason Jupp himself? And why would drug dealers have all these neat traceable transactions through bank accounts?

My brain cried out for coffee to kick-start it. At the machine, I pressed the button for cappuccino, but instead a vile diarrhoea-like liquid spurted out.

'Oxtail soup,' said a passing secretary, spotting my disgust as she put envelopes into the nearby pigeonholes. 'They got the buttons mixed up when they serviced it.'

'So if I press soup do I get cappuccino?'

'Nah—not so simple—you have to press the button for black coffee.'

'OK,' I said.

'Oh—while you're here, this is yours,' she said, handing me an envelope with the Vodafone logo on it.

All the bills on the corporate phone account came round shortly after the end of the month.

All the bills…

The same brain that minutes before had been struggling whirred unbidden into action.

'Is there one of those for Isabelle?' I asked, endeavouring to hide my excitement. 'We're sending a few bits on to her parents.'

'Sure,' she said, rifling through the pile and handing it to me.

I poured away the soup and rushed off—the need for coffee forgotten.

***

By sheer good luck, I now possessed a log of all the calls Isabelle had made up from 1st June to 14th June, the date she'd died.

I worked backwards.

She'd last called Ryan, presumably trying to track him down. An earlier call to Greg must have been made for the same reason. Before that, she'd rung a number with a

Llandudno dialling code—her parents, I guessed, to share the joyous tidings of her promotion.

But she hadn't called Smithies.

That was disappointing—after all the shenanigans over the tax losses I still favoured him as number one suspect. If he'd somehow got wind of what Isabelle had discovered, then he had a motive. It was possible he'd called her—I recalled that the police list had included his number. Also Ryan had told me Smithies' number had come up when he'd checked Isabelle's phone. But that might have been days or weeks earlier. I contemplated several devious ways to get my hands on Smithies' phone bill, before concluding that the task was impossible.

She'd called another mobile number Friday lunchtime. I googled the number, but to no avail.

'*Dial it.*'

I used my landline, so whoever answered would see "number withheld".

'Hello.'

'Uh—who is this?'

'Thomas Evans,' came the reply. 'Who are you?'

I resisted the urge to ask directly if he was connected with Evans Haulage.

'Jan Brady,' I said, making a rapid decision to impersonate my personal assistant. 'I'm a secretary where Isabelle Edwards used to work and I'm calling round everyone who knew her—we're having a collection for a memorial fund…'

He cut me off abruptly.

'I'm not that close to Isabelle.'

'But your number's on her phone, so I assumed…'

'We went to school together, but I haven't seen her since—well not much. We exchanged a few words in the local now and then when she visited her parents. To tell the truth, I was surprised to hear from her.'

'Did she say why she was phoning?'

'Said she wanted to pick my brains about the business.'

My ears pricked up.

'What business?'

'Why, the family haulage company.'

'*Well, well, well,*' said Little Amy.

'What did she ask you?'

'Nothing—but she asked to meet up the next time she came back to Llandudno. That would have been last weekend. But then she went missing and the rest…I already told the police all this…'

'Sorry,' I said. 'Just being nosy.'

I reckoned the police weren't aware of the link between Evans Haulage and JJ. And even if they were, Carmody and co had been focussed single-mindedly on their prime suspect Ryan Kelly.

'So will you donate to the fund?' I asked him, deftly reverting to the lie I'd spun.

'Go on then,' he said. 'Put me down for fifty pounds and text me where to send it. You sure you didn't want anything else?'

His tone of voice suggested he'd twigged that the memorial fund story was a complete fiction.

'Quite sure—thanks so much.'

Without thinking too hard, I dialled the number on the Evans Haulage invoices.

'Good morning,' I said smoothly, 'Please may I speak to your accounts department.'

'The bookkeeper, you mean?'

'I guess so,' I replied and with a click, the receptionist put me through.

'Hi there—I'm the temp up at JJ Slate and I have a query on some invoices,' I began. If they were involved in the scam, this would undoubtedly rattle them, but it was a risk worth taking.

'I usually deal with Trevor.'

No alarm, just natural caution.

'Yes I know. I'm calling on his behalf.'

He appeared to accept this without question.

'If I give you invoice numbers can you check them back to your records?'

'Sure I can.'

I read out the numbers of the suspected counterfeits.

'They're ancient,' he said. 'Two years at least.'

He gave me the dates from his files, which were markedly different from those on the invoices, as was the customer name, delivery address and invoice amount. As I'd thought, someone had photocopied old invoices and changed the details, but forgot about the serial number. Careless.

'*Ask him if they ever deliver to the East Grinstead address?*' urged Little Amy.

They did.

'From the slate mine?'

'Why yes—but that's on a different arrangement—we bill a company called Parallax Projects.'

'Ah,' I said, 'maybe that's where the confusion's come.'

'No confusion here,' he replied defensively.

'I realise that—I'm checking from our end.'

'As a matter of fact,' he said, 'we've got another load going out there on Wednesday.'

Five days' time.

'What of?' I couldn't resist asking.

'Empty crates, of course. Parallax is the company that repairs the crates.'

'*Cannabis leaves. The crates would be too light to pretend they were full of slate, so instead they pretend they're empty.*'

As if she feared she wasn't making her points forcefully enough, Little Amy had put in an appearance. She sat perched on the table in the corner of my office, in a hideous yellow jumpsuit I didn't remember at all. The kid might be correct about this, even if her fashion sense hadn't fully evolved yet. Crate repair using the usual haulage company would be a great cover for transporting drugs.

I took stock.

There was likely a counterfeit haulage invoice to correspond with each fictitious slate sale to Parallax, and probably forged delivery notes and other documentation too. Meanwhile, genuine invoices had been raised to Parallax, allegedly for transporting empty crates.

But I kept revisiting the same uncertainties. If the slate sales were non-existent, why had the invoices been paid? And how were Jason Jupp and Parallax connected?

As ever, I had more questions than answers but I'd gleaned some useful information—a load of something en route to East Grinstead on Wednesday evening.

'*Why don't you find out what*?' said my gutsy alter ego.

32

It was a lunatic idea, dreamt up by a fourteen-year-old.

Although in her defence, it didn't seem lunatic at the time—more like the next logical step in a voyage of discovery. I'd found a link between Jason Jupp and drugs, but had failed to establish a connection between Jason and Parallax. If I could tie in Parallax to the drugs this would scarcely matter. I'd have enough evidence to move forward.

Common sense should have suggested that whatever evidence I obtained during this ill-judged expedition might be of limited use. Strictly, I'd still be obliged to report to Smithies' chum the MLRO. And I'd have the additional challenge of inventing a rationale for my unorthodox initiative.

But common sense lay dormant as I changed into jeans and drove down straight to East Grinstead from work the next Wednesday. The merits of action versus inertia outweighed all other considerations at this point.

On the way I called Lisa. The assessment centre normally wrapped up Wednesday lunchtime, but I'd heard nothing from her. We would go together to learn her results tomorrow morning, but I'd hoped for a debrief before then. Her phone rang twice before switching to voicemail. I left an upbeat message, hoping that all had gone smoothly and she was out enjoying herself. Once she would have called me the minute she'd left the centre, I reflected bitterly. Once she would have been out enjoying herself with me.

A quick recce confirmed that my Merc was far too conspicuous to be left anywhere near the industrial estate. I parked discreetly in a residential road half a mile away, and made my way on foot.

Unit 29 was a warehouse with a deserted air, no name above the entrance, nor any evidence of any manufacturing or processing activity. Nervousness inhibited me from trying the handle of the roll-top door or ringing the bell. Anyway—it was too early. By calling Evans Haulage and pretending to be from Parallax, I'd found out that the delivery wasn't due for another half an hour.

I waited in the bushes at the edge of the business park, racking my brains for a reason to justify my presence if someone challenged me. I would have asked Little Amy, but she'd gone silent on me, as though having spurred me on she now wished to distance herself from the project. Typical.

After nearly an hour, my feet had numbed from inactivity, and still there'd been no delivery. How silly—I couldn't wait all night—five more minutes, and I'd abort the mission.

I was on the verge of leaving when the Evans truck turned in and stopped outside unit 29. The driver climbed out and rang the bell I'd declined to press when I'd arrived. Up went the roller door. I moved in closer, hidden by the shadow of an adjoining building. Shaking with fear, I slipped unnoticed inside while the truck driver talked to the man helping to unload the crates. I hid in the corner, my heart thumping.

They finished the job quickly. I stayed in place, listening for any clue as to the contents of the boxes. But all I heard was some banter between the men, and a discussion about what they should watch on TV later.

Ultimately, the roller door went down and the truck departed.

And then silence.

I waited, unsure if I was alone, far longer than necessary. Then I moved towards the stack of crates.

A hideous wailing began. I cursed myself—how could I have been dumb enough not to foresee that the warehouse might be alarmed?

I thought fast. How long before someone came? Without question, the system would be wired to a security company. They would notify the key-holders, possibly the guys who'd just left. That gave a matter of minutes to achieve my goal. But I only needed minutes. Using a screwdriver as leverage I prised open the top of a crate.

Empty.

Another one.

Empty.

I couldn't check them all—I had to leave.

But there was one small difficulty—I was locked in.

What an idiot. I'd embarked on this wild goose chase for nothing. The goods being delivered appeared to be exactly as claimed and I was about to be discovered somewhere I had no business to be. Either my judgment had deserted me or I truly had lost my mind.

I heard voices, which I recognised as belonging to the men from before. I scurried back to my original hiding place and held my breath.

I was far from ideally positioned, but I couldn't change that now. I waited until they were at the opposite end of the warehouse and sprang out from my lair.

For an instant I believed I'd got away with it—but no.

'Oi, you—what are you doing here?'

As if propelled by a powerful force, I bolted.

A shot rang out. I figured it must be simple to hit a target at this range, and they were gaining on me. I tripped, skidding along the tarmac and skinning my knees through my jeans. Without checking for damage, I pulled myself upright. A bullet whistled past me—they were closing fast.

I charged out of the estate into the road and narrowly avoided being knocked over by a white van. The driver opened the window.

'Alright, love?'

'Those men are after me,' I said, gesticulating wildly before pulling open the door and leaping into the passenger seat. I had no clue who this guy was—he might even be a member of the gang, or a random serial killer. But for the moment he represented my best means of escape.

The driver didn't wait for any further explanation but floored the accelerator and squealed off into the darkness.

My heart pounded like a sledgehammer.

'Police station for you,' he pronounced, taking in my dishevelled state.

'No—it's a private matter. My car's down the road, can you drop me there?'

'Are you sure you're OK?'

'Certain,' I said, endeavouring to sound normal. 'And thanks.'

My Good Samaritan wished me all the best. Who was he and what must he be thinking? Certainly, he'd asked fewer questions than I'd expected. But what did it matter? I was safe.

'*That went well, didn't it?*'

Typical—now the danger was past, Little Amy had chosen to reappear.

'Hoped you'd gone for ever.'
'*Oh no—I'm always here, whether you realise it or not.*'
And whether I liked or not, it seemed.
Weary with relief, I started the ignition.

33

The physical aftermath was bad enough. Embryonic scabs on my knees cracked open with every step and discharged a clear liquid that soaked straight through the dressings I'd applied. My shins throbbed insanely.

Worse was the self-loathing and disgust at my own stupidity. Last night the relief at having escaped in one piece had trumped every other emotion. Now, I realised the ordeal was far from over. If the delivery was innocuous, they'd report the incident to the police. It wouldn't take much to track me down—my car registration would have been caught on CCTV somewhere. But if the crates I hadn't opened contained drugs, those bad guys would pursue me, perhaps with greater zeal than the Sussex police. And thinking about it, why would they have shot at me if they had nothing to hide?

I would have rung in sick, but as Lisa's sponsoring partner I was supposed to collect the result of her assessment with her. She'd think even worse of me if let her down.

As she bounded into my office I didn't need to ask how it had gone—she radiated optimism.

'Hi,' I said. 'Tried to call you yesterday.'

'Yes,' she said. 'Sorry. Went out and got blind drunk.'

Who with, I asked myself.

'Oh, that's good.'

'Amy, you look awful,' she said with warm-hearted malice as I hobbled along beside her en route to the meeting. 'What the hell happened?'

'I hurt my knee,' I replied, in a statement as true as it was incomplete.

'Fell down pissed somewhere, eh?'

Even a month ago, I would have taken this remark as friendly teasing and given a flip response back. Now I suspected this was no joke. The balance of power in our relationship had shifted.

'No, actually. Anyway, you're in fine shape after your big night out, and I'm assuming you're quietly confident?'

'Yep,' she said. 'Went amazingly.'

Instead of expanding on this she remained silent as we walked to the meeting room.

On entering, I drew back as I spotted Greg sitting at the other side of the table.

'Uh—uh—wrong meeting.'

'Not at all,' he said. 'Didn't Lisa tell you I was her lead assessing partner at the centre?'

'No,' I said with barely suppressed umbrage. 'She didn't.'

Despite Lisa's recent coolness towards me, I hoped she'd pass, but Greg's involvement surely didn't help her chances. Smithies had to have nobbled him beforehand.

'Your secretary told me you were on holiday.'

'I was until Monday, but I came back to sit on the assessment panel. Why did you want me?'

'Oh,' I said. 'Only checking how you were after the funeral.'

There was no point in discussing JJ with Greg now, useless to take any action. I'd swung back from a determination to sort things out to a weary apathy. From the moment I'd become involved in JJ, my life had fallen apart. It had to stop.

'That was thoughtful. I'm OK, I think. Nothing beats work for taking your mind off your problems.'

Except when your problems began and ended at work.

'You're not in great shape,' he observed, eyeing me with sympathy as I winced from the pain when I bent my knees to sit down.

'Minor knee injury.'

And I could somehow tell he thought I'd fallen down drunk too.

Undeniably, Greg possessed all the gravitas needed in an assessing partner. His face gave nothing away, as he went through the exercises one by one, picking holes. By contrast, Lisa's crestfallen expression suggested she'd been blithely unaware of these perceived weaknesses. Her interaction with the others in the team exercise had been "borderline acceptable". Why? Because she hadn't attempted to conceal her impatience with the other candidates. Greg didn't reveal which side of the border she'd fallen—he seemed to relish putting her through the wringer, and continued with his litany of complaint. On finding out in the in-tray assignment that her secretary planned to be on holiday the next week, she'd responded with a pithy 'bloody typical'. This had not met with the assessors' approval. I thought of the ice melting in the champagne bucket back in my office. By the sound of it, we wouldn't have anything to celebrate today after all. I glanced at Lisa, still able to empathise with her even though she'd cast me aside—why didn't Greg just put her out of her misery?

But unexpectedly the tenor of his comments changed. Lisa had demonstrated a formidable intellect, with incisive analysis of the hypothetical client situation and she'd handled the role-play meeting with poise. There'd been some doubts about her judgement on the risk management exercise but unlike some of the other candidates, at least she'd reached a decision.

All in all, he said, it had been a tough call, but they'd passed Lisa, subject to her having individual coaching in the weaker areas after appointment. And, as with everyone else, provided she passed the final interview with Pearson Malone's Executive Board.

'Well whoop de doo!' said Lisa as we emerged from the meeting, but with a strange note of sarcasm in her voice.

'I've got some champagne in my office for you.'

She shook her head.

'Nah—not right now. Got stuff to do, but cheers anyway.'

She walked off purposefully, as though in a hurry to get somewhere else. How on earth had our friendship deteriorated so fast?

***

Smithies did one aspect of his job magnificently—he sure as hell knew how to celebrate a success. As soon as he'd heard Lisa's news, he'd thrown himself enthusiastically into organising an impromptu champagne knees-up downstairs in Daly's. I'd seldom been in a less celebratory mood, but to duck out would be unsupportive of Lisa. Although she had a down on me, or even especially if she had a down on me, I didn't want people thinking I resented her achievements.

A champagne drunk is a happy drunk. After I'd downed the first two glasses, I felt appreciably better. I decided I should drink it more often, instead of the gin that stoked my paranoia and deepened my depression.

I'd been watching Smithies carefully as he'd worked the room, full of sham bonhomie and sipping daintily at his glass. The man was a chameleon, charming one moment, venomous the next, and someone so duplicitous could easily be a killer.

But I'd resolved not to involve myself with any of this. Sure, one of my clients might be running a cannabis farm on the side, which might be connected with a colleague's death, but how was that my business? Let some other bugger sort it out. I'd gone way beyond the call of duty already.

Little Amy was disappointed by my devil-may-care attitude.

'*You're drunk again*,' she told me severely as I paid a visit to the Ladies.

'Since when were you such a Puritan?' I hissed. 'What about the time you drank five pints of cider and puked all over Miss Hope's doorstep?'

'*That was you, not me*.'

I despaired of the kid—she attributed all her mistakes to me, and took no responsibility for mine. I so wished she'd piss off back to the hoard house—it was all she deserved.

Champagne happiness comes at the price of suspending judgement. Consequently, I left Daly's with no sense of danger, even when my phone rang and JJ's personal number showed up.

'*Go on then—answer it*.'

You should never speak to a client when drunk, unless he's drunk too, but I kidded myself I could handle it. I wasn't a lightweight like Little Amy, vomiting after a few pints of cider. I was a mature woman who invariably remained firmly in control—especially after champagne.

'Amy?' said JJ. I wondered who else he might be expecting to answer my phone.

'JJ, how are you?' I tried hard not to slur my words.

'Fine,' he replied, sounding doubtful. 'And you?'

'Great, thanks.'

That was the champagne talking.

'Can you come over tomorrow afternoon? Something's cropped up that I want to run by you.'

His casual tone suggested it was nothing important. And at least he'd not sprung some technical question on me without warning, as he was prone to.

'*He's going to kill you.*' There was a note of glee in Little Amy's voice. '*He's found out you're onto him.*'

How was that possible? Would he really invite me to his offices to bump me off? Paranoid as I was, the idea seemed farfetched.

'Sure,' I said. 'What time?'

'About three?'

'Let me double-check my diary…'

'*Don't say I didn't warn you.*'

Distracted by my calendar, I disregarded the roar of the car coming up behind me, until it was almost too late. At the last minute a primal instinct kicked in and I threw myself into a nearby doorway. The car mounted the pavement, missing me by inches, before swerving back onto the road and screeching off into the distance. I lay on the ground, shaken, bruised and no doubt resembling a homeless wino. Amazingly though, I still held my phone and JJ was still at the other end of it.

'Hello.'

'Amy—are you OK?'

He sounded surprised to hear my voice.

'Yes, thanks,' I said, breathless and stunned by the brutal jar of the attack. 'I must have tripped over something.'

I staggered to my feet and dusted myself down—my knees smarting badly. Surely, he couldn't be responsible for my mishap from the other end of a telephone line?

'*Come on—JJ has people to do whatever he wants. They followed you and arranged for JJ to distract you at the crucial moment.*'

On reflection, she could be right. Funny, wasn't it, how the call had come as I walked down Arundel Street to the Tube, a street where there wouldn't be many eyewitnesses?

But they'd botched it.

'Are you sure you're OK?'

'Yes, no worries—see you tomorrow.'

I shook uncontrollably. Good sense, let alone paranoia, suggested this was no coincidence. My plan to steer clear of all this nonsense had run up against a major hitch—I knew too much already to be safe.

Without thinking I hit Carmody's number on the phone.

'*Uh, uh,*' said Little Amy. '*I can't believe you still trust that creep.*'

What did she know—silly little bitch? She still trusted our mother to clear up the house.

He answered on the first ring.

'Amy?'

'Somebody tried to run me down.'

'Where?'

Incredibly, he didn't sound shocked—but I suppose nothing fazes police officers.

'Arundel Street.'

'Are you hurt?'

'No—no—I'm OK, sort of.'

'Did you get the registration number?'

'No—too quick...'

'Type of car?'

'I'm not sure—some big SUV?'

'Any witnesses?'

I looked around me. The few people who'd been in the street had all hurried on, as everyone does in London.

'No... not any more. It was JJ—he called me while they tried to kill me. He must have found out I saw a drug farm at the slate mine. Maybe he knows about the warehouse at East Grinstead too—that's where they deliver the cannabis. I didn't actually see it, but I'm right. Why else would they try to shoot me? And that's why Isabelle was killed—she had all the same information as I did—the phony invoices, the bank statements, the whole blinking lot. So I got it wrong—it's not Smithies—it's JJ, or his son—I guess you realise his son's a drug dealer. But I worked it out. The drug money paid those invoices off, though I can't fathom how they got the cash back. So there was a fraud after all.'

This deluge of information made total sense to me, but Carmody sounded less convinced.

'Amy,' he said. 'Don't take this the wrong way...'

A 'but' was coming.

'But have you been drinking?'

'Yes, but not much, I only...'

'You're not making much sense and you sound kind of drunk...'

'So you don't believe me...'

'I believe you're telling the truth as you see it, but it does seem astonishing that someone would try to mow you down like that.'

'But someone did—you *must* treat this seriously.'

'I wish I could.'

'You have to do *something*.'

'You're not hurt, so in the absence of further evidence there's nothing I can do.'

'Ah, I see.'

And indeed I did see—he had no intention of potentially making a fool of himself by acting on the ranting of a hysterical drunken woman.

'I suggest you jump into a cab back to Chiswick and sleep this off...'

The patronising git.

'I suggest you get stuffed,' I said, and hung up.

'*Told you.*'

***

Whatever Carmody thought, I hadn't drunkenly stepped in front of an oncoming car. No—this had been a serious attempt to eliminate me. I did know the difference.

They'd pulled a gun on me the previous night and now they'd discovered my identity and location. I hurried to the Tube station, ears pricked and eyes casting neurotically around for any sign of a repeat attack. Despite my fears, I made it onto the train safely and flopped down in a seat, still shaking, with relief now rather than fear. But a sense of realism tempered my relief. They'd botched this attempt to kill me—next time I might not be so lucky.

'*Carmody doesn't give a shit. And you gotta ask why.*'

'His promotion, obviously. He doesn't want anyone to find out he arrested the wrong person.'

'*No—there's more. He's hiding something from you.*'

'But what?'

Without thinking, I'd been speaking out loud, and people in the carriage were staring at me oddly. I'd have to be more careful. And for once, Little Amy must have agreed with me, because she didn't say another word on the journey home.

34

Four weeks ago, my only worries had been Smithies, the upcoming pay review and Lisa's promotion. I hadn't yet slept with Ryan, Isabelle was alive and my mother's hoarding out of sight and out of mind. I still had my job as group leader and Lisa was my friend. And I had no idea that the new clients I'd taken on were fraudsters. Best of all, a pesky little kid who claimed to be my past self wasn't yet hounding me.

She was onto me again as I picked up the gin bottle on arriving home.

'*Not a great idea*,' she said, shaking her head. '*Honestly, an old biddy like you should have more sense.*'

'OK, Miss Goody Two Shoes—I'm fed up of your pious twaddle. Do you ever consider that you might be responsible for how I've grown up?'

'*Bloody typical—everyone always blames me for everything. Anyway, even it is my fault I can't help it. I'm an abused child—you told me so yourself.*'

'I despair! I cannot believe I'm here talking to you—you're not real.'

'*Oh—I disagree*,' she said, smirking. '*I'm the most real person you know.*'

'Well, I've had enough of you. I'm ordering you to go away and leave me alone—forever.'

'*OK—OK. I know when I'm not wanted. But remember—I told you—I'm always with you.*'

I made to pour out my gin, but thought better of it. When I looked again, she'd gone.

I checked and double-checked all the doors and windows, then set the alarm. Though I was as secure as possible in the circumstances, I didn't feel safe at all. I fell into bed fully clothed.

I lay in the darkness, buzzing and unable to settle, certain that Little Amy was close by, watching me and judging. And I wasn't wrong.

'*Use your brains, for fuck's sake.*'

Language, please, child, although who was I to talk. I sat up, switched the light on to find her critically appraising the contents of my wardrobe. How dare she, in that yellow jumpsuit—a garment so hideous she must surely have broken the rule of a lifetime and discarded it.

Still, the little bitch had a point. I'd missed something, and for my own safety, for my own sanity, I needed to find what it was.

'If you're so smart,' I said. 'How come I grew up so dumb?'

'*I dunno*,' she replied. '*You do realise these clothes are extremely boring. I think I'll kill myself if I grow up into you.*'

Go ahead, I thought.

'So where do I start, clever clogs?'

'*I'd get rid of the whole bloody lot.*'

What a cheek, especially coming from someone who had no concept of throwing stuff out.

'Not with the clothes, with JJ.'

'*You have to connect JJ with Parallax.*'

Sure. JJ was behind the attempt to kill me, without a doubt. It couldn't be a fluke that I'd been on the phone to him when the car had come at me. But how had he tracked me down?

And then I twigged—Smithies—they were in cahoots. Yes, Smithies had tipped them off when I left the party.

'Have a safe journey home.' Smithies' parting words played back inside my head. And all the while he'd been aware of JJ's plans for me. Heartless—utterly heartless.

Somehow I must find the evidence to join the dots. Without question, proof that JJ was connected with Parallax would be useful. And yes, I'd tried and failed before, but perhaps I hadn't tried hard enough. In retrospect, most of my failures had arisen because of lack of effort and willpower—even clearing up the hoard.

'*So who* are *the directors of Parallax?*'

Great question, kid. I should revisit the register of directors and shareholders.

One director's name stood out as unusual—Roderick Lavender. I googled him.

First up was a Facebook page.

'*Check his friends*,' urged my pesky alter ego. Her astute suggestions narked me immeasurably. Had I really been so annoying at her age? For a nanosecond, I sympathised with my mother.

'What do you know about Facebook?' I chided. 'It didn't exist when I was you.'

'*So what*,' she said. '*It exists now*.'

Roderick had been savvy enough to set up his privacy settings so only friends could see what he posted. However, like many Facebook users, he hadn't restricted the visibility of his list of friends.

One of them was Jason Jupp.

I was in business. Easy to have your chums front you as a company director, or as a shareholder. And how would anybody find out unless they trawled through social media sites? Why hadn't I thought of that before?

Impatient for more, I clicked the link to Jason's page. He too allowed open access to his friend list. And up popped the names of the remaining two Parallax directors.

Result—I'd made connections between Jason and drugs, and Jason and Parallax.

All I needed was a way to link Parallax with the drugs, apart from another abortive trip to East Grinstead.

'*Bank statements.*'

I wanted to tell her to shut up, but I needed her. She was my brain—she was guiding me.

All the deposits in the Parallax account came by BACS from a company called Impex Ltd. It was odd for a company to have one customer, and as I'd spotted before, even odder for drug transactions to be paid for by bank transfer. I mean, with all the anti money laundering rules, it must be a real challenge to introduce drug money into the banking system. Yet Impex had coolly wired millions to Parallax over the last few years.

In the beginning, most of the money had been paid away from Parallax by cheque. It was impossible to tell where without Chloe Fenton's assistance, which I felt certain wouldn't be forthcoming. But then a couple of months ago a flurry of BACS payments totalling three and a half million to JJ Resources had cleared all the amounts owed.

But once again, why pay drugs money to the JJ company? And who was Parallax's mysterious customer?

'*Time to do due diligence on Impex.*'

This mini-me was amazing. I'd never heard the words 'due diligence' at her age.

I fully expected Impex Limited to be a shell company with nominee shareholders and directors, but there I was wrong. The company described itself an import-export agent, with a proper website, and a business established for several years. A company search revealed they'd filed accounts, all meticulously set out and audited.

This threw me. Were they after all genuine customers of a genuine firm?

'*Import export agents are prime fronts for money laundering*,' Little Amy informed me.

How the hell did she know? My fingers flew as I called up a search on the directors.

There were two of them—Darren Mayhew and Carol Andersen. They had everything you'd expect, down to their professional profiles on LinkedIn. Darren's photograph stirred a vague memory, but I struggled to place him. The address on the register was the same for both, and it checked out to the electoral roll too.

'*They're aliases, obviously*.'

But if they were, they'd been elaborately and comprehensively constructed. Darren's biography gave his education as being Oldham Grammar, a school which no longer existed. I checked Friends Reunited—nothing doing, but far from conclusive—the network had fallen out of favour in recent years.

'*When were they born?*'

My mind now hared ahead of Little Amy's. Of course—Genes Reunited lets you search for birth and death records. I had Darren's date of birth from the directors' register so away I went. I clicked on "search all records"—only one birth with that name and surname in the relevant year, but in Slough, not Oldham. Oddly, there had been a death in the same year. Father, grandfather perhaps.

'*Nah*,' said Smarty Pants. '*Old men weren't called Darren then*.'

I downloaded the certificates. Darren and Carol were both real enough, until that is they'd died in infancy.

'*Wow, they're using the identities of dead kids*.'

I clicked back to LinkedIn. I figured it must be tricky to fabricate a whole profile, but both seemed to have a comprehensive list of contacts. Neither had any jobs listed before Impex, though, which I guessed would make the task of constructing a mock persona easier.

This was significant progress, but I'd gone as far as I could tonight. Tomorrow I'd take a trip to Impex's business premises, or maybe the directors' home, but for now I must try to get some sleep. Nobody can run on empty forever, however wired.

As I attempted to settle back down, I remembered. Darren was the guy I'd met in Daly's the first evening with Carmody. They'd worked together, Carmody had said.

In an intense flash of lucidity, I finally understood the truth. Carmody had been hiding something. They were all in it, Smithies, Jim Jupp, his son and a bent policeman. And Ryan had been their scapegoat.

35

I woke with a start at eleven-fifteen, seized by a conviction that I must go into work immediately so as not to raise their suspicions.

In hindsight, this belief had little logical merit. It certainly didn't warrant flying out of the house without showering and still wearing the same clothes as the night before.

Smithies was after me before I'd even grabbed a coffee.

'Can you spare me a few minutes?'

'When?'

'How about now?'

I shook with fear as I replaced the phone in its cradle.

No doubt Smithies was disappointed not to be announcing my untimely demise. But now what would he do?

'Come in, Amy, and sit down,' he said. His calculated gentleness made me shudder.

'Now—do you have any idea why I wanted us to meet this morning?'

I shook my head, although a connection with their failure to kill me seemed probable.

'Don't look so worried. My turn to be worried today.'

'Why's that?' I asked, a shade too belligerently.

'I'm concerned about your mental health.'

He sounded for the world as though he meant it, which disturbed me more than anything.

'It's clear that relieving you of the stress of the group leader role hasn't done the trick.'

I knew it. He was unveiling Plan C. Plan A had been to make me so insecure I wouldn't dare delve into JJ. When he'd failed, Plan B had been to kill me. And Plan C was what?

'I'm fine,' I snapped.

'Sadly I fear not,' said Smithies. 'Look at the state of you.'

I glanced at my reflection in the glass walls of his office—not a pretty sight. Only now did I realise I was wearing yesterday's clothes, with unwashed hair, dusty from last night's tumble. How could I have forgotten to change and shower? A lack of make-up and a wild, glassy-eyed stare completed the picture.

'And since we lessened your workload, I've continued to hear disturbing reports as to your state of mind.'

'From who—who?' I demanded.

'This morning Eric Bailey took a worrying telephone call from JJ. Jupp says he spoke to you last night and that, frankly, you were three sheets to the wind.'

'That's a lie.'

'Amy—it's useless to deny it. Even I noticed how much champagne you quaffed at the party.'

'We were celebrating,' I protested. 'At the last do you reckoned people hadn't drunk enough—remember? And anyway, I wasn't drunk...'

'If you weren't drunk on the amount you put away then I'd say you'd developed a worrying tolerance.'

So I couldn't win either way. It was unacceptable to be intoxicated and sobriety only proved I was a soak.

'And if I was drunk, it was out of hours.'

'But we are all ambassadors of the firm twenty-four-seven,' he replied. 'Particularly if you take a client's telephone call.'

Perception is reality. You could be slated for being under the influence, but it was perfectly acceptable to cover for your brother-in-law in a drug-related swindle. Killing a colleague and colluding in the attempted murder of another were also tolerated, as long as nobody found out.

'It wasn't like that. While I was talking to JJ on my phone, a car nearly ran me over and…'

As he well knew.

'I have to say I'm beginning to think your alcohol abuse may be at the root of your psychological issues. Your ex, Greg, mentioned you'd been hitting the bottle. He's worried about you too.'

I hated the way he said "your ex". Did he think I'd forgotten I'd been married to him? Or maybe such a vast number of Gregs were concerned about me that he needed to clarify which one he meant. The grins of the water-skiers mocked me as he continued with his monologue.

'And Lisa tells me, in the strictest confidence, that you've not been yourself for a while.'

'How loyal of her,' I said. 'After everything I've done for her, she goes sneaking behind my back grassing me up.'

'To be fair to Lisa,' said Smithies. 'I did ask her to keep an eye on you, when I began to suspect you might be on the verge of a breakdown.'

It hardly seemed credible. They hated each other—why would they form this unholy alliance against me?

'But you hate her so much you tried to hold back her partnership for no reason. Why would you suddenly rely on her except because you loathe me even more?'

'Now there you go,' Smithies replied. 'The very use of such emotive and unprofessional language gives us a window into your mental state. And besides—Lisa has passed the assessment—how can you say I held her back?'

'But you didn't want her to *go* on the assessment,' I reminded him.

'I had no part in that decision, as I made clear at the outset. In fact I'm pleased for Lisa. And I've been so impressed by what I've seen of her, I'm contemplating a bigger role for her.'

'Yes?'

I guessed from the queasiness in the pit of my stomach what he had in mind. And I finally understood what had lain behind Lisa's aloofness—she'd sold out to the enemy for her own personal gain.

'But we're not here to discuss Lisa. We're here to talk about you. And we cannot go on like this.'

No—we could not. It was the first statement he'd made I agreed with.

'Now we do appreciate you've had a tough time with Isabelle and Ryan's deaths, and your mother's illness. But you're not your usual self at the moment and as responsible employers, we must help you through this trying phase.'

This sounded suspiciously like the beginning of a firing or "asking for resignation" speech.

'What did you have in mind?'

'It may be helpful if you saw the firm's doctor…'

'I don't think that's necessary,' I said, desperately trying to regain control of the meeting.

But I could no longer hide from the truth. I was broken—after all the shit life had handed me, I had finally buckled and lost the fight. Despite my fear of ending up like my mother, a different kind of craziness had sneaked up on me while I'd struggled to be normal. And if I was too spineless to face it, I was as bad as my mother—in denial.

'I'm afraid we must insist. So I suggest you go home, contact HR and consider yourself signed off sick until further notice.'

'But I have to see JJ this afternoon, and there are some big events coming up soon, including the JJ completion meeting on Monday.'

I tried forlornly to keep up the pretence, to convince him I was sane and no threat to them. I so didn't want the stigma of mental health issues. It would be the end of my career, the end of everything I'd fought for so hard over the years. Every day I'd stood in front of the mirror and talked myself up, but for what? At least my mother had succeeded in keeping her foibles hidden. Mine were there for all to see.

'Please don't worry,' he said. 'Everything will be taken care of. Lisa is quite capable of handling both of those, and if you let us have a note of any other upcoming appointments…'

'Tell me straight. Are you putting Lisa into my old job? And don't you dare lie to me.'

He appeared to be gauging whether I was strong enough to bear the answer.

'Well, we *are* considering giving Lisa an early shot at a leadership role. Nothing's been decided yet, but there's a vacancy, for sure. I have far too many other responsibilities to continue in that capacity myself.'

I knew he'd planned from the beginning to install one of his sycophants as group leader. But to find that Lisa *was* one of his sycophants—a nasty, sneaky undercover one—represented the ultimate betrayal. I'd trusted her as a friend, dammit, but she'd stabbed me in the back while standing on my shoulders. And she'd had the gall to heap guilt on me for our cooling friendship.

'Plus she has the confidence of the team—they tell her everything.'

Yeah—and then she tells you.

Tears pricked at my eyes. I wouldn't let the bastard Smithies see me cry, no matter how I hurt inside. I dug my nails into the palms of my hands, using physical pain to negate the raw emotional anguish. Little Amy never cried and I wouldn't either. Where was she now, I asked myself? I missed her.

'You could have asked *me* for information,' I countered, battling vainly on.

'Would you have told me the truth? I think not, even assuming you knew. Ever since I arrived, I've seen you becoming more and more isolated and suspicious of everyone. These are not signs of sound mental health as I'm sure you're aware.'

But *he'd* made me paranoid—I'd been OK till he arrived, hadn't I—or had I?

'I could go on,' said Smithies, 'but I sense you're becoming emotional. And I can see this has taken you unawares. Would you like someone to be with you—your mother perhaps?'

Enough.

'You must be kidding!' I screamed, so loudly that the people sitting near Smithies' office all craned round to see what the commotion was. The dam broke and the tears flowed—tears of anger and frustration, rather than sadness.

And I saw it all now in the utmost clarity. No one needed to kill me for my knowledge about the activities at JJ Slate, because nothing I said in future would be taken seriously. I'd been totally discredited and written off as a crazy bitch. That was Plan C.

This was the end game, his final victory. I'd been so strong, yet he'd brought me down in a few weeks. And it was my fault for letting him spook me. That was the beauty of his strategy. He'd spotted my weakness and allowed me to reduce myself to this crumbling wreck with little intervention from him.

'I'm so sorry it's come to this,' said Smithies, in the syrupy pseudo-sympathetic voice he did so convincingly. 'I do hope you're back to your old self before long.'

Undeniably, his final statement was true. For nothing would give Smithies greater pleasure than to see me sufficiently recovered to attend a firing meeting.

***

I composed myself in the Ladies for a few minutes, and when I stepped out of the stall the tsunami of emotion had passed. Then I noticed Lisa hovering.

Intuition told me she had a detailed knowledge of my discussion with Smithies, because he'd told her what he planned to do. Oh yes—she'd sold out to the enemy alright.

'Thanks, bitch.'

'Amy—what are you talking about?'

She put on her most innocent face, but I wasn't fooled. I now understood the full scale of her treachery. She was not only a barefaced liar, but a liar who'd sneakily hidden behind a façade of total honesty. Though the betrayal was just about bearable, her double standards stank—I'd believed she was a better human being.

'You're spying on me for Smithies. And don't try to deny it, because he told me himself.'

'It isn't what you think. You've got hold of the wrong end of the stick. If you calm down for a moment, I can explain.'

'Go on then,' I challenged her. 'And it had better be good.'

'Look, I'm a chavvy Essex girl and it's been tough for me to get so far. And when Smithies came on board, everything changed. I didn't have a cat in hell's chance of making it unless I did something different. I was all set to leave, as you know, but when I thought about it, I decided there was another way. There's nothing wrong with building bridges with him—heck, I advised you to do the same.'

'OK—I get that, but you could have done it without wrecking my life in the process.'

'It had nothing to do with you! You've been so self-centred recently—everything is always about you. This is about *me*—right? I didn't have to wreck your life—you did it all on your own.'

'With a little help from my friends,' I added.

'Will you listen to me, please? When Smithies bounced me off the assessment centre, I went to see him.'

'And told him he'd better promote you because I was an unstable neurotic untrustworthy bitch and you wanted my job.'

'He's giving *me* the group head job?' she gasped.

The Shirley Temple naivety would have been utterly convincing if I hadn't known better.

'Don't pretend you don't know—give me credit for some intelligence.'

'No—honestly—I had no idea. So what's happening to you?'

'Signed off long term sick, as you're well aware.'

'It's probably for the best,' she said, abandoning any attempt at feigned ignorance.

'Best for you, you treacherous cow.'

'No—you, stupid. You're not well—I've been trying to tell you for weeks, but you wouldn't listen.'

'You said nothing, apart from some hypocritical advice to cut down my drinking. You—who nailed your colours to the mast of total truth—you've lied and lied and lied.'

'There you go again. You know, Amy, the last few months you've been a complete bitch to work with, seeing people plotting against you all the time.'

'Because they *were*!'

'No—it was all inside your head—the head that's so comprehensively messed up you can't see anything straight. All I did was point out to Smithies how uniquely valuable I would be to him as a partner, because the whole team trusted me.'

'And spying on me.'

'No not spying on you—helping him to do his job, giving him essential information.'

'And he said?'

'He blustered as you'd expect—said he had excellent sources already. But I told him that everyone was so suspicious of his brown nose snitches they were useless as informants. What he *really* needed was someone who had everyone's ear and who was known to be his enemy.'

'And he asked you to spy on me.'

'No—honest to God he didn't. I admit he did ask me to watch out for you, but only because he was worried and he knew we were friends. He's not as bad as you paint him—he *couldn't* be that bad. As a matter of fact it was when you started saying he'd killed Isabelle that I decided there was something seriously wrong with you.'

'You told him *that*,' I said, aghast.

'No, of course not.'

But I didn't believe her. The trust between us had snapped

like a neck in a hangman's noose the moment I'd discovered she'd been angling for my job.

'But Smithies was dead against your promotion. I made them change their minds. I met with Townsend…'

'Smithies didn't want to lose face, as you can imagine, but all the same I'd struck a chord. He predicted that you'd leap into action to rescue me.'

So Smithies had persuaded Lisa to plant the idea of a brewing equality issue in my mind. He'd actually sat there and taken a bollocking for sexual and racial discrimination for what he saw as a greater benefit. And they must have staged Lisa's argument with him at the drinks party to perpetuate the myth that they were sworn enemies. Then her "job interview" must also have been a fiction designed to spur me into action.

Clearly, the pair of them could have enjoyed stellar careers in MI5, or maybe on the stage.

'And all so he could have a spy in charge of the group.'

'It truly wasn't that way. And I do appreciate all your efforts on my behalf...'

'You used me.'

'No, no I didn't. I wish you'd listen.'

Despite everything, I envied her cunning. I'd been so busy fighting Smithies that I'd failed to recognise the advantages of having him on side. Lisa had provided *egg-zackly* what he needed at the appropriate time. But the cleverness of her plan had to be seen in context, because she'd made a pact with the devil. And something in her story didn't ring true—nobody manipulated the Machiavellian maestro Smithies quite so easily. He must be gaining some additional benefit, even if Lisa hadn't yet figured out what it was.

'I've heard more than enough.'

'Oh come on, Amy—lighten up. This is no big deal.'

'Not to you, evidently, but for me… I can't trust you anymore. You do realise that?'

'I seem to recall that you advised me never to trust anyone at work.'

The tidal wave of anger welled up again. How dare she, how fucking dare she, throw my own advice back at me?

'If you're a chavvy Essex girl,' I said. 'You'll understand this.'

And I socked her one, full in the face.

I'd blindsided her. She stared at me blankly, not even registering shock, blood trickling from her nostril. But before her jungle instincts kicked in to deliver her retaliatory blow, we heard the door.

Both of us quickly straightened up as Jan, my secretary, walked in.

'Lisa has a nosebleed,' I said. 'Perhaps you could call a first aider.'

'Won't you stay with her?' asked Jan, with alarm.

'No,' I said. 'I'm going home—I've been signed off sick.'

I wondered if Lisa would rat on me. Frankly, I didn't much care—it was hard to see how things could get much worse.

But every time I caught myself thinking that, they did.

36

'Can you spare me a minute of your time, sir?'

Dave Carmody looked up from the stack of paperwork on his desk.

'Sure.'

'About Amy Robinson—Isabelle's boss.'

Carmody's stomach lurched. Had something terrible happened to Amy? She'd sounded pretty wild the previous evening, and he feared the worst.

'You'd better take a seat,' he said. His calm demeanour belied the turmoil within.

'She seems to be in a spot of bother, one way and another, sir.'

'Yes?' The fear ratcheted up a few notches as Carmody fought to keep his voice steady.

'A guy from Croydon division called. Her mother has filed charges against her for forging her signature on a contract with a house clearance company. This apparently resulted in all her mother's possessions being taken away.'

Carmody relaxed slightly.

'How come they called you?'

'Her neighbour practically frogmarched the mother into the station, and she mentioned Amy's connection with the Isabelle Edwards case. They asked if we'd interviewed Amy—if we'd formed a view of her.'

'And what did you say?'

'I said she was a thoroughly professional and upright woman, and the whole story sounded most implausible. I hope that was OK, sir.'

'Yes, very good—thank you.'

Carmody had little respect for DS Holland's intellect, but the guy was endowed with a shrewd perception of emotion that was equally useful. Without anything having been said, he was all too aware of Carmody's attraction to Amy.

'I expect they'll ask her a few questions,' Carmody went on. 'I bet it's all a silly misunderstanding. She did tell me in passing that her mother's a hoarder.'

'Ah I see, sir. But the weird thing is, they're not the only ones who're after Amy. They called me back afterwards and told me they discovered NCA have been making enquiries about her.'

'What?'

Carmody sat bolt upright.

'Connected to an undercover operation they've been running jointly with various forces around the country. They wouldn't give any details—said it's top secret. But they're scared stiff she might undermine whatever it is they're trying to achieve.'

'Really?'

'So it's been agreed that Ms Robinson's to be arrested for the forgery and brought in for questioning. They've been told to hold her as long as possible.'

'Sweet Jesus, what's that all about?'

It had to be serious, though. The National Crime Agency only involved themselves in the most substantial organised crimes, such as major drug dealing. Last night, when she'd called him, he'd been absolutely convinced that Amy was gripped by drunken paranoia. Now it seemed there might be some substance to her wild allegations. Had Amy attempted to do her own sleuthing and run up against an existing investigation?

Somehow, he must find out.

37

I'd just returned to my desk to collect together my things when my landline rang.

'Reception here. There's two policemen downstairs asking for you.'

My mind hared through the possibilities. Assault on Lisa? No—too quick—she must still be ineffectually blotting her nose in the loo. Trespassing at warehouse? No—drug dealers would shrink from involving the police. Accessory to murder? Ancient history. I took my handbag with me though—instinct told me I might be gone some time.

Two plainclothes detectives waited for me in the foyer. They flashed identification, which might have been gym membership cards for all I knew.

'How can I help you?'

'We must ask you to accompany us to the station,' said the younger of the two men, stony-faced, 'to assist us with our enquiries.'

'Enquiries into what?'

'Amy Melissa Robinson, I am arresting you for forging the signature of your mother, Mrs Pauline Robinson, on a document. You do not have to say anything, but anything you do say may be taken down and used in evidence against you in court.'

The astonished expression on the receptionist's flawless face said it all—to my knowledge this was the first time that an arrest had taken place on Pearson Malone premises. But she couldn't have been more staggered than me. As I'd said to the Cynthia Hope, there was no way on God's earth my mother would report me to the police.

The conclusion was clear—these were not real policemen—they were JJ's people faking it. If I accompanied them I'd be dead meat on the slab.

'Do I have to come now? This isn't a great time...'

'I'm afraid so.'

My mind raced—how on earth had JJ's crew got wind of the forgery? But then I remembered, I'd told Lisa, who must have helpfully informed her new best buddy Smithies.

'Can I see your ID again please,' I asked, playing for time. Strangely, I felt calmer than I had in weeks, ready to use all my wits to rescue myself from this predicament.

'Sure.'

He let me peer at it for longer this time. It seemed genuine enough—they looked policeman-like. But still I had doubts.

'You'll have an opportunity to give a full statement at the station,' said one. But that failed to reassure me.

'Listen,' I said, thinking fast. 'Can I pop to the loo? I've been sitting in a meeting for hours and I'm absolutely desperate. It's just over there.'

'I suppose so,' the older man replied uncertainly.

I was desperate not for a pee, but for a few seconds to consider my options.

I didn't have many. The only exit was the door I'd come in by, which they'd be watching assiduously.

If I hauled myself up above the suspended ceiling and crawled along the ducting...

I stood on the loo and pushed, but the ceiling panel stuck fast. Even if I'd been able to dislodge it, the athletic demands of the plan would have been far beyond me, especially with my scabby, purulent knees.

No—I'd have to exit the way I'd come in. And they'd spot me for sure.

Unless…

At lunch hour, people came and went all the time. A secretary I recognised emerged from one of the stalls and put on a cerise raincoat with a black baker boy cap.

'Could you do me a huge favour?' I asked her.

'Sure,' she said, studiously ignoring my unkempt appearance.

'Can I borrow your coat and hat? I know it sounds absolutely ridiculous but some bad men are waiting outside for me and I need to escape.'

As a partner, people automatically do your bidding and don't ask too many questions. I counted on that now. And although she plainly thought me deranged, she reluctantly handed over both items of clothing.

'Thanks,' I said. 'I'll make certain you get them back.'

I exited the Ladies, covering my face with a handkerchief as though blowing my nose. It was vital to walk assertively, as if I had every right to be hurrying along. I averted my head from the bogus detectives as I scuttled across reception.

Unobserved, I stepped out into the normality of a Friday lunchtime in London.

***

Once clear of the building I fled, running faster than I knew, the scabs on my knees cracking open as I went. It would be dangerous to stick to the main streets—already I'd drawn too much attention to myself—so I left Fleet Street as quickly as I could. I dived into a narrow passageway, which led to a labyrinth of further walkways and courtyards, and thinking quickly, jettisoned the borrowed coat. It was too conspicuous and before long, the two fake Plods would discover how I'd escaped.

Was it my imagination again or did I hear someone behind me? I scurried round a corner, into another ginnel and then another. Still I fancied I heard indecisive footsteps going this way and the other as my pursuer tried to find me.

I tiptoed into a new section of the maze and through an alley containing the back entrance to a pub. The bar was packed with grey suits drinking mineral water with their lunch. I wriggled past the heaving throng and exited by the main door on Shoe Lane, before hailing a taxi on Farringdon Street.

'Where to, ma'am?'

Good question. I needed to hole up somewhere while I worked out my next move, but I couldn't risk a trip home.

'Heathrow Terminal 5,' I said in a flash. Airports were anonymous—and anonymous equalled safe. Plus I could leave the country—someone could fetch my passport—no idea who, but that was tomorrow's dilemma.

After a few hundred yards, I asked the driver to stop by an ATM and I withdrew five hundred pounds from each of my three cards. I didn't know much about being a fugitive but avoiding leaving a financial footprint seemed like a sensible precaution.

There was plenty of time for rumination in the hour and a half it took to reach Heathrow, and plenty of issues to ponder. How had I ended up in this mess in the space of four weeks? How much of it was my fault? What was real and what was imaginary?

None of the questions had an easy answer.

Fraud in a respected Pearson Malone client seemed unlikely enough. But cannabis growing in a slate mine—possible police involvement in money laundering—a partner murdering a junior colleague—all this sounded crazy and delusional.

'*Come on. You know it's real.*'

Great—so a figment assured me all the rest of it was genuine. What sense did that make? And wasn't that the whole point? People with delusions *believed* them.

And if it was real, which I now doubted, that didn't necessarily mean I was OK—far from it.

I'd dreaded anyone seeing the muddle inside my head, or the mess in the house. For years I'd striven to present a polished image to the outside world. But now the madness had seeped out through the veneer of sanity, as an unchecked hoard would eventually spill outside the house. The prospect of being crazy terrified me, but equally I'd seen all too graphically where the path of denial led. So I had to ask myself—was it possible I needed help?

'*No—no!*' Little Amy shrieked.

***

I'd last stayed at the Sofitel hotel with Greg when we'd flown to San Francisco in a last-ditch attempt to save our flagging marriage. With hindsight, the futility of the endeavour was clear, since he'd already lined up my replacement by then. But at the time I still harboured an irrational hope that my perfect life was salvageable. My decision in the taxi might have seemed random, but now I saw a depressing logic to it. Perhaps deep down I sensed that I was doomed to failure once more.

Reception seemed reluctant to take a walk-in for cash—even asking had evoked a defensive, suspicious response. Being memorable might be more dangerous than being traced through a credit card, especially as the two goons were not real police. So I reluctantly handed over my Premier MasterCard, which the receptionist swiped, eying me curiously. With luck, the hotel wouldn't charge it till I left, and not at all if I paid in fistfuls of notes at the end. Besides, I'd be long gone before anyone identified the Sofitel as my destination.

But gone to where? And who could I trust to assist me?

Not my mother, for sure. Nor the colleague who'd betrayed me. Not the boss who'd killed Isabelle and plotted to get rid of me. Or even the police. As I mentally ran through my pathetically short list of friends, I realised they were all acquaintances, work colleagues and business contacts. But whose fault was that? Isolation was the reward for distancing myself from everyone.

The room was a standard, far less plush than the Prestige Suite I'd booked for the last visit, and noticeably smaller. The poky bathroom lacked the opulent marble finish I remembered, and the absence of a minibar was an additional irritation I could have done without. I sat on the bed, exhausted by the physical and mental exertions of the day, and flicked on the TV. At least I saw no announcement about a hunt for a deranged woman—something to be thankful for I supposed.

After few minutes I'd recovered enough to run a bath—there could be no doubt I badly needed one. I also hoped relaxing in a hot tub might coax my brain into action. I gasped in agony as I submerged my scabby knees—how could they ever heal when every action triggered a relapse?

Despite my valiant efforts to stay alert, I dozed off and woke nearly submerged in the now chilly water, amazed to find it was nearly eight pm. Shivering, I wrapped myself in a fluffy white towel and padded back to the bed, where I found seven voicemails and five missed calls on my iPhone. Two from Greg—the other three, worryingly, from Carmody. I daren't listen to the messages.

In the midst of my aching loneliness, a sudden nostalgia for the times I'd spent with Greg swept over me, together with a recognition that the break-up had been my fault. My secret had been the cancer in our marriage, his betrayal merely a symptom. All he'd wanted was a normal girl to share his charmed life, and superficially I'd fitted the bill. How was he to have suspected the crumbling wreck that lay behind the elegant façade? How frustrating for him, living with a shadow, my big secret tethering us to a half-lived life filled with unspoken fears. Hardly surprising that he'd sought solace elsewhere.

Of the people Smithies had mentioned who allegedly had my welfare at heart, Greg was possibly the only one who truly cared. Reluctant as I was to show him the depths to which I'd sunk, I guessed he was the one person who would help me. I waited for Little Amy to pipe up with her opinion, but she'd slunk away. Anyway, I'd run out of options. I hesitated, but not for long, before dialling his number.

'Amy—thank God. Are you OK? I've been so worried.'

'I need your help. This sounds ridiculous, but…'

'It's fine, I know what you're going to say,' he said, cutting me off. 'You were right—there *is* a fraud at JJ Slate. I'm so sorry I didn't listen to you in the first place.'

The relief was overwhelming. At last someone other than me was prepared to face the truth. Better still, everyone would take Greg seriously—he had gravitas.

'Why did you change your mind?'

'Call it an accountant's nose, but something made me uneasy about those debtors and I asked some more questions. I've put in a preliminary report to Potter, and he'll need much more information. But don't worry—we can sort everything out. Look—where are you?'

The place likely evoked the same unhappy memories for him as for me, but he didn't sound surprised when I told him. He simply said he'd meet me in the bar in half an hour or so. I guessed he was coming from Chiswick, and wondered what he'd tell Tiffany about where he was going.

38

I dressed quickly. My clothes smelled pretty rank, but I had no others. I turned my knickers inside out—depths to which I'd never even sunk in the hoard house.

By the time Greg rolled up forty-five minutes later, I'd downed two large G and Ts—but hey—I was celebrating. I wasn't as flaky as I'd thought—a result in all the circumstances.

He bought me another drink, and a beer for himself, and although I detected some disapproval at the empty glasses on the table, he said nothing.

'Tell me what you discovered,' I began.

'The more I chewed over it, the more suspicious it seemed that those debtors had been cleaned up just before our audit. So I checked more thoroughly and one account, Parallax Projects, seemed especially dodgy.'

'Yes, completely.'

'I can't prove it, but I suspect Parallax may be a related party to JJ. But in a nutshell, all those invoices were forgeries. No slate was ever supplied to them. I can't think how the audit team didn't pick it up.'

'Pearson Malone will be on the hunt for a scapegoat,' I said gloomily.

'Well, they can't hold me responsible—I'm only the corporate finance partner.'

'Will the deal fall through?'

'I expect so, but I don't care. I'd much prefer to be on the straight and narrow ethically than cover my arse. If I'd listened to Ryan…'

A sad, faraway look clouded his eyes, something I'd not seen before.

'You can't change what's past,' I said, putting my hand on his.

'Shame about us too,' he went on. 'If only we'd been able to communicate better. It was down to me—I felt under such pressure to be perfect, and in the end I had to escape.'

'*You* felt under pressure?' I echoed.

'Yes—however hard I tried, nothing I did could make you happy.'

'It was the same for me—I wanted so much to be the ideal wife.'

'Yes, and I found it impossible to live up to that. I knew something was wrong in your family, but I couldn't bring myself to ask. If it was out in the open it would have finished us—we wouldn't be the dream couple any more. And I couldn't tell you about my family situation either.'

I almost asked what situation he was referring to, when the image of his father drunk at the funeral popped unbidden into my mind. In fact, he'd been plastered at every family occasion we'd attended, at our wedding even. And I'd never stopped to consider the effect that must have had on Greg—I'd been so wrapped up with my own issues.

'I know. Your dad's an alcoholic, but no one ever mentions it—you all cover for him and pretend it isn't happening. And everyone covered for my mother. See—we're quite similar really.'

Greg squirmed uncomfortably.

'So tell me about JJ,' he said, pointedly switching the topic of conversation.

'Right, for starters Parallax *is* a related party and I can prove it.'

He listened in amazement as I described unearthing the link between Parallax and Jason Jupp, the drugs farm and the probable source of the debt repayments.

'I'm amazed,' he said. 'I'd never have thought of using Facebook like that. And as for the money, I assumed it was all old man Jupp's dosh—he hated his son, and he hated drugs.'

Crucially, though, Greg believed me, which meant so much I almost cried.

'But I still don't understand,' I said. 'Why funnel the money into JJ? It wouldn't be easy to extract it again.'

'Do you really not get it?' he said in disbelief.

'No—I don't.'

'You'll kick yourself when I tell you. It's obvious. JJ Resources is selling out on a multiple of fifteen times profits—it was all a scam to inflate the value of the shares. You do the maths—JJ shells out a few million to pay off those dodgy debtors and gets the money back many times over.'

Yes, it was obvious now, but I saw trouble looming post-completion.

'Won't Megabuilders twig that the slate division's generating less income than they expected?'

'That concerned me too,' Greg admitted, 'but I imagine they'd continue to put some invoices through to Parallax, and pay them, then taper it off over a few years. They'd still have made a killing. And remember, nobody will be scrutinising the books too carefully. It's a small business division—that's how they got away with the scam for so long—and it'll be an even smaller part of Megabuilders.'

'So you do believe me—about the cannabis?'

'Of course I do—you saw it, didn't you? Do you doubt your own eyes?'

'Not at all,' I said hurriedly.

'I feel so bad,' said Greg, swigging the remnants of his beer. 'We should have listened to Ryan.'

'You shouldn't beat yourself up. How were you to know? The auditors didn't spot it, and neither did Megabuilders' due diligence team.'

'The audit partner says it's not his fault—says he can demonstrate they carried out a thorough audit programme. I have my doubts though. They queried those debtors, but hey, when they were cleared all in one go, it didn't ring any alarm bells.'

'But why didn't the Parallax guys clear the debts as they went along—avoid any suspicion?'

'They probably didn't want to put the money in until they were pretty sure that the company sale would go ahead. Like you say—it would be tough to get it out otherwise.'

Which sounded plausible enough.

'So what else did you find?' he asked, trying to catch the waiter's attention to order another beer.

'Why do you think there's more? Isn't that enough?'

'No—there's something else you haven't shared with me—I can tell.'

There was no harm in coming clean, I decided, so it all spewed out. I described the papers Chloe Fenton gave me, the fake haulage invoices, and my fruitless visit to East Grinstead.

'Ah, so that's why you looked so rough at the meeting with Lisa,' he said.

'It shook me up, as you can imagine.'

'You should have rung in sick.'

'I would, but I didn't want to let Lisa down in case she needed some support.'

'I think she had enough support from Ed—she could hardly fail with his backing. I was pretty much told we had to find a way to pass her.'

That didn't shock me as much as it ought to have done, not even that Greg had taken the expedient course.

'Oh, don't worry,' he said, suddenly concerned that I might have the wrong impression. 'Fortunately she *was* up to the required standard.'

But what if she hadn't been?

'Anyway,' he went on, avoiding the question I hadn't asked. 'We digress. You hadn't finished.'

For the dramatic finale, I added that the bank statements appeared to implicate former officers of the Metropolitan Police in a money laundering operation.

At the point, for the first time, I'd shocked him. Perhaps I'd hit him with too much at once.

'So in your opinion, who killed Issy?' he asked.

I hated Smithies so much I was still tempted to say his name, even though there were other, more convincing suspects.

'Someone connected to JJ, maybe the son. They're the ones who had most to lose.'

'I've been working with JJ for several years, grooming the company for sale. I'd be amazed if he would...'

'Who else if not him?'

'Search me,' he said.

'He's not acting alone, though. He employs all sorts of goons. Those policemen who came to arrest me—they definitely weren't real.'

'How can you be so sure?'

'My mother would never complain.'

A cold shot of realism ran through my veins, as I remembered the missed calls from Carmody. Could my mother have changed in the last ten years?

'Let's deal with one problem at a time,' said Greg, sensing my panic. 'It can all be sorted out. Might even be an opportunity for you to patch up your relationship with your mum.'

'I sincerely doubt it.'

At least he hadn't said she was the only mother I had.

'And if you need medical attention, we can fix that up too.'

'Oh God. I'd forgotten I'm supposed to be crazy in all the excitement.'

We laughed together—the first time in two years. And I glimpsed for an instant what I'd seen in him in the beginning.

'By the way,' he said. 'Where's all the paperwork, the invoices and so forth? I'll have to go through it to update my MLRO report.'

'At the house. In the drawer of my bedside cabinet.'

'OK—I can pick it up if you give me the keys. Safest if you stay here, in the circumstances.'

'Another drink?' he asked, as the waiter approached.

'Why not?'

It would be my fourth double G and T, but hey—I had a head for it. And anyway, a minor celebration was in order. Greg had accepted what I'd told him. And who better than him to spur the bigwigs into action, willingly or unwillingly?

I popped to the loo and reappraised my appearance. All in all, I'd scrubbed up reasonably presentably and looked considerably perkier and less deranged than earlier in the day. Things were on the up.

Greg had his phone to his ear when I returned.

'Potter,' he mouthed at me.

I envied the sure-footed way Greg dealt with the situation. Compare and contrast with gutless little me, unable even to begin the reporting process.

'Yes, yes—having spoken to Amy, there's significantly more information than I realised. Your judgement call, but I fail to see how you can avoid making a report.'

Greg took a swig at his beer, as Potter responded, probably reinforcing the need for concrete evidence.

'I'm not scared of Eric Bailey,' said Greg, with striking bravado. 'Anyway, let's speak again when I have the papers.'

'Well done,' I said.

'And well done you too. I feel terrible—if I'd paid attention to Ryan, I'd have been onto this much sooner—why he might still be with us…'

He kept revisiting the guilt that was eating him—I feared it would haunt him forever.

'We were all reluctant to recognise the truth—you weren't the only one.'

'But you stuck with it, like a dog worrying at a bone—at considerable personal cost. You were brave—I'm just picking up the pieces on the back of your tenacity.'

'In fact, they played it pretty cleverly—the deception wasn't that easy to spot, even down to those counterfeit haulage invoices.'

'Yes,' Greg agreed. 'The quality amazed me—impossible to tell them from the originals, except for the serial numbers. How on earth did Isabelle get them?'

'I bet she blagged them off the client, using her unquestionable charms.'

Greg shook his head sadly.

'Both dead,' he said. 'Tragic.'

He excused himself, ostensibly to go to the Gents, but I'd caught a glimpse of the little tear in his eye. He was a kind man underneath all the corporate finance bluster, and I'd let him get away.

I sat, substantially more woozy than I expected after three and a half large gin and tonics. It could have been lack of sleep, or relief at the way everything was panning out, or shock at Greg's staggering revelations of his perspective on our marriage.

No—no it was more than that.

My fingers tingled—the room swam. Something was wrong—very wrong.

And then it hit me. How could Greg comment on the quality of the forged invoices? He hadn't seen them yet.

I vacillated. Could I have mentioned it without realising? It seemed a tiny inconsistency…

'*Tiny!*' piped up a familiar shrill voice. '*It's absolutely enormous.*'

She sat on the arm of the sofa in a denim mini-skirt and a Breton top, and those frightful hooped earrings.

'*Check his phone,*' urged Little Amy. '*I'll bet he wasn't really talking to the Potter guy.*'

He'd left it on the table with his car keys. My head swam as I typed in his pass code (the same as it always had been) and tried to focus on the call history.

In the past two hours, he'd made or received no calls. The last but one call had been to me, and the final one I recognised as JJ's personal mobile.

And I recognised, in a flash of insight, what had been staring me in the face. Chloe Fenton had told me Isabelle planned to talk to someone she trusted. Not Ryan, because she'd been reluctant to disclose how she'd conned her way into a double promotion—not Smithies, because she reckoned he must be involved. No—she'd chosen to confide in Greg. That's why she'd called him the night she died.

But Greg hadn't been a safe confidant. Maxed out on his borrowings, he depended on the deal completing to avoid incurring Bailey's wrath and keep his job. It was much easier for him to eliminate the threat than address the issue properly. And Greg was in an ideal position to set Ryan up. Even Ryan's suicide now made sense—he'd guessed the truth. Faced with the impossible choice of taking the rap for a crime he hadn't committed or destroying his adored elder brother, he'd opted out altogether.

Yes—it was obvious now. Greg had killed Isabelle to save his deal…

And I was way, way too woozy—he'd spiked my drink.

I saw in shocking clarity how this would play out. He'd help me back to my room—witnesses would testify as to how drunk I'd been. And he'd run me a bath and let the water lap over me—leaving me to drown in the tub—a tragedy involving a drunken and unstable woman. I pictured him at the inquest in his pinstripe suit, white shirt and shiny black shoes. He'd describe how he'd pleaded for me to get help, how distraught I'd been, how he'd hated to leave me. But his heavily pregnant wife was home alone. He'd wipe a little tear from his eye and everyone would agree that he'd done everything possible, more than could reasonably have been expected, for a crazy ex-spouse. Death by misadventure—case closed. I'd be eliminated—permanently.

Well, I was damned if I'd let him do it.

There was no time for analysis. I had to get out and quick—before whatever he'd drugged me with took full effect. Already my eyelids felt heavy...

I grabbed his car keys, hoofed it down to the hotel car park and clambered into his precious Ferrari. I reversed into a pillar before clipping the edge of the ramp at the exit, but who cared. As I floored the accelerator, the car set off shrieking like a banshee.

***

I'd gone a few hundred metres when the wailing siren and flashing blue lights started up behind me. Shit—everyone after me. Faster, faster...

How'd they found me? They couldn't be everywhere after all.

I slowed too late for the rapidly approaching roundabout, misjudged my position and caught the edge of it with my rear offside tyre. The car rocked and snaked and bounced off the barrier at the roadside. They were gaining on me. For future reference, a powerful car is pretty useless when driven badly.

Concentrate, must concentrate... Must lose them....

At the next roundabout I swung the car off to the left, back towards the other airport terminals. I cursed this poxy Ferrari with a mind of its own. Still the blue lights and siren dogged me.

Another bloody roundabout...

Knickers inside out...

39

I screwed up my eyes against the bright light and tried to sit up, but without success. Clearly, a herd of wild elephants had stampeded over my comatose body during the night.

Gradually I focussed on a white-coated woman at the foot of my bed.

'Where am I?'

This unoriginal question was justified in the circumstances. At that point I recalled nothing since my spectacular exit from the Sofitel car park.

'Hillingdon Hospital near Heathrow. You've been in an accident.'

Now I remembered *why* I'd been in such a hurry to leave the Sofitel.

'Oh God—Greg. He mustn't find me.'

'Don't worry.' She placed a reassuring hand on my arm. 'Everything will be OK.'

That's what Greg had said.

'How are you?'

'Terrible. Am I badly hurt?'

'Surprisingly little, given you rolled the car. There's plenty of bruising, bump on the head, a gash on your leg, some minor grazing to your chest from the seatbelt, but nothing too drastic.'

As the memories flooded back, I felt compelled to explain the danger I was in.

'Greg, my ex-husband is after me. He's killed once—he'll do it again… They're all out to kill me, my client, my boss. My friend betrayed me—she might try to kill me too…'

'There's nothing to worry about,' she said in a soothing voice. 'The police said they'd be along to talk to you later this morning.'

I didn't find this particularly heartening, as I recalled Carmody's chum Darren's involvement.

'No—no—you mustn't leave them alone with me. The police are out to get me too.'

'Hardly surprising in the circumstances.'

I got it. To her, I was not the victim of a massive conspiracy, but another drunk driver who'd come to grief.

'You think I messed up, don't you?'

'It's not our place to judge.' Her tone seemed chilly and disapproving. 'You didn't kill yourself or anyone else at any rate, so you can thank your lucky stars.'

Luck didn't come into it. Death, even if it had come hanging upside down in a drunken car wreck with my inside-out knickers, would have been a doddle compared to survival. Today would have dawned and the world would have continued without me. And who would care?

Not Greg—I should have let him do his damnedest anyway. Not Lisa, not my mother, not Smithies.

Ah yes, bloody Smithies. How tragic that poor Amy should have ended up like this, and for the avoidance of doubt we must put in place procedures to avoid this from happening in future. With a company wreath and some faux soul-searching, he would hastily reassemble the pieces of the jigsaw puzzle. Lisa would find someone else to chew up and spit out. Greg would slither off scot-free, and nobody would do a damned thing about the activities at JJ, or those corrupt ex-policemen. And my mother would happily rot in her own filth.

I was inconsequential—just like everyone else. And in attempting to outrun my enemies, I'd finally outrun myself.

Maybe it wasn't too late to die—if I held my breath and wished hard enough.

'*Egg—zackly.*'

Oh shit—look who's back.

'*You can't die*,' she said. '*I have to grow up into someone better than you.*'

Egocentric as ever. Didn't she realise that if I died she died too? And good riddance.

I dozed on and off for a few hours. Nurses bustled in and out, but without engaging me. Then I heard a familiar voice talking to the nurse in the corridor.

Carmody.

Based on his facial expression, I concluded that he hadn't seen the light and arrested Greg. But on the other hand, sending over a chief inspector for a motoring charge seemed like overkill—akin to a Pearson Malone audit partner attending a stocktake. But he was part of it, wasn't he—the money laundering and all the rest? Though he couldn't know that I was onto him, surely…? Still—better not to mention it, just in case…

'Go on then,' I said. 'Get it over with—charge me with drunk driving and driving without insurance to add to the trumped up forgery charge.'

Carmody viewed me quizzically.

'What makes you say the charge is trumped up?'

'Under no circumstances would my mother report me to the police—it's not in her nature.'

'Apparently her neighbour insisted.'

Ah yes, of course. Once again I had underestimated the tenacity of Cynthia Hope.

'I see.'

'Anyway, even if you believed the charges were unreasonable, what on earth made you cut and run?'

'I thought...' I paused—it sounded stupid now. 'I thought the detectives might be JJ and his crew impersonating policemen, after they failed to run me down.'

He shook his head, despairing at the drivel I was spouting.

'And what about last night?'

'Greg tried to kill me. And I'm *certain* he killed Isabelle. I had to escape—that's why I was driving drunk. Why else would I be going like a bat out of hell in someone else's car?'

'I don't know,' he said. 'So far, I've understood little of what you do. Still, you'll have an opportunity to defend yourself at the appropriate time. Although I think it fair to warn you that Mr Kelly's version of events is significantly at odds with yours.'

'Well it would be, wouldn't it—why would he own up to murder after so successfully framing his kid brother?'

I fancied that only Carmody's innate professionalism prevented him from rolling his eyes.

'I'm sorry, Amy, but I'm struggling here. First it was Ed Smithies, then the other night you accused JJ. And now it's your ex-husband's turn to be cast in the role of villain.'

'This is different. Don't you see? He killed Isabelle because she was investigating the racket at JJ Slate, and foolishly confided in him. He *needs* the company sale to Megabuilders to go ahead and he'll go to any lengths...'

'Can I stop you there,' said Carmody. 'Mr Kelly has been very compassionate, taking everything into account.'

Such as his crazy ex-wife totalling his Ferrari, I guessed.

'Compassionate, my arse—he drugged my drink!'

'I understand you drank at least four double gin and tonics.'

'*Only* four.'

'That's a fair amount of alcohol for someone of your body weight—it would easily put you over the limit for driving.'

'But that's irrelevant.'

'With respect—it's highly relevant, because you got in the car and drove.'

'IT WAS AN EMERGENCY,' I shouted.

He sighed.

'Mr Kelly tells us you were extremely agitated. If you hadn't bolted, he would have sought medical attention for you. He's been worried about you, as Ed Smithies confirmed.'

'Bloody Smithies,' I said. 'He's in this somewhere too.'

Another barely repressed eye roll.

'Now—you can't have it both ways.'

'Why not?'

'It's called paranoia,' he said.

'Oh well. You're going to charge me anyway, so why don't you get on with it?'

'I'm not allowed to charge you while you're in hospital.'

'OK then—interview me, or whatever.'

'Later—for now I must inform you that we took a blood sample last night.'

'And you can do that without my permission?'

'Yes—leaving it until you came round wasn't an option. But we do require your consent to analyse the sample.'

'Can I say no?'

'You can—but you'll be committing an offence.'

'You go right ahead,' I said. 'And I'd suggest you test the sample for drugs at the same time, then you'll realise I'm telling the truth. But I *must* make a statement.'

'As I said, we'll be inviting you down to the station in due course.'

'There is nothing I can do—*nothing*!' I shouted. 'Why don't you at least check Greg's bloody alibi for the night of Isabelle's murder! Don't accept what he says at face value just because he's so bloody plausible. I'm telling you Greg is a killer and you've let him bamboozle you with all his smooth talk. Why don't you use your brains instead of acting like PC Plod!'

I would have screamed the place down if a nurse hadn't interceded on my behalf.

'DCI Carmody,' she said. 'I cannot have you upsetting Amy. Can't you see she isn't up to being interviewed by the police?'

'This wasn't an interview,' countered Carmody. 'We were only…'

'I don't care what it was—you're leaving now anyway. The doctor's on her way round.'

'But…'

'No buts—out!' she told him firmly.

'I'm sorry I upset you, Amy,' he said, I suspected more for the benefit of the nurse than because he meant it.

'Nobody bloody well believes me,' I ranted at the consultant, who'd swept into the ward with a bevy of medical students as Carmody left. 'My ex tried to kill me, and so did my client. My client's got a bloody great cannabis farm and everyone's covering it all up, including the police.'

'Do you mind,' she said, ignoring my diatribe, 'if these students observe you while I examine you?'

Not at all—the more witnesses, the more chance someone might take me seriously.

The doctor gave the history of my case in a deadpan fashion, describing how I'd been heavily intoxicated on admission, but was still worryingly incoherent even after sobering up. She ran through my injuries with poker-faced professionalism, and asked them what they would do next.

One of the students, a black guy built to be a nightclub bouncer rather than a medic, looked me up and down appraisingly, before saying.

'Hey—possible psychotic episode here. I'd say full psychiatric assessment for this dude.'

'Spot on,' said the consultant, before turning to me. 'That's the plan. And we'll take a urine sample—a high earning professional like Amy is a prime candidate for drug abuse—most likely cocaine.'

'No drugs,' I said, appalled. 'Although you should definitely check for whatever that lying bastard put in my drink.'

'So we'll keep her in for observation,' she continued, ignoring me again, 'and do a psych evaluation on Monday morning.'

'But I don't need one,' I protested. 'Do I have to?'

'It would be advisable—your belief that people are trying to kill you is worrying.'

'It worries me as well,' I wailed. 'Especially as it's true. Anyway—you can't keep me here against my will.'

'Actually we can,' she replied, a cruel smile playing across her face. 'We can make an order under Section 5(2) of the Mental Health Act and detain you for up to seventy-two hours. But I'm sure you'll agree that it'll be much easier all round if you cooperate.'

I opened my mouth to argue, but she'd already moved on with her entourage. The black guy spun back and winked at me—another hallucination perhaps.

Weighed down with despair, I closed my eyes and tried to sink back into oblivion.

40

Dave Carmody left the hospital disappointed by how badly he'd handled Amy. Maybe it would have gone better if he'd brought flowers, but somehow that hadn't seemed appropriate. After all, it wasn't entirely a personal meeting. He'd volunteered to be the one to tell her they'd taken a blood sample.

It had been a frustrating twenty-four hours all round. To say NCA were being tight with their information was a gross understatement. Then to find out from Ed Smithies via Greg Kelly that Amy lay unconscious in hospital…

For all Amy's crazy ranting about Greg, she had undoubtedly stumbled on some kind of wrongdoing at JJ Slate. Once Carmody had learned of NCA's involvement, he'd checked what she'd said. Jim Jupp's son did indeed have form for drugs. And he recalled the valid point she'd made on their disastrous dinner date. If Isabelle had unearthed a crime, someone other than Ryan had a reason both to kill her and frame Ryan.

He'd come to the hospital with the ulterior motive of asking Amy about what she'd discovered, but instead she'd started raving like a lunatic about Greg, forcing that officious old dragon of a nurse to call a halt to the discussion. He comforted himself with the thought that it wouldn't have made any difference anyway.

On balance, he was still reluctant to accept Ryan's innocence, but this new evidence of an NCA investigation tilted the odds. He now felt obliged to double-check to square his conscience. But all the same, he hoped to allay his unease. Allegedly his promotion was "in the bag", but a disaster before the final sign off might change that.

He reviewed the story as they'd understood it. Ryan's car had been caught on CCTV several times that fateful evening. He'd first driven over to Chiswick around seven pm and, finding Greg out, he'd enjoyed a few drinks before driving back home at around ten-thirty pm. Within half an hour, Ryan had killed Isabelle, whereupon he'd bundled her body into his car and made his way back to Chiswick. He'd visited Amy, leaving in the dead of night to dispose of Isabelle's body in the canal.

If someone else had taken Ryan's car, first they would have had to locate it. They couldn't have known he would be in Chiswick. That meant following the car or, less likely, putting a tracker on it. Second, they would have to steal his car keys and then replace them after. Frankly this seemed like a ridiculous amount of effort. Why hadn't they grabbed Isabelle on her walk home? Why frame Ryan? Wouldn't it have been easier to stage an unplanned attack by a stranger?

Amy had exhibited more paranoia than ever at the hospital—whatever she'd discovered about JJ had only fuelled her fears. But it was even more ludicrous to accuse Greg than Ed Smithies. Why, the guy had bent over backwards to help him understand Amy's delusions.

Maybe he should let it go. Yet Amy's parting words rang in his ears.

'Why don't you use your brains instead of acting like PC Plod?'

And in that instant, he saw what he'd been blind to before.

41

No other visitors came. I'd half expected Greg to show up, full of false solicitude as he evaluated the prospects for another murder attempt. But it seemed that even Greg's chutzpah had its limits.

I longed for a friend who cared enough to bring me grapes and sympathy, but I only had myself to blame for my isolation. However, according to the senior nurse, my mother was threatening to visit.

'She sounded ever so guilty about what a struggle it was for her to come over after her broken hip. But if you're still here on Monday she'll do her utmost. And she wanted to tell you she forgives you for everything. What a sweet lady she is.'

She forgives me—outrageous.

The need to avoid seeing my mother would in itself have been sufficient motivation to pass the psychiatric evaluation with flying colours. But other, stronger impulses spurred me on too. It incensed me that Greg had hoodwinked Carmody into accepting his story without question, while everyone always mistrusted me, whatever I said. On Monday afternoon, Greg would sit down at the JJ completion meeting, his squeaky-clean image intact and unsullied.

I had no doubt he would try to kill me again, unless I got in first. Quite simply, it was him or me.

Little Amy popped up at the end of the bed.

'*You have to lie on the test*,' she said baldly. '*Just tell them everything's OK now. Come on—you can do it!*'

I didn't reply. With an upcoming psychiatric evaluation, I had no wish to be observed speaking to a hallucination.

If only it was possible for Little Amy to take the test for me. She was supremely accomplished in sustaining the illusion of her normal middle-class life in that pebble-dashed Croydon semi. This was the girl who'd gone swimming five times a week to use the shower at the pool, who wore fashionable clothes all immaculately clean and pressed. If no one had intervened to save her, it was due in large part to her consummate ability to pretend she didn't need saving.

But if Little Amy had been capable of that then logically, passing the evaluation must be within my own grasp. Especially as failure was not an attractive option.

'*Yeah—you escape and kill the bastard*,' she said.

And on that, we were both in total agreement.

***

It was no different from preparing for any other meeting. Do the research, keep your head straight and act the part.

After googling 'psychotic episode', I concurred with the medical student's provisional diagnosis, although there was a certain irony in the diagnosis being made on the basis of my "delusions" of being persecuted, rather than the hallucinations I'd carefully avoided mentioning.

The psychiatrist was a delicate Indian woman with compassionate eyes who nodded sympathetically at everything I said, but spoke little herself, maybe because I didn't let her get a word in edgeways. She wore impeccably tailored trousers and a lightweight cashmere sweater, with gold bangles and red patent peep-toe shoes—not a white coat in sight.

I read the jottings on her pad upside down. 'High-functioning alcoholic'. 'Psychotic episode?' At least the high-functioning part seemed encouraging.

'OK, so why don't you start off by telling me a bit about yourself, Amy.'

There was a balance to be struck here, between being crazy and in denial. So my strategy was to make such a full disclosure that she would never guess I was holding anything back. We covered the hoarding—my father's death—the breakdown of my marriage—workaholic tendencies—hostile atmosphere at work—Isabelle—Ryan—my mother's illness.

I noticed, with mixed emotions, that she'd added 'Complex PTSD?' to her list. Ah well, that figured—nothing was ever simple with me.

She listened carefully to my confession, smiling slightly by way of further encouragement. But I needed no prompting—the words flowed freely.

I admitted I'd been drinking too much because of the stress at work. I even suggested that the alcohol and stress might have triggered my delusions of persecution.

'And how do you feel now?' she asked.

'OK, except I'm a bit embarrassed about having made such a fool of myself. I realise now that everything was in my head ... but it felt so real, and so scary...'

And especially scary because it *was* real.

'Do you ever take any recreational drugs?'

'Never.'

'Odd because your urine sample tested positive for ketamine.'

I was about to suggest that Greg had used the drug to spike my drink, but checked myself at the last moment. I'd already conceded that the spiked drink was part of my delusions.

'Look, I know have a few mental health issues which need to be addressed…'

Little Amy sat calmly on the end of my bed, wearing a gold lamé dress (where the heck had that come from?) and smoking a Sobranie cocktail cigarette. She worried me—was anyone who could conjure up that image in any position to judge between real and imaginary?

But obviously I hid her from the shrink, together with my murderous plans to stop Greg in his tracks.

'That was interesting,' she said when I'd finished.

'So what's your diagnosis?'

'I think you've had an acute psychotic episode—do you understand what that means?'

I denied all knowledge, so as not to alert her to my pre-meeting research. She explained it in terms of being disconnected from reality for a spell. She agreed that it had likely been brought on by a combination of stress and misuse of alcohol, possibly with an element of Post Traumatic Stress Disorder, although strictly I didn't meet the diagnostic criteria for PTSD.

'Do I need any treatment?' I asked. 'I have private medical insurance.'

Surely a willingness to cooperate would improve my chances.

'Well, you seem to have made a rapid recovery and regained full insight into your mental state. That's good news, but as a precautionary measure I'm prescribing some antipsychotic medication to reduce the risk of recurrence. I'd also strongly advise you to avoid alcohol for the time being, if you can manage that.'

'Of course,' I said indignantly. 'I know I've been drinking too much but I'm not an alcoholic.'

'OK, I hear you,' she replied. 'And no drugs either.'

'What about work?'

'Ah yes, as work stress has been a major trigger, I'd suggest you take a couple of weeks off at least. We'll review you in the clinic in a fortnight and reassess the position then.'

A fortnight—I couldn't think so far ahead. All my energy was focussed on the JJ completion meeting that afternoon.

'So am I free to leave the hospital?'

'Why yes,' she replied. 'Why ever wouldn't you be? After all, it's not as though you're a danger to others.'

Little did she know.

42

The sudden flash of insight had shifted Carmody's perception. Now he saw there was a far stronger case against Greg Kelly than anyone else.

Greg claimed to have arrived home at nine-fifteen pm—a time consistent with the CCTV images of him at Turnham Green Tube Station ten minutes earlier. Isabelle had called Greg at around nine pm, he claimed, and left a message asking where Ryan was. Nothing wrong with any of that.

But Ryan had parked his car on the route from the Tube station to Greg's house—they hadn't picked up on that before. Suppose Greg spots it. He's already listened to Ryan's message—he knows Ryan's drinking in some local bar passing the time until he arrives home. So Ryan can wait a bit longer, while Greg takes care of the troublesome business with Isabelle.

But no—Greg doesn't have Ryan's car keys. OK—he doesn't need to—he has his own car. The Ferrari's as distinctive as the Triumph—they can check CCTV. Or ask Isabelle's neighbours.

Greg kills Isabelle, sometime around ten pm—comfortably within the pathologist's window. Either he planned it, or they argue and it gets out of hand. But either way, he strangled her, and quickly figures how he can set up Ryan to take the fall.

So he takes the spare car keys from the hall table and drives back to Chiswick, then swaps over his car with Ryan's. He returns to Isabelle's flat, loads up the body and comes back, switching the cars around each time, so no one else pinches Ryan's parking space. Then—at the dead of night—he dumps her in the canal at South-

all. And on Monday, he even puts the car keys into Ryan's desk drawer at the office, so we all assume Ryan had forgotten where he left the second set.

It was a theory, at least. Now he should check the CCTV.

43

Although no bones were broken, I found movement far more painful than I'd expected—but just about possible. The mirror confirmed my worst fears—raccoon eyes, bird's nest hair and a swollen lip worthy of a professional boxer.

The clothes did not inspire confidence either—trousers soaked in more or less dried blood, and a bra and top shredded by the paramedics. I'd have to button my jacket and wear nothing underneath it. I checked my watch—two hours till the meeting—time to go home and change first.

The driver of the taxi I'd called eyed me dubiously, but flashing my wads of cash had a calming effect. Less than half an hour later, I was back in my house, having instructed him to wait outside and keep the meter running.

Although I'd been away for a mere three days, spots of mould had appeared on my coffee cup from Thursday night. I rinsed it out carefully, and emptied the espresso machine, aware that I could be away some time.

'*Yuk.*' Little Amy wrinkled her nose. '*Like at home.*'

I had no time to argue with her, and extracted a large carving knife from the big wooden block on the counter.

'*Straight through the heart. Why ever did you marry the creep? He deserves to die.*'

My phone rang—Carmody.

He couldn't conceivably have any idea what I planned to do, but even so I jumped back guiltily as I recognised his number on the caller display.

'Hi,' I said casually.

'I heard you left the hospital.'

'Yes—amazingly enough they pronounced me sane.'

'Great news,' he replied, without any enthusiasm. 'And where are you now?'

It seemed like a strange question to ask—unless they planned another attempt to arrest me.

'Why, at home.'

Although I'd be gone by the time they arrived.

'Good. And you're not planning on doing anything rash?'

'Dave, I'm black and blue from head to toe and utterly worn out. A cup of tea and daytime television is as rash as it gets.'

'Excellent,' he said. 'And when you're better, we'll get you down the station and see if we can't sort out all the confusion.'

His lies were as blatant as mine. He had no intention of sorting out the confusion, only adding to it—especially if he was protecting his chum Darren from a money laundering charge.

'Great,' I said, before hanging up.

I put the knife in the zip compartment of my handbag. It would be straightforward taking it into the meeting. A bunch of accountants is not exactly a strategic target for terrorists or crazed assassins, so security was lax in the Pearson Malone building. In future that might change, I guessed.

'*Kill the bastard.*' An evil grin spread across Little Amy's face.

I managed, with difficulty, to put on a teal jersey dress from Jaeger and scrape my hair back into a tight bun. With some judiciously applied concealer and slap of lipstick, I almost passed as normal, even though passing as normal was a joke now. Ironically, an incredible sense of liberation surged through me. As an officially crazy woman, I had carte blanche to do absolutely anything.

The meter showed nearly a hundred pounds by the time the cab rolled up outside the main Pearson Malone Office. No matter. I gave the guy a fifty pound tip.

I blipped my security pass against the reader. Nothing happened.

Hell—they'd put a stop on it.

'Having problems?' asked the commissionaire. 'These new readers are so temperamental.'

Without further investigation, he pressed a button to release the gate.

Nobody paid me any attention as I hobbled purposefully across the atrium. I hoped to God I wouldn't see anyone I knew, even though I had every right to be there. But if they played the crazy card against me, this time I would trump it.

Buoying myself up with that thought, I pushed open the door to Room 38.

44

All the suits were there, and Lisa with her busted nose all taped up. I wondered what yarn she'd spun to explain it away.

The room fell silent when I entered.

'Amy,' said Greg, with authority. 'We were given to understand you were unwell. Lisa is taking your place at the meeting.'

Lisa gazed at me, shocked that I'd been insane enough to show up.

'I'm absolutely fine,' I assured them. 'I was involved in a minor road traffic incident on Friday, but I wouldn't have missed this meeting for the world.'

Greg licked his lips nervously, assessing his options. He flashed an apprehensive glance at Jupp. I reckoned I'd been formally fired as JJ's tax partner, so why didn't they come out and say so and shoo me out? I guessed they were keen to avoid rousing Megabuilders' curiosity.

'Amy—it's brave of you to battle on,' he said, full of simulated kindness. 'But for the sake of your health we must insist that you step down from this meeting.'

I fancied I heard the cogs in his brain whirring. A thought balloon above his head might have read 'What the hell is she planning?' He surely realised that I had no intention of sitting the meeting out in silence. But on the other hand kicking up about ejecting me might raise eyebrows.

JJ himself had no such inhibitions.

'Ms Robinson has been removed from the Pearson Malone team. She has no role in this meeting.'

'Why has she been removed?' asked the lead partner from Megabuilders' lawyers—Kevin, the shrewd little Scouse guy with the big mouth who I remembered from the last all-parties meeting.

'Owing to ill health.'

'*Do it—do it now.*'

I reached for my bag, and stopped myself. I shouldn't let him off too easily. These guys needed to understand my motives. They might choose not to believe me, but that was their funeral.

'*Now—now!*'

Little Amy stood behind Greg, wearing her school uniform again, perhaps in recognition that she was attending a formal meeting. She had no place in my life. I willed her to go away, but she stuck there resolutely.

'Fair enough,' I said. 'I'll leave. But before I go, let's clear up a few loose ends.'

'This is grossly inappropriate,' roared JJ. 'I'm the client and I don't want this woman here. Call security.'

Which would without question have been the outcome, had Kevin not intervened.

'It might be easier to hear her out, don't you think?'

'But who can say what rubbish she might come out with—she's been diagnosed with psychosis, you know.'

Quite how JJ had discovered this was a mystery to me.

'We're intelligent people,' said Kevin. 'If she's talking rubbish then we'll all recognise it as such, won't we, Ms Robinson?'

I could have hugged him. In retrospect, I feel he suspected something was amiss.

'As you're all aware,' I began, 'there's been some discussion on the availability of tax losses in the slate mine division, culminating in our conceding them to HMRC. You need to understand why.'

'Pearson Malone got it wrong,' said JJ triumphantly.

'Did you ever consider why the Megabuilders tax due diligence team didn't pick up on the issue?' I asked Kevin.

'I'm told it was highly technical—easily missed.'

'Maybe so,' I agreed. 'But there is another reason they didn't spot it.'

I paused for dramatic effect.

'What?'

'There was no mistake. At first I suspected that the JJ finance department had screwed up in implementing the reorganisation but I checked that out too. Those losses were available.'

'What rot,' said JJ, with total conviction.

'I can prove it.'

'But what would be the point of disclaiming usable tax losses?' asked Kevin, his brow furrowed.

Blimey, if I'd written the script for this guy I couldn't have done better myself.

'That is a very pertinent question—one I asked myself. And shall I tell you what I found?'

Greg and JJ exchanged agonised glances, and Goodchild looked none too comfortable either.

'Can we please take a break for five minutes,' said Greg. 'I need to have a private word with Amy.'

'Not a chance—there'll be no private word. Everyone in the room should hear what I have to say.'

'*Before she kills you,*' added Little Amy.

'But she's in no state of mind to...' JJ blustered.

'No—let her speak,' Kevin cut in. Whether or not he thought me crazy, I had his full attention.

'What I found was strong indications of a fraud, which would be quickly exposed if the HMRC enquiries were allowed to run their course. Once the losses were disclaimed, the questions no longer needed to be asked.'

They stared at me as if I'd peed on the lawn at Wimbledon. I studied their faces intently. JJ was squaring up for a big shouting match, the power of his voice being his preferred weapon in any dispute. Goodchild tried hard to suppress his squirming, but didn't succeed. He glanced anxiously at JJ and Greg, as though hoping one of them would salvage the situation. Greg tried his damnedest to stay in control. And Lisa, absentmindedly shredding a paper napkin, peered nervously at the others.

JJ broke the silence.

'How ridiculous,' he said. 'These are serious allegations. How dare you bring this nonsense up at this late stage in the proceedings?'

'I'm afraid Ms Robinson is, as we warned everyone, ill,' added Greg. 'I think it would be appropriate if you left the meeting, Amy.'

'No—she should stay,' said Kevin.

'That's not your decision,' said JJ.

'OK, but I'm left worrying about what you guys have got to hide.'

'Well let me tell you,' I chipped in. 'JJ Slate has been raising bogus invoices to artificially inflate the company's share price.'

Now everyone listened intently. While these might be the ravings of a madwoman, they indisputably livened up the meeting.

'Now this is some lunatic idea Amy's raised before,' said Greg, at his most patronising. 'And I can confirm that the debtors she's referring to were all paid post year end.'

'But on Friday you *agreed* with me.'

'Hardly. We never discussed the matter—you were far too agitated to have any kind of rational conversation. You must have imagined it, along with all the rest of your delusions,' he lied.

The Megabuilders team viewed him with suspicion. The cracks had begun to show.

'You might ask where the money to repay the debts came from,' I went on.

'Where?' asked Kevin.

'Incredible as it sounds, there's a cannabis farm in a disused shaft of the slate mine. The drug money was funding the fraud.'

The tension snapped and everyone roared with laughter, although I fancied the merriment to be somewhat artificial in the case of Greg and Jupp. Goodchild laughed too, in amazement. Judging from the expression on his face, unless he was an Oscar-winning actor, he'd known nothing of any dope growing before now. The professionals relaxed—the deal was safe—I was after all a crazy woman spouting off her stuff.

So what—I hadn't expected them to believe me.

'Gentlemen,' said Greg, ignoring the presence of Lisa and two other women. 'I'm sorry you've had to listen to this arrant nonsense. Amy, regretfully I must ask you to leave. You're plainly unwell.'

'Top man,' said JJ. 'Never heard such gibberish in the whole of my life.'

'Yes, this woman is *insane*,' agreed Goodchild.

I didn't care anymore. Crazy bought me the freedom to say and do what I liked. Hell, I might be wrong about all this but it didn't matter. At last I'd been released from the tyranny of passing as normal.

'I shall be complaining in the strongest possible terms to Eric Bailey,' JJ blustered on.

'Don't worry,' I told them, as I observed Greg dialling for security. 'I'm leaving in a moment. But I haven't finished yet.'

'No—you are done!' cried JJ.

'I'm not done by a long chalk. Finally, I want you to know that this man Greg Kelly is a murderer. You see, I wasn't the first to notice the anomalies in the slate mine accounts. Isabelle Edwards got there first and now she's dead. An innocent man committed suicide in prison while his brother, the real killer, went free. And all because he didn't have the guts to come forward when he discovered the scam—because he was determined to save his own career.'

Greg shrugged off the comment—he'd recovered his composure now everyone had decided not to take me seriously.

'Well your career is over, I shall make sure of it,' said JJ. 'I've never seen such disgraceful, unprofessional behaviour in all my years in business. You won't work in the City again.'

'So what?' I said. 'I don't give a shit.'

'*Now—do it now.*'

The moment had come.

I reached for my bag, and stopped myself. A harsh realisation brought me up short. Something about being egged on to kill by a figment jarred. In its own way, the idea was just as nuts as hoarding up a house with junk and blinding yourself to your kid's discomfort. They'd allowed me out of hospital because I recognised I had issues, not to embark on a nihilistic orgy of destruction.

'*Now—now! The bastard deserves to die. And you'll get off anyway, because you're crazy.*'

I reached into my bag. My hand gripped the handle of the knife...

45

It hadn't been plain sailing. The CCTV data showed no sign of Greg's Ferrari and it was only at the last moment that Carmody had realised why. Of course—Greg had used his wife's car, a Ford Fiesta—far less conspicuous than the Ferrari. After re-checking, Carmody was now armed with enough evidence to arrest Greg Kelly.

His boss hadn't been overly enthusiastic, though.

'Shame you didn't think of this before,' he'd said, leaving Carmody fearful his promotion might be in jeopardy.

So be it.

Out of courtesy, he'd informed NCA of his plans, in view of the potential link to their operation. They'd freaked when he told them—they weren't ready to pounce on JJ and his son quite yet—hoped to suck some others into the web. But pragmatism had won the day.

They'd also been more forthcoming with information than before. They'd had the warehouse at East Grinstead under surveillance for a while, in addition to infiltrating the slate mine. Their sham company Impex was the jewel in the crown of their ambitious operation, set up to offer money laundering services to drug barons while gathering information for their prosecution. Darren had been working undercover, posing as a company director.

Carmody questioned the legality of it all—perhaps that's why NCA had been so coy. After all, where do you draw the line between crime detection and using illegal entrapment? He felt relieved he didn't have to answer that question.

Amy's antics had been most impressive though. Effectively, she'd single-handedly exposed a covert operation which had fooled an army of sophisticated criminals. They'd only latched onto her for two simple reasons. Firstly, Amy's car registration had been logged down by the van driver who'd picked her up in East Grinstead—one of their surveillance team. Secondly, her searches on Impex and its directors had generated an alert.

And she'd been right about Greg Kelly too—eventually.

He didn't believe for a moment that Amy planned to spend a quiet afternoon watching the television. As a woman of action, it wasn't her style. So they'd put a tail on her, and sure enough, she was headed to the Pearson Malone offices, probably to confront Greg.

Anyway, whatever she planned to do, they wouldn't be far behind.

46

Carmody burst into the meeting room, accompanied by an entourage of other officers and two security guards. That moment of vacillation had cost me dear.

I couldn't begin to imagine how he'd caught up with me so quickly, but I was resigned to my fate.

'Ah, well done, Chief Inspector,' Greg said smoothly. 'Ten out of ten for anticipation.' Relief was etched deep into his face.

'Ms Robinson,' Carmody said. 'Would you kindly allow me to pass?'

I stood, stunned and cowering as the party advanced past me and towards Greg. He froze, horrified—no surely not.

'Greg Kelly, I'm arresting you for the murder of Isabelle Edwards. You have the right to remain silent, but anything you do say may be taken down in evidence and used against you.'

'There,' he said softly to me as Greg was led out by his subordinates. 'I knew you'd want to see me do it. Although I wish to God you'd stayed watching the telly like you promised.'

The remaining participants in the meeting stayed rooted to their seats, mesmerised by the unfolding drama. Even JJ's blustering spluttered to a halt as the inevitable consequences of Greg's arrest began to dawn on him. Goodchild sat, rigid and ashen. And Lisa, shaken to the core, quietly sobbed into her handkerchief.

And me—I silently thanked whatever deity had intervened to save me from myself.

'Ladies and gentlemen,' I said, smiling sweetly. 'This meeting is now concluded.' And I hobbled out, without looking back.

47

I hailed a taxi from the rank outside the office and switched off my phone before it began buzzing. I had zero desire to speak to Smithies, Lisa, Bailey, HR, Potter, Carmody, the psychiatrist, the press, or any other bugger who believed they had a claim on my soul. Sod them all—I was the only person who mattered now.

The cab driver waited as I nipped into Sainsbury for the essentials of life – pizza, gin and cigarettes. On finally arriving home I deadlocked the front door behind me and unplugged the landline.

Despite the dire warnings, the meds combined with the gin quite nicely as the pizza cooked. The analytical part of my brain switched off and an eerie calm descended over the rest.

The outcome of the day had evidently disappointed Little Amy, but I knew now that she wouldn't be happy until I'd destroyed myself.

'*You fucked that up*,' she scolded.

OK—time to take a firm line with her.

'Politely—will you please piss off? You must realise I don't need you anymore.'

'*But you do—see how I've helped you.*'

'*Helped* me—because of you I nearly killed a man.'

'*Don't you think he deserved it?*'

'No—actually I don't, and I can't believe I was ever so brutal as you.'

'*Well you were.*'

'I don't care—I want you gone—now.'

Somehow this was different from all the times I'd dismissed her before. She pouted, but she'd got the message alright.

'Don't forget, I'm always with you, even if you can't see me.'

But she'd already faded and her voice was dying away as she said it. And I knew for sure she wouldn't be back.

After dinner, I smoked eight cigarettes, one after the other. Why had I ever given them up? You can die anytime, whether you smoke and drink or exercise like a demon and eat five portions of fruit and vegetables a day. And my body felt marvellous, as did my fucked-up bombed-out crater of a mind.

I passed out on the sofa and woke at eleven in the morning, with a euphoric sense of freedom.

***

Like so many of my recent experiences, the freedom was illusory. Consequences had to be faced, apologies made and bridges rebuilt. That was reality.

The doorbell rang. I ignored it. It rang again, repeatedly and more insistently.

I dragged myself up and hobbled to the door, trying to ignore the crippling, almost overwhelming, physical pain. I scooped up the post from the mat and reluctantly, I opened the door a crack, on the chain, as I had the fateful night when Ryan had called.

Carmody.

OK, squaring the circle with law enforcement was a reasonably sensible place to start dealing with the fallout of the past few weeks.

'Thank God you're OK,' he said. 'We were on the verge of breaking down the door.'

I didn't see anyone with him—he was as bad as Smithies with the 'royal we'.

'No need for that,' I told him brusquely, showing him in.

'So how are you?'

With a practised sweep of the eye, he took in first my crumpled dress; followed by the pizza remnants, dirty glasses, half-empty gin bottle, and overflowing ashtray. Finally, his gaze came to rest on the charred silhouette of a cigarette on the otherwise immaculate beige carpet.

'Pretty good, in the circumstances.' Especially as I'd narrowly avoided being burnt alive.

'I didn't realise you smoked.'

'I quit five years ago.'

'Looks like your carpet's ruined.'

'Nah—must be possible to have it repaired. And if it can't be I'll buy a new one. Coffee?'

'Please.'

His wandering into the kitchen after me caused me no anxiety—the pills I'd been prescribed worked like magic.

'Fab kitchen.'

His gaze came to rest on the knife block with the carver missing—but nothing was said.

I sniffed the milk and poured it down the sink.

'Milk's off—you'll have to drink it black.'

'No worries.'

'Why you did come here?' I asked when we were back in the lounge.

'Just curious about how you were doing.'

'I wish I knew.'

'Also I wanted to inform you that in all the circumstances we won't be proceeding with the drunk driving charges, or pursuing your mother's complaint.'

'Am I supposed to be pleased?'

Frankly, I'd reached a point where I simply didn't care.

'You've been through a lot. I'm sorry I didn't listen to you earlier.'

'What made you listen in the end?'

He told me how he'd taken my comments about using his brain to heart, his issues in dealing with NCA and the CCTV evidence which finally nailed Greg.

'I imagine he's weaselled his way out of it though. He's a slippery bastard.'

Even as I said it, I pictured Greg coming up with a plausible and perfectly innocent justification for everything.

'As a matter of fact, no—he's confessed—seemed glad to get it off his chest. But he's hoping to plead guilty to manslaughter. He says he went there to talk to Isabelle and play down her disquiet, but she argued with him and insisted he should file a report with the MLRO. And he lost his temper and put his hands around her neck then she went limp... He claims it was a terrible accident...'

'Do you believe him?'

'Perhaps. But given the way he tried to frame his brother afterwards he'll struggle with a manslaughter plea. And Isabelle's family will object like crazy. But to his credit he's been helpful in filling us all in on the accounting anomalies and the drugs.'

'But Greg told me the purpose of the invoicing scam was to increase the value of the company. He didn't seem to know anything about the drugs.'

'Not true—he's given us the full story. A few years ago Jason Jupp hit on the bright idea of using his father's slate mine to grow dope. It was a big scale operation producing around two million pounds street value every quarter. The manager and staff took a cut, but they were worried Head Office might decide to sell the mine if it wasn't profitable enough. So they started raising fake invoices. After Megabuilders put in their bid, Greg somehow discovered the false invoicing and alerted JJ. JJ dug deeper, found out about the drugs and hit the roof with Jason. Both Greg and JJ realised they'd lose the sale if the irregularities came to light, or at best there'd be a substantial price reduction. So Greg suggested coercing Jason into putting the drug money back into the company. He'd worked out they'd get it back many times over when the deal went through.'

It was worse than I'd thought. Greg had been instrumental in perpetuating the crime, rather than merely turning a blind eye. And I now remembered the conversation I'd overheard between Jason and his father way back at my first meeting with JJ—something about taking his dirty money. If only I'd listened more intently.

'JJ was arrested as soon as he stepped out of the meeting room, at the same time as his son and the team at JJ Slate,' Carmody added.

'And Goodchild, the finance director?'

'No—Goodchild's still free—no evidence. He claims to have been unaware of any wrongdoing, and no one's suggested otherwise.'

'Bollocks,' I said. 'He was the one who disclaimed the tax losses.'

'Yes, yes, but proving it is a different matter. And frankly, most people are not as hung up as you on esoteric aspects of tax law.'

Carmody had a point, but a piece of shit like Goodchild deserved to cop it, if only as an indirect blow to Smithies.

And an indirect blow was probably the best I could hope for. I now supposed Smithies must be beyond reproach, despite my paranoia.

With some trepidation, I raised the subject of Impex and Carmody's dodgy ex-colleague Darren. I was now almost sure that Carmody wasn't himself involved, but the events of the past few weeks had shaken my sense of certainty about everything.

He explained the internecine politics with the NCA that made the inter-departmental rivalry at Pearson Malone seem good-humoured by comparison.

'So basically, I was investigating a law enforcement sting?'

'Yes—and astonishingly well, I might add. Mind you, even you wouldn't have put together the whole picture if we hadn't seen that guy Darren—he was working deep undercover.'

'So was it coincidence we bumped into him?'

Carmody cleared his throat nervously.

'That bugged me too. I shouldn't say this, but I'll level with you. I have a hunch that those bastards at NCA knew all along I'd arrested the wrong guy and let me go ahead anyway.'

'Why?'

'Because they were so determined to keep their covert operation on track at all costs.'

'Now *that* does sound paranoid,' I said. '*I'm* supposed to be the one with the mental problems.'

He gave a lukewarm smile.

'I hope you're charging Greg Kelly with my attempted murder too,' I said.

Carmody shook his head.

'I shouldn't think so—it's all a bit awkward for us—you understand…'

I understood all too well—once again he'd prioritised his own concerns above mine. Still, what did I expect? Everyone treated me like that.

'He will be charged with conspiracy to defraud, though,' Carmody added in a vain effort to soften the blow.

'Well, that's a comfort.'

He hesitated.

'If you must know, I feel dreadful. I should have listened more carefully, not been so ready dismiss your ideas. Hard as it is for you to accept, I really do like you and I wondered...'

'No.'

The word came out with such vehemence he must have instantly recognised that changing my mind would be impossible, at least in the short term. I felt sure we were fundamentally unsuited to each other on any level. Because I understood now the real damage my mother's hoarding had done. It wasn't the mess, or even the shame, but the indignity of having my feelings, opinions and desires invalidated time after time. Just as I wasn't important enough for my mother to clear up—I was less important than Carmody's promotion. And that wasn't good enough.

'Fair enough,' he said, backing away apprehensively. 'Maybe I'll see you around.'

'Maybe not,' I replied.

After he'd gone, I opened an official looking envelope that had come in the post. It was the psychiatrist's report to my GP. The last paragraph read as follows:

On admission she believed that she was the victim of a conspiracy involving business associates who were attempting to kill her and this included her ex-husband who she believed had spiked her drink. She had acted in response to these beliefs driving while intoxicated. At the time she believed her life was in danger so she may have a defence to the drink driving charge and I would recommend she seeks expert legal advice. By the time I assessed her several days later these delusional beliefs had resolved and she had regained full insight. She appears to have had an acute psychotic episode from which she has made a rapid recovery. She acknowledged that she has been drinking hazardous quantities of alcohol but strenuously denied recreational drug use, however her drug screen was positive for Ketamine which would be consistent with her drink having been spiked though it is not clear how reliable her account is. She has been under considerable stress at work which may be a contributory factor. I have strongly advised her to moderate her alcohol consumption and avoid recreational drug use. I have prescribed a modest dose of antipsychotic medication and on balance suggest she continues this for the present to reduce the risk of recurrence. I have arranged to review her in the clinic in two weeks and recommend she does not return to work until after the review.

Despite everything, I had to laugh.

Epilogue

I'd been eagerly anticipating my scheduled "return to work" meeting with Smithies. He didn't know it yet, but this time I had the upper hand.

'Amy, *how are you*?'

His solicitous tones confirmed that he was still playing the old game, but he would discover soon enough just how dramatically the rules had changed. In fact, everything was different. I'd never noticed how strained the grins of the water-skiing party were, particularly Smithies' wife. It was obvious now how she gritted her teeth and feigned happiness for the sake of her fancy lifestyle.

'I'm on top of the world,' I informed him.

'I suppose it's the medication you're on,' he replied, no doubt searching for some rational explanation for my change in attitude.

No way would he cope with the new improved Amy. After all, how do you psych somebody out who's invincible? Undaunted, he continued on his pre-prepared script.

'As responsible employers we'll fully support you in your return to work. If there's anything we can do to assist you, please let us know.'

'For a start, I'm not at all happy with these alleged breaches of the money laundering regulations everyone's banging on about. Anything you can do?'

Predictably, Pearson Malone had been left with egg on its face. A partner of the firm was up on charges of murder and conspiracy to defraud, and questions were being asked on the quality of the JJ audit. Private Eye had run a whole series of articles highlighting the close relationship between Bailey and JJ the drug baron. And because I'd brought the scandal to the fore, I was in line for all the flak.

During my absence, emails had flown around whipping up a ferment of condemnation at my failure to make a timely money laundering report, as though this had caused the whole debacle. Smithies was the prime mover, naturally. He'd latched onto this as a much quicker and more reliable method to see me off than long term sickness due to poor mental health. The final email from Smithies stated, ominously, that "the appropriate steps" would be taken in due course.

'Well, it's not *me*,' he said apologetically. 'And you're lucky no other action's being taken. Eric Bailey found various other aspects of your unprofessional conduct most disturbing.'

'Did he?'

'But I've fought your corner and we're down to this minor compliance breach.'

'Technically it's not minor at all—potentially non-compliance with the money laundering legislation carries a prison sentence…'

'I take your point, although you don't seem too worried.'

'Actually, I'm pretty sure the police won't be taking any action.'

'Ah yes, your friend Dave Carmody—very much on your side now he realises you have the power to queer his pitch. However, our internal disciplinary procedures are an entirely separate matter…'

'But surely you can do something…'

'I'm afraid that's impossible.'

'But I'm not the only one who failed to report my suspicions, am I?'

He gave a nonchalant little smile.

'I can't imagine who you're referring to.'

'If you listen to this you'll find out,' I said, pulling out my laptop from my bag and inserting the CD Smithies' predecessor John Venner had given me.

Smithies' brow furrowed, but bewilderment quickly gave way to alarm as he heard the familiar whiny grating of his own voice. He listened with mounting apprehension as he calmly advised Goodchild how to conceal the fake debtors he'd discovered from the auditors.

Goodchild had fallen on his sword, resigned and forfeited his precious share options, but had wriggled out of prosecution, because nobody could prove his involvement. Significantly, neither JJ nor Greg had ratted on him. He wouldn't be safe, though, if this recording came to light.

Cut to a later conversation—where Goodchild expressed his relief and puzzlement at the debtors having been repaid. This didn't mean Goodchild knew about the drugs, of course, and on balance I suspected not. Most likely he'd found the false debtors and tried to hide them from JJ, while JJ had been simultaneously concealing them from him. What a pair.

Still, whatever the truth, Smithies would be mightily embarrassed if the recording became public.

'Where did you get this?' he asked, his face contorted with anxiety and coated in a film of sweat.

'Not telling.'

I would never disclose that his predecessor had been so suspicious of Smithies that he'd bugged his office. Venner described it to me as a kind of insurance policy he hadn't needed to claim on once his job offer from the client had come through. But he'd been so appalled by what he'd heard, he'd let the recording continue after he'd left. He figured it would always be useful to have the dirt on an unscrupulous bastard like Smithies. But ultimately, hearing about the mess I was in, and outraged by the rumours Smithies had started about the child-porn, he'd contacted me and handed me the evidence.

'It can't be genuine,' Smithies protested lamely.

'It is,' I said, 'and you know it. By the way, it gets worse.'

I honestly thought he might keel over and die as we listened to the next snippet, where Lisa coldly used the knowledge gained from Isabelle to blackmail Smithies into reinstating her promotion.

Her account of offering to be the eyes and ears of the group had always rung hollow to me. She'd simply gone to Smithies and threatened to expose his brother-in-law. It was *Lisa*, not Greg, who Isabelle chose to take into her confidence, and in doing so signed her own death warrant.

The final discussion was between Smithies and Greg. He mentioned how Isabelle had become a bit over-enthusiastic about the anomalies at JJ and warned Greg not to take any notice.

'So you see,' I said to him. 'There were plenty other people who knew.'

'But I had to alert Greg to these ridiculous allegations…'

'Aha, so the conversation *was* genuine,' I said triumphantly. 'And the allegations weren't ridiculous, were they?'

I removed the CD from the disk drive.

'What will you do with it?' Smithies asked, in a panicky voice.

'Well, let's see. I could take it to your mate Potter, or Bailey, or the BBC. Or I might even hand it into the police—they haven't found enough evidence to arrest Goodchild yet.'

'I was trying to help him out of a spot,' said Smithies, as though this exonerated him. 'Wouldn't you do the same for your sister's husband?'

'No—I wouldn't,' I said, surprising myself at the force of my denial.

'But it would be a tremendous own goal for you if you made this public,' he said, still attempting to press my insecurity buttons in the old way. 'The firm's reputation should be paramount in your thinking.'

The buttons didn't work anymore.

'Why should I care? You guys are squaring up to fire me anyway.'

'I can categorically confirm that nobody's ever suggested firing you.'

'Your assurances count for nothing. But there is another way…'

'What?' he demanded eagerly, like a drowning man snatching at a twig.

'If you could overlook my failure to report…'

'I *do not* give into blackmail threats.'

'Oh yes you do,' I said, raising my eyebrows a fraction.

'But it's out of my hands…'

'OK, let's put it this way, you may have significant influence over the matter…'

'And if I do what you want will you destroy the CD?'

Oh dear. Was that born out of blind optimism or hopeless naivety? He didn't seem to recognise that he no longer had the power to manipulate me.

'No, I won't.'

'No deal then.'

For all his acuity, he failed to appreciate the weakness of his own negotiating position.

'OK—no deal. This goes public. I'll take my chances over the minor compliance issue.'

'I *need* the disk.'

'Sure, but I'm not giving it to you. I want you to sweat over it, to be looking over your shoulder, knowing I can bring you down any time I choose. Because that's how I felt when you victimised me.'

'It wasn't like that, Amy. I've always had your best interests at heart, but you were ill and too insecure and paranoid to see it.'

'Well,' I breezily replied. 'Let's see who's insecure and paranoid now, shall we?'

***

I had one more person to confront.

'Are you sure they have your meds right?' said Bailey when I handed in my resignation.

I understood his surprise. There were two ways of playing the firing game if you were on the receiving end. The first was to fight and try to prove them wrong, and act like you were desperate to hang onto your position. Only losers played it that way. Alternatively you could sit on your arse and wait for them to make the moves. The "tough guys" favoured this approach, and generally secured a bigger pay-off to go away and stop bugging everyone. Ideally method two could be combined, as in Venner's case, with a timely and lucrative job offer.

But giving them the finger and walking away from five hundred thousand a year with no compensation and no job to go to featured nowhere in the corporate games manual. It was akin to throwing the chessboard up in the air in a fit of petulance rather than figuring out the moves in a game you knew you'd ultimately lose.

Unsurprisingly, Smithies had backtracked on the "minor compliance breach". But they'd find something else later. Bailey wielded the ultimate power and he didn't care for me much either.

I guess he liked me even less after I'd explained why I was leaving.

Greg had been scared to disclose what he'd discovered at JJ, so he'd ended up helping the client to conceal it, with disastrous consequences. The money laundering reporting officer wasn't truly independent. And when I'd raised a few enquiries, I'd been pressured to stop. This was not a healthy environment for anyone, leaving aside the numerous corporate governance issues. And I told him so.

'Fear runs through this whole firm like a cancer,' I concluded, with a dramatic flourish. 'Fear of making a mistake—fear of being fired because we don't fit in—fear of telling our people the truth—fear of facing the truth ourselves. And the rot starts from the top.'

'That's only your perception.'

'Ah yes, but perception is reality, isn't it?'

'Those meds you're on certainly pack a mighty punch.'

I noticed for the first time what a nervous, wiry little man he was without his bully-boy henchmen to prop him up. And he was wrong about the meds—I'd stopped taking them—who needed antipsychotic pills to deal with reality?

'You were a sensible partner before all this nonsense. But if your mind is made up…'

I understood—there was no place in Pearson Malone for someone who had the guts to speak the truth about the organisation's weaknesses.

'It is.'

I stood up to leave and he rose to shake my hand. Then he paused.

'One last thing before you go, Amy. I'd value your opinion on something. I believe you're the one person who won't try to bullshit me.'

'You can count on that.'

'It's about Lisa Carter—you were her sponsoring partner, weren't you?'

How quickly he'd slipped into the past tense.

'Yes.'

'She had her executive interview yesterday.'

Ah yes, the final hurdle in her unseemly scramble to partnership.

'I take it she passed?'

I didn't care either way now.

'Not necessarily. Having Kelly as her assessing partner didn't help her cause, but to be frank a couple of the board expressed some doubts.'

'Doubts about what?'

'Her judgement.'

'Really?'

To my mind her judgement of how best to progress in the toxic cesspool of Pearson Malone had been spot on.

'Yes, the view is she should have spotted the irregularities at JJ.'

'Did you ask her about it?'

'Yes—she said she'd suspected nothing.'

'And your problem with that is?' I asked warily, unsure of his agenda.

'She might be lying, afraid of admitting to having suspicions and then doing nothing…'

'Yes,' I agreed, still apprehensive about where this might be leading.

'But the real worry is she genuinely didn't suspect anything. And there's the nub of the matter. In this job we need a sixth sense to sniff out trouble. And if Lisa lacks that, she doesn't have what it takes.'

He seemed blithely oblivious to the irony of this statement.

'Quite,' I agreed. 'So fail her, if that's how you feel.'

'The board is split,' explained Bailey. 'Everyone agreed that if she failed to smell a rat, she shouldn't be promoted, bearing in mind the concerns at the assessment centre over her risk management. But several board members suspected she might be lying to protect her own position, and they had a degree of sympathy.'

'Yes,' I said. 'I can see that they would.'

This shocking attitude only vindicated my decision to quit. I'd no desire to be part of a culture where lying might be justified but an honest failure to identify a fraud was regarded as a major weakness.

'So you know Lisa better than anyone—and you voiced suspicions about the JJ account, so it can't be unreasonable to expect her to have spotted something too. What do you think?'

Giddy at the power that lay in my hands, I didn't hesitate. Lisa had ruthlessly exploited the frailties of those above her to get to the top, in spite of her claims to moral superiority. Why even the assessment centre had been fudged, and I reckoned she knew it. No one more richly deserved to be hoist by her own petard.

'In my opinion, she's definitely telling the truth. And there's no need to rely on me—read her application papers. Honesty is one of Lisa's major strengths. She'd never tell a lie.'

'That's what I thought too,' said Bailey. 'Thank you, Amy. And goodbye.'

We shook hands and I walked away, certain we would never meet again.

THE END

Thanks so much for reading CONCEALMENT. I hope you enjoyed it and if so, I'd very much appreciate a few words of support on Amazon or Goodreads!

You can continue following Amy's adventures in EXPOSURE and then RESTITUTION. Both books are available from Amazon in ebook or paperback form.

You may also like to join the Crazy Amy VIP Fan Club. As well as being able to keep up with all the latest news, you will have free access to a series of short stories which run in parallel to the books. They are free, and are available exclusively to club members. Further details can be found at www.roseedmunds.co.uk

Finally, if you check out the Mainsail Books website at www.mainsailbooks.co.uk, you'll find many more tales of corporate skulduggery, and an exciting free offer!

Rose Edmunds
Brighton, UK

OUT NOW ON AMAZON
EXPOSURE BY ROSE EDMUNDS
CRAZY AMY BOOK 2

City high-flyer Amy has crashed and burned. Fresh out of rehab and with her career in tatters, the sudden death of an old friend propels her into an illicit undercover fraud investigation.

But Amy's in way over her head. The assignment quickly turns sour, pitching her into a nightmare where no one can be trusted and nothing is what it seems.

In mortal danger, and with enemies old and new conspiring against her, Amy's resilience is tested to the limit as she strives to defeat them and rebuild her life.

Printed in Poland
by Amazon Fulfillment
Poland Sp. z o.o., Wrocław